THE DAY OF THE FIFTH MOON

BY THE SAME AUTHOR:

Novels

THE LAST SURRENDER
SOMETIMES AT NIGHT
ACQUAINTANCE WITH GRIEF
THE REVOLUTION
THE WORLD OF LUKE SIMPSON
THE EMBASSY
THE HAPPY HOSTAGE

Biographies

H. G. WELLS
FREUD AND HIS EARLY CIRCLE
JUNG — MAN AND MYTH
HAVELOCK ELLIS
ERNEST JONES — FREUD'S ALTER EGO
THE WAY BACK

History

THE INTERNATIONAL BRIGADES

Essays

WE HAVE COME A LONG WAY
THE PROBLEM OF PROGRESS

THE DAY OF THE FIFTH MOON

by

VINCENT BROME

LONDON
VICTOR GOLLANCZ LTD
1984

First published in Great Britain 1984
by Victor Gollancz Ltd,
14 Henrietta Street, London WC2E 8QJ

British Library Cataloguing in Publication Data
Brome, Vincent
The day of the fifth moon.
I. Title
823'.914[F] PR6052.R573

ISBN 0-575-03494-7

Typeset at The Spartan Press Ltd.,
Lymington, Hants
and printed in Great Britain by
St Edmundsbury Press, Bury St Edmunds, Suffolk

To Angela

AUTHOR'S NOTE

Vincent Brome has used multiple sources — biographies, diaries, letters, histories — in recreating the historical basis of this novel, among them Peter Fleming's *The Siege at Peking* (Hart Davis, 1959). All the main characters are fictional.

CHAPTER I

FOR ALL HIS haste he was very aware of the vast walls of the Tartar city heaving fifty feet into the air, the ring of fortifications, the yellow-gowned priests, the temples and canals.

He was late and the barbaric grandeur of the city was all too familiar, but no one could ignore the Soochow harlots or the Mongols hawking venison. They plied their trades with a special kind of Chinese persistence.

He was late and the Minister would be furious if he arrived after the Queen's birthday party had begun. And then he stopped abruptly, frozen in his tracks by what seemed a sudden apparition. It materialized beside the vermilion pillar of a Manchu palace, a demon from some Grand Guignol pantomime. Its face was a peasant's face and its eyes gleamed with something between cunning and intelligence. The white tunic was caught in at the waist by a flaming red girdle, the hair tied in a red cloth, red ribbons flowing from wrists and ankles. Sitting on the off-side shaft of a cart, it began ostentatiously sharpening a weapon, which was something between a sword and a knife, as it saw him approaching. Then came the words, spat out as Kershaw hurried past: "Old hairy one."

In 1900 they were familiar words, but Kershaw had never heard them delivered with such venom. As he threaded his way swiftly through the camels he became aware of the pink walls of the Forbidden City high in the background. Once upon a time there was no connection between this apparition and the Empress, but now . . . As he hurried on he wondered what intrigues were afoot at that very moment among the sleek eunuchs, the grand councillors, the Empress and the shadowy red-ribboned figures who came and went outside the city.

Ten minutes later he approached the Legations, crouching under the vast Tartar wall—somehow, today, it seemed to him, miserably. The English Legation was relatively lavish. Two great tiled pavilions dominated the Minister's oriental house with its handsome halls looking out on the theatre, the student quarters and the bowling alley.

When he heard the strains of music Kershaw knew that he was indeed late, and as he approached the fives court he could see the weird combination of Chinese musicians desperately trying to cope with their Western instruments, rendering a Strauss waltz with a rhythm unknown to Strauss. Everywhere the grounds were lit with beautiful Chinese lanterns, thick clusters of them surrounding the entrance to the theatre.

In the theatre the tables, covered with spotless napery and silver cutlery, were already filled with members of the British community and selected guests from other legations. They all sat stiffly, waiting for the first course of dinner to appear, with Sir Archibald Angus Mainwaring in full dress uniform, his decorations falling away in waves from his gold brocaded collar. Baron von Ketteler sat to Sir Archibald's right, literally at that moment flourishing his fine moustaches, and the American Minister, Edwin Conger, to the left. Monsieur Bleriot wore his own peculiar brand of French evening dress, and his wife was elegant in black taffeta with long white gloves and pearls round her throat. It should have been a festive occasion but Kershaw at once detected a muted note. It was not only his own vacant place, the undelivered first course and the confused Strauss rhythm. Something deeper was troubling this tiny gathering of European men and women surrounded by the seething life of the Chinese capital, Peking.

Half bowing to Sir Archibald, Kershaw made elaborate apologies which Sir Archibald ignored, and Kershaw realized that he was in for a not very happy evening.

The superficial buzz of social exchanges hesitated for a moment on his arrival and then flowed on again. As an official interpreter, Kershaw's ranking was not very high, and Monsieur Bleriot on his left continued to address the elderly Irish bachelor, Sir Robert Hart, directly across from him.

As the cold consommé came at last, Bleriot turned to Kershaw and said: "You've been to the London Mission, I hear. How are zey?"

"As well as can be expected," Kershaw said.

Monsieur Bleriot leaned closer to Kershaw and dropped his voice. "You know ze Chinese better than most. What — as you say in English — are zey up to?"

"Do you mean the Chinese, the Empress or the Boxers?"

"All three."

"The Chinese couldn't care less, the Empress is listening to the wind and the Boxers are trying to create one."

"What do zey think in the Mission?"

"They put their faith in God, the British Empire and Sir Archibald, in that order."

Bleriot made an elaborate gesture with his small white hands. "How many names, Mr Kershaw, do zee English missionaries have for God?"

"They teach the godless Chinese five different names for a god they don't believe in."

"Why?"

"Each denomination clearly has exclusive rights in God — the Catholics refuse to concede to the Protestants, the Methodists to the Jesuits, the Jesuits to the Baptists. Each has to have an exclusive God with an exclusive name.

"How do zee Chinese take zat?"

"As always, the Chinese are puzzled but accommodating."

Bleriot's eyes blazed. "Monsieur. You are as blind as Sir Archibald. Accommodating — do you tink zee Boxers are accommodating?"

"The Boxers are not the Chinese."

"Zen what are zey?" Monsieur Bleriot put Gallic attack into his words and such a sweep into his gestures that he nearly knocked the plates from the hands of the servant who suddenly appeared behind them.

The plates, which were slipped with such skill before them, contained an extraordinary hybrid dish which tried to reconcile something resembling roast beef with bamboo shoots and many another Chinese delicacy. Monsieur Bleriot did not trouble to conceal a sickly distaste for what he saw.

As he began eating, Kershaw became aware of Lucy Shelham, wife of the Deputy Minister, signalling to him with her green eyes from across the table. For once he could not decode the message. As their eyes met and concentrated in an effort to communicate his pulses quickened. He never quite understood why anyone so — the word he always used was a male word — handsome should have chosen his own lean, haggard, slightly stooped person to entrust with the secrets of her body.

The husky voice of Baron von Ketteler broke across the table. "Sir Archibald, I and my colleagues from the legation would like to congratulate you on the great news of the relief of Mafeking." The news of the relief had arrived that morning.

"That is most gracious of you," Sir Archibald said. His voice was thin and high like his long face. There was a kind of vacancy in his face, as if God had thought it sufficient to grant him fine eyes, a straight nose and noble brow without adding too much mind to the final construction.

"Ee hasn't learnt a thing," Bleriot muttered. "Ee doesn't realize we're going to see another Mafeking if ee 'as his way."

Baron von Ketteler suddenly broke into fluent German and left Sir Archibald floundering in a welter of portmanteau words. Monsieur Bleriot said in a louder voice to Kershaw:

"What is your personal view?"

"I'm just an interpreter," Kershaw said. "I'm not expected to have a view."

"Mr Kershaw, if you can be interrupted," Sir Archibald said, as if a Niagara flow of talk was falling from Kershaw's lips, "would you be so good as to translate what the Baron is saying."

The Baron repeated his words and Kershaw translated: "I cannot see the symbolic head of a culture reaching back thousands of years into the past allowing herself to become the ally of a barbaric brutality which belongs to the Tartars who once invaded China."

Bleriot made a loud sound of disgusted disbelief. "I disagree with you, zir," he said. "I 'ave continuously pressed for a request to be sent to Tientsin for a naval detachment to guard the legations. And what 'as 'appened? I 'ave been ignored. Simply ignored. I must remind you gentlemen that only two years ago when disturbances arose we asked for naval detachments. When we got them order was restored. Sir Archibald, why don't you ask Mr Kershaw what ee thinks? Ee 'as just come back from the London Mission and ze missionaires know what they are talking about."

Sir Archibald directed an icy stare in Kershaw's direction. Unpunctuality on the Queen's birthday was unforgivable, and he was not prepared to have a mere interpreter up-ranked to diplomatic utterance.

Baron von Ketteler took the initiative again. "Tell us what you have heard, Mr Kershaw."

"They think," Kershaw said succinctly, "that the outlook is black."

"Characteristic," exclaimed Sir Archibald. "Missionaries are always alarmist. I've never known them be anything else."

"Alarmist," Bleriot said, pushing back his chair abruptly. "If zey are alarmist then so am I." He wavered for a moment as if he were about to leave the table and then with a heavy sigh he returned to the roast beef and ate a few mouthfuls. Conversation ran on but all attempts to steer it away from the Boxers simply brought it back — circuitously — to the same subject. Twenty minutes later Sir Archibald announced that they were overlooking something much more important than the Boxers. Bleriot again exploded. "More important! Nothing is more important!" He came to his feet. "I do not think I am in ze right mood for zis company tonight. If you will excuse me, Your Excellency. . . . " Waiting for his wife to adjust her jacket, he escorted her with quick short steps round the table, half bowed at the door and disappeared through it. There was a brief uneasy silence. At last Sir Archibald came to his feet. "Ladies and gentlemen, we are forgetting ourselves. . . . We are forgetting the day and the occasion. . . . Pray charge your glasses. Today, ladies and gentlemen, is the twenty-fourth of May in the year 1900, the eighty-first birthday of our most glorious Queen, Queen Victoria, and I give you the toast. . . . "

They all came to their feet, the Ministers and their wives, the representative of *The Times* newspaper, the Captain of American Marines, the young English doctor, Baron von Ketteler, the Deputy English Minister and his wife Lucy, Kevin Kershaw and a score of others.

Extending his glass to the full length of his arm Sir Archibald gazed a moment at the winking champagne bubbles and then spoke in a voice as sonorous as he could make it:

"I give you the toast — to Her Imperial Majesty, Queen Victoria."

The guests took up the words in a half chant — "The Queen, the Queen." The words echoed out into the soft warm Chinese night. Peking was not yet into the hot season, but already the heat was taking its toll of Lucy Shelham's mascara, and small beads of sweat ran down Sir Archibald's left cheek into the gold brocaded collar of his uniform. Kershaw suddenly wanted to escape from the room, the heat, the ritual, the artificially generated emotion whose patriotic basis was spontaneously available only to the English — and he was certainly not English.

As Sir Archibald turned towards the tennis court where the Chinese band awaited his signal, he failed to notice that two of its members were asleep. Sir Archibald duly made the pre-arranged signal but the silence continued. His face stiffening, Sir Archibald raised his hand and gestured a second time, so vigorously he might have been firing a pistol. There was a shuffling of feet and instruments, a muttered Chinese imprecation and at last, a little raggedly, the National Anthem began.

Thousands of miles away in Balmoral the octogenarian Queen was also enjoying "some nice music after dinner", and no slightest trace of the tension among the staff of her Legation in Peking troubled Her Majesty in her beautiful castle set in its emerald lawns, despite the strange rumours which filtered through to her.

Half an hour later Sir Archibald called for silence once more and announced, "There will now be dancing on the tennis court." As they poured out on to the lawn, it presented the usual contradiction between the Eastern and Western culture: the court steam-rolled to perfection with its net swung to one side, the trees hung with Chinese lanterns whose soft light made small pools of illumination surrounded by darkness. The cosmopolitan throng broke into groups, waltzing, talking, gossiping and drinking one glass of champagne after another.

Kershaw detached himself and remained aloof with his back against the wall of the theatre. It was eight years now since he had come back to China from America. Perhaps . . . come back . . . was a falsification of the facts. They had, after all, practically driven him out. His Chinese mother was dead and his American father had disowned him after the scandal. . . . Scandal. Once again what an absurd word to use. Western culture which prided itself on civilized values could hound a man, if he broke its more sacred codes, with a ferocity which was no less savage psychologically than the physical horrors now threatened by the Boxers. Or was he once again exercising that dangerous streak in his thinking which constantly sought for polarized analogies capable of destroying an opponent's case? After all, he was biologically prescribed to polarize, with his Chinese-American origins, and as the thought occurred he knew that it, too, was false. Only the jet black hair and a certain pallor in his face hinted at his Chinese mother, his physical frame conforming to the heavy-shouldered American footballer. Physically the clash was there, but not pronounced. Mentally, complicated conflicts arose. The oddest resonances of another culture could break into his American thinking, to produce the withdrawn person whose stoicism when confronted with material disasters had infuriated at least three women in his life. His gentleness, the soft mellifluous voice and the sheer grace of the way in which he carried his big body drew him so easily into their lives and even beds, but he lacked the American vitality which faced and overwhelmed difficulties, allowed himself to be carried along by what he too easily regarded as the inevitable. He remained too often a spectator of his own and others' lives. He lacked what he regarded as vulgar American drive.

Under the big plane tree, away from the dancers, in the far corner of the court he overheard von Ketteler saying, "We must get this railway concession fixed within the next month — if we're all still alive."

"Still alive," a figure, anonymous in the darkness, said, "you're worse than Monsieur Bleriot."

"Just realistic," von Ketteler said.

"One just has to get the priorities right of course."

"And which comes first in your view?"

"Oh, the concessions of course."

Priorities, Kershaw thought. The first priority among the

Ministers in the Legations was rapacity. The network of protocol which ruled their daily lives made possible social and professional exchanges which appeared highly civilized. Penetrating its inner workings he knew that civilization as something quite different: an elaborate façade covering conspiracies to outwit one another on concessions, commercial deals, building contracts, and all the profit-making processes which Ministers affected to despise. Even now, with the worst threat to their security daily becoming more intense, under the cover of deputies and lesser minions, they were competing for favours with the ruthlessness of gold prospectors in a Klondyke saloon. It was a necessary part of their culture. It clashed with everything Kershaw drew from his Chinese past.

He became aware of someone standing beside him and suddenly realized that Lucy Shelham had left the dancing to join him.

"You're mad," he said.

"Why shouldn't I talk to you?"

"Where's your husband?"

"He's drinking with Sir Archibald. When can we meet again?"

"Not this week."

"There may not be another."

"You're worse than Bleriot."

She dropped her voice to a whisper and leant towards him. "Something terrible's happened to me."

"He's threatened to leave you?"

"No — I've fallen in love with you."

"Oh, my God — not that!"

"I knew how you would react."

"I can't afford to have . . . " Kershaw stopped as he saw Sir Archibald coming towards them. "Do forgive me, Mrs Shelham," he said, "but I did need Kershaw to do some interpreting for me. Can I drag you away, Kershaw . . . I really am sorry to interrupt. . . . "

As the night advanced Lucy Shelham made several attempts to see Kershaw alone again but without leaving the tennis court and retreating into the inner rooms of the Legation it proved impossible. Hour after hour the dancing and gossip continued.

No one seemed anxious to leave the security of the English Legation to return to music-less rooms and isolated apartments where anxiety returned with all its subtle interactions of class, nationality and creed. And then, quite publicly, towards three o'clock in the morning, Lucy Shelham sought out Kershaw and said in a fierce undertone, "There's no law that says you mustn't dance with me."

"There certainly is," he said. But she had already half drawn him on to the tennis court and before he could recover he found himself dancing. Her breath smelt strongly of drink and her movements were so bold he realized she was slightly drunk. At thirty-five she had carefully preserved the voluptuous lines of her figure and now her breast brushed his chest with an effect which was not altogether unintentional. Her wide-swung eyes were softly troubled, the line of her neck slender but she exuded above all the kind of sensuous warmth which only a woman could achieve.

"Keep your distance, for God's sake," he said, disengaging his body and straightening her arm until it was stretched horizontally beside them.

"You're drunk."

"Do I disgust?"

"Yes, you do."

She drew back.

"I'm sorry." She turned away unsteadily. "Forgive me — I'm so miserable — "

"So am I," he said.

"You!" she exclaimed. "Miserable? You're always so self-contained, so damnably well adjusted. Why should you be miserable?"

"Because," he dropped his voice to the shadow of a whisper, "I should like to make love to you and can't."

"What did you say?"

"Nothing," he said. "You must go home. Shall I get you a chair?"

Once again a voice broke in on them — there was no escape. "Ah, there you are my dear. Really must be going . . . nearly four o'clock. Thank you Mr — er — "

"Kershaw."

"Thank you Mr Kershaw. Keeping wife company." He looked such a travesty of a diplomat with his carefully controlled pomposity, his drooping chaps and wide moustache. He took his wife by the arm and she tried desperately to conceal the unsteadiness of her steps. "Ah ha — a little too much?" As they moved away, he said over his shoulder, "Goodnight, Mr Kershaw — rather, good morning."

"Goodnight."

It was almost dawn as Sir Archibald's last guests climbed into their sedan chairs and set out on the swaying journey through the straight, silent, empty streets. The golden lanterns paled, the music ceased, the servants began to clear the tables and collect the glasses.

Another cloudless day broke, with no hint of rain. The drought seemed endless and the great parched plain stretched around the city. Sir Archibald referred to it when reporting on the situation, the following day, to the Marquis of Salisbury at the Foreign Office in London. Such was his reputation that the Foreign Office seldom questioned his memos. . . . Educated at Harrow and Sandhurst, served in Afghan War 1879–80, mentioned twice in despatches — Boer War 1881 — medal with three clasps — Consul-General Cairo 1890–5 — Envoy Extraordinary and Minister Plenipotentiary Peking 1898.

As Minister Plenipotentiary he now wrote in longhand on official parchment paper: "I am convinced that a few days' heavy rainfall to terminate the long-continued drought which has helped largely to excite unrest in the country districts would do more to restore tranquillity than any measures which either the Chinese Government or foreign governments can take. . . ."

CHAPTER II

When Lu-Ching, the deputy magistrate of Fengtai, heard that there were crowds of Boxers in the Eastern Gardens calling upon the common people to follow them, he knew it would not be long before they were asking for — or demanding — audience with him. He consulted his legal colleagues and they were deeply disturbed at the news. "We must take great care and we earnestly beseech you not to anger them for they have so many ways in which to make of trouble a mountain that may crush us. . . ."

Lu-Ching was a proud man. He had resisted the rise of the Boxers with all his magisterial powers and was known to have issued the edict: "Those whose misdeeds are light I beat. Those whose misdeeds are heavy I behead." Instructions had been given to the village headmen to exercise as many restraints as possible on the Boxers and their doctrines but the tide of red-heads had multiplied and now they were clamouring within earshot of the very yamen itself.

Looking deeply into the heart of his ancestors he sat in contemplation for two hours within the yamen and when no clear message emerged from such meditation came sadly to his feet and began to don his official robes. There was the big mortar-board hat with its golden band which clamped it to his head, the voluminous under-tunic, richly brocaded and reaching to his ankles, and the inner tunic with blue and gold patterns woven gorgeously into its arms, the arms themselves coming down over his hands to conceal them completely. Finally he pulled on the special black paper-soled shoes of double thickness which gave him an extra inch of height, since he was a short man and the occasion needed every inch of authority which he could summon.

At two o'clock that afternoon the request for audience was delivered and Lu-Ching settled himself on the official bench, a large black marble chair with sides curved like a cup. He ordered the main gate to be opened wide, but his heart shook a little as an immense crowd of chattering Boxers, each flaunting red head-scarves and weapons, surged in and overwhelmed the courtyard.

Six men detached themselves from the crowd and moved forward, one by one, to pass singly through the inner door into the yamen. As he entered, the first one drew himself up, paused for a moment and in a voice meant to be thunderous said "I am Ho-Li-Chung, the Great One from the Chung Dynasty". The second said "I am Han-Mia-Shih the Great Immortal", and a third announced himself as "Chang Lu-Fi of the Lame Leg".

Lu-Ching's face remained impassive but his mind smiled to see what need they had to try so many tricks to aggrandize insignificance.

The ritual words of etiquette came naturally to his lips, and then he said with elaborate politeness, "Assembled holy saints, for what purpose can I turn my skills to your service?"

Someone in the restless crowd of flashing head-scarves cried: "How do we know this magistrate is not a Secondary Hairy One?" Then Han Mia-Shih the Great Immortal spoke. "He is polite and reverential to us but we must not be deceived. We have come to invite you to our altar to burn incense."

"It is not customary for me to burn incense in such circumstances," Lu-Ching said, but immediately a growl of such power came from the crowd he regretted the frame he had given to his words.

"There is much business needing my attention," he said, "but I will come to your altar tomorrow."

The Great Immortal spoke again. "It is written in the sky that you come today and without your soldiers."

"You must give me time to consider the matter."

"There is no time."

Lu-Ching knew that thirty soldiers were concealed in an inner courtyard and to summon them needed the smallest gesture of his arm for which signal his secretary waited fearfully in the background of the official chair, fiddling nervously with his green tunic. But thirty soldiers. What could they do against this mob, and why invoke premature bloodshed when, with all his skill in handling people and knowledge of the trickery of incense burning, he might convince them of the simple truth — that he had nothing to do with the Secondary Hairy Ones.

There was a pause, charged with small whickering noises from one section of the crowd which had already grown impatient. Lu-Ching bent and held a swift exchange with his secretary. "Let the soldiers surround me and I will go," he said, but at once the Immortal One replied:

"Magistrate, you need not soldiers who may provoke us."

"I will take ten," Lu-Ching said and the Immortal One considered his words.

"So be it magistrate. You shall take ten. Now we must go."

As Lu-Ching rose there was a surge of Boxers waving spears and knives towards his chair and he felt the sweat break out under his armpits. Perhaps this was the chosen day for his retreat into the lands of his ancestors, but the Immortal One intervened.

"Wait!" he said. "We have yet to burn incense."

Lu-Ching's secretary went swiftly to the stables and returned with his favourite black horse Pu-Jo, gaily caparisoned in crimson. Ten soldiers surrounded Lu-Ching as he mounted, and the confused entourage, led by the six Immortals, moved out of the yamen towards a decaying temple whose three tiered dome of yellow tiles had many gaps in its roof.

Approaching the forecourt Lu-Ching was addressed by his secretary, a short fat man from another province who regarded his master as divinely inspired by the Dowager Empress.

"Make no traffic with them or you will lose all rank," he implored, but the scene which now opened before Lu-Ching's eyes gave him no choice.

The Immortals led them into a double row of men lining the approaches to the temple and every man held a sword, spear or knife. The mob quickly jostled his ten soldiers aside and Lu-Ching found himself, alone with his secretary, being propelled by force down between the double ranks guarding the temple. The impulse to set his horse at the charge and attempt an escape was almost overwhelming but the disciplines which had kept his mind cool served him well. The sweat of fear accumulated on his brow and something stirred deeply in his viscera but nothing showed in his face or manner.

Forced to dismount at the terraced steps before the altar he climbed them slowly, led by the Immortals and followed by the mob. As they entered the temple he saw at once an image, incongruous to its surroundings, standing four-square in his path. The pain stabbed again in his viscera as he recognized Kuan Ti, the god of war. Before the ferociously challenging image stood an incense table and as they approached it the cry went up inside and outside the temple — Kowtow! Kowtow!

Custom made surrender easy, for all paid homage to the god of war, and now carefully playing each part of this ordeal in the hope that if the steps were correctly interlocked he would survive, he said: "I worship Kuan Ti because the government which I represent would approve such worship."

While his secretary muttered the incantations he went through the ritual nine kowtows and three kneelings but as he tried to rise from the third kneeling the powerful hand of the Immortal One fell upon his shoulders. "We must burn a memorial to the gods to know whether you are a Secondary Hairy One before you rise," he said.

All suspected Christians were now submitted to this test by which a piece of parchment, lit from the altar candles, was burned to ashes and if the ash did not rise from the ground then the man was guilty of being a Christian and was beheaded.

Lu-Ching controlled his fear as they prepared the ceremony because he knew that the merest puff of wind or Boxer trickery could take his life from him, now, at this very instant, when he was in the full flush of manhood and success. Especially Boxer trickery in controlling the ash could be so fatal.

With many graceful gestures the Great Immortal took a parchment from the altar and lit it from the solitary candle. As he placed the parchment on the altar everyone fell silent. Long afterwards Lu-Ching remembered the terrifying speed with which the flames licked their way down its yellow length, leaving the delicate lacework of ash as if the inner reality refused to be consumed. Involuntarily he was tensing his body to will the ash to rise but it lay there inert. The shouts broke out at once, shouts of triumph and revenge.

"The gods have spoken!"

"Secondary Hairy One!"

"Kill! Kill! Kill!"

Lu-Ching felt his blood freeze momentarily and then he knew that his life depended on challenging their deeply ingrained fear of power, authority and the Empress.

"We know now your heart," the Great Immortal said. "Certainty comes from the gods. They have spoken. We are not stupid mandarins making slovenly judgments and killing. There is no doubt in our evidence even by the breadth of a silk thread."

Impassivity — control — clear unequivocal judgments — the training from his days in the service of the Empress and before that the school of Chinese law must be evoked and paraded with all the authority that went with his office. His voice shook a little as he began to speak but he quickly recovered its full power.

"I came to you freely because I am not a Secondary Hairy One. I came expecting real evidence — but you do not render it. You say you enter my heart and know what happens there. But that is not real evidence by which judgments are made. You must examine these matters with greater care. To kill is bad. To kill an imperial magistrate — that is rebellion against the Empress. She will mete out such punishment for such an act as you will not be alive to remember. That punishment may mean death to every inhabitant of this city and that includes — all of you. Think on these things before you act."

There was a silence and in the silence, the ash moved slightly on the altar. "See — it rises," someone shouted. But it did not rise. Some undetected whisper of air was playing with the ash and Lu-Ching's life. The ash crept an inch or two along the surface of the altar and seemed to struggle to free itself from the bondage of physical matter. Then it broke in many pieces and was dead again.

It surprised Lu-Ching that his speech had silenced the multitude because he knew that these people believed themselves to be the possessors of supernatural powers. Above all they were granted invulnerability against any chosen enemy once they had been initiated into the Boxer's creed. But what if the Empress were that enemy. Everyone knew that once a Boxer had undergone the requisite training, and had developed his faith to the right pitch, bullets passed through his body and left him unharmed, sword thrusts did not wound him and even cannon-balls lost their destructive power. Many a demonstration had proved this beyond doubt. Once the celebrant had been possessed by the spirit of the Boxers' god, Mi T'o, that spirit could deflect bullets by the wave of a hand, or heal instantaneously a sword thrust capable of killing the uninitiate. What power had the Executioner's sword against such magic? How could the Empress behead any one of those who were truly confirmed in the faith?

The Great Immortal One suddenly spoke again.

"That we may be sure of protection from mandarins and their like we will consult the god Mi T'o," he said.

He moved with slow measured steps to the altar, turned to face the mob and swaying slightly began to intone like a litany:

"The instructions from the god Mi T'o to his disciples has been proclaimed upon every mountain by the Ancient Teachers. . . . We reverently invite the Gods from the central southern mountains, from the central eight caves to preserve China and destroy the foreigners." As he spoke several Boxers took up position facing away from the altar towards the south-east, genuflecting every few seconds, knocking their heads on the ground and making cabbalistic signs. Others brought out two Christian crosses and placed them beside the worshippers' feet to be stamped upon as and when the impulse took them.

"We ask your protection now, god Mi T'o, from acts we carry out in your name. The Iron Lo Han if cut with an axe, or chopped with a knife, will show no trace. Cannon cannot injure, water cannot drown. If I urgently invite the Gods they will quickly come, if I tardily invite them they will tardily come from their seats in every cave in every mountain. Ancient teachers, Venerable Mother, do swiftly as I command and bring us your protection."

Two of the Boxers had increased the speed of their genuflections and head knocking until they were in a rhythmic trance and now it was evident that the Great Immortal One had invoked the dark gods to overwhelm the power of fear and reason, to overwhelm Lu-Ching's warnings. If he did not break into the spell he would certainly die, but how to break such a spell which mounted in power every moment? He must wait. Wait for what was called the moment of release.

It came very quickly. The two Boxers suddenly went into violent spasms, their limbs twitched, their eyes rolled and they began to foam at the mouth. They were indeed possessed, lost to all reason, given up to some demonic force self-generated by maniacal fervour. And then abruptly they were still again, converted into sculptured silence, with glazed eyes staring unseeing above the heads of the crowd.

Everyone remained in silent awe. The Gods were working their way with two of their number while they watched and none dared interrupt. Suddenly one of the two Boxers came out of his trance and said: "It is written that we try again."

"Try again?" the Great Immortal asked. "Is that the message?"

"That is the message."

The Great Immortal hesitated. At last he said, "So be it."

He took another parchment, lit it and waited. As the sides curled in upon themselves and blackened, Lu-Ching felt his own body curling from the flame and blackening as it burnt. The pain which moved over his skin was excruciating. Only long years of training kept his face impassive as his mind and body seethed.

And then the ashes stirred and rose, drifting away on a sudden movement of air whose origin no one knew, or was it the Great Immortal who had created the wind deliberately? There were so many trickeries for making the ash rise and fall. Could it be that the Great Immortal feared the vengeance of the Empress but did not want to admit it to his acolytes? Had he deliberately framed the message and created the wind to escape from the situation in which he found himself trapped and in fear of beheading?

So great was Lu-Ching's relief that he found himself momentarily paralyzed, and then he heard the Great Immortal say:

"We leave you now. . . . We go to the Legations. We intend to kill all Secondary Hairy Ones. We must exterminate. There is no other way. But we will be back — and we shall expect you, magistrate, to pass sentence on the Secondary Hairy Ones. Not on us."

With that he led the Six Immortals back down through the double line of guards and the crowd surged after them.

Lu-Ching stood there, still paralyzed, and he seemed not to hear his secretary when he said "Excellency — we must fly at once — they may come back." The secretary untethered the horse and brought it to Lu-Ching but when he addressed His Excellency it was useless because he drew no response.

Lu-Ching's body was shivering slightly as he released control over it. His mind was offering thanks to his ancestors that whichever of them had intervened to save him from the most painful death should gain recognition from the others. As he rode slowly back to the yamen his thoughts at last broke free and almost at once he remembered the American-Chinese gentleman whose name was Kevin Brandon Kershaw. Years ago he had reason to incur a great debt to Kevin Brandon Kershaw and now he thought of him in the British Legation and was afraid for him.

CHAPTER III

LADY MAINWARING HAD furnished her oriental bedroom with materials from England which almost reconstructed her bedroom in Cadogan Square, London. The same long crimson curtains with patterned pelmets, closely similar brocaded chairs and exact replicas of the solid mahogany chests of drawers. Her dressing table had in fact been shipped out intact, and as she sat in front of the triple mirrors with their ornate silver fittings she wrestled hopelessly with a new pimple at precisely that part of her neck which, when dressed, was not covered by her ropes of pearls.

"I don't care what you say," she said to Sir Archibald. "I don't think we should send the children out to the bungalow — it's too dangerous."

"Everyone's so alarmist," Sir Archibald said as he tightened the inner cummerbund to check the threatened middle-aged spread.

They rose without fail at 7.30. Between 7.30 and 8.00 both went through the rituals which checked the inroads of middle age, Lady Mainwaring handling her make-up with skill to disguise the wrinkles under her eyes and Sir Archibald battling with the faintest beginnings of a paunch. The face which stared back at Lady Mainwaring from her mirror was suddenly joined by Sir Archibald's gaunt visage. One was haunted by the ghost of disillusion, the other by indecision. Both were handsome in their different ways.

She picked up the whalebone corset, fitted it round her body and said, "Lace me." Sir Archibald exerted considerable strength to close the corset and her drooping breasts were pushed back into spherical solidity.

As each step towards the final image was taken, another year fell away. They retreated from middle age to the almost young couple who had not so very long ago been so much admired, dancing to Strauss, in their Cadogan Square drawing room. As she took up the scent spray she said, "You were very restless in the night. What were you muttering about?"

"I had that damned dream again," he said as he slipped on the tunic of his uniform.

"I don't know why you worry about it," she said. "Just accept it."

Throughout their married life she had preached the philosophy of acceptance and on most occasions of stress failed to practise it.

The dream varied in form and intensity and had two parts. First he saw an enormous fountain with coloured spheres held like a conjuring trick in the thrusting arcs of water, but one of the spheres became a human face and the face had resemblances to himself. The spray in the second part of the dream fell slowly and solidified into a beautiful broad crimson carpet which stretched away into infinity and there, walking towards him, a tiny figure slowly grew into an enormous magisterial person with knee breeches, silken stockings and a blue brocaded uniform, while a great voice announced, "Pray Silence For His Excellency Her Imperial Majesty's Ambassador to God." It was his wife who read the obvious meaning of the dream when it first occurred. He was one of the spheres trapped in this forgotten outpost of the British Foreign Service when he always hoped he would have become at least Britain's Ambassador to Washington.

Now she said, "Dream or no dream, I don't care what you say. I'm not sending the children to the bungalow."

He leaned over her and gently kissed her still bare shoulder.

"Why didn't you want to make love last night?" he said, with the same formality he might have brought to bear upon the next question on the agenda.

She flinched slightly under his kiss. "I must say," she said, "you have a gift for inappropriate moments. We're all about to be murdered in our beds and you are worrying about making love." She turned and looked at him with big sad eyes. "And really, Archibald, we're getting a bit old for that, aren't we."

He knew what she meant. He knew that, strive as he would, he had never mastered the art of being a satisfactory lover, but why did it continue to worry him? After all, sex did not mean very much to a woman once the first flush of youthful passion had spent itself. It was different for a man. He had to find release from these constantly renewed tensions, but sex was not his main problem with Lucilla. She had changed. From being the background compliant figure he had married she had slowly discovered his weaknesses, and now frequently asserted herself in circumstances unbecoming to the Minister's wife. She was unorthodox in her dress, too. She refused to clutter herself with unnecessary petticoats and long drawers, and in the hot season in Peking wore dangerously little.

She was fanning herself with the beautiful Chinese fan he had given her for her thirty-third birthday.

"I'm perspiring already," she said. "It simply shouldn't be as hot as this so soon. Help me, Archie, will you?" As he patiently dealt with the row of buttons at the back of her dress, he wondered all over again why she couldn't be like all the other wives and use the services of the Chinese maid. After all, Pretty Poo — as they had nicknamed her — was devoted to her. Twenty minutes later, with their public images resurrected from the ruins left by sleep, they went in to breakfast.

Sir Archibald sat in the Minister's office frowning over Edict 421 which the Empress had issued three days earlier. Rumour and counter rumour had poured in that morning compounding the confusion in his mind. The provinces were in a state of anarchy, dominated by the Boxers, and the Empress had the situation completely under control. The Legations should send to Taku for troop reinforcements at once, and there was no reason to think the Boxers would be allowed into Peking. Sir Robert Hart, wise in the ways of the Chinese, a scholar reputed by the Foreign Office to be the best adviser any Minister could have, had read Edict 421 and regarded it as "not unreasonable in the circumstances". Sir Archibald tried to concentrate his mind on the meaning of the Edict.

There was a knock on the door. His secretary opened it and said, "Mr Kershaw is here, sir."

"Show him in."

Sir Archibald greeted Kershaw with that subtle combination of patronage and respect which he reserved for the lower ranks of the Legation.

"Take a seat," he said. "I wanted a small translation confirmed for me. These Chinese Edicts are full of such subtleties . . . you never know when to read between the lines. What do you make of that paragraph?" He passed the Edict across his leather topped English desk; it had two paragraphs underlined in red.

Kershaw was surprised. "I didn't realize," he said, "that you read Chinese."

"I have a smattering," Sir Archibald replied.

Kershaw picked up the paper and with occasional hesitations translated: "Of late in all the provinces brigandage has daily become more prevalent. Most critics point to seditious societies as the cause, and ask for vigorous suppression and punishment. But reflection shows that societies are of different kinds. When worthless vagabonds form themselves into bands and . . . create disturbances, the law can show absolutely no leniency.

"On the other hand when peaceful and law abiding people practise their skill in mechanized arts . . . this is in accord with public-spirited principle. . . ."

Kershaw finished translating and replaced the paper on the Minister's desk.

"I read that to mean," Sir Archibald said, "that the authorities will suppress real brigandage which includes the Boxers."

He made it a statement of fact, not a question, but his eyes conveyed the hint of a question to Kershaw. He could not bring himself directly to ask Kershaw's opinion, but such were the uncertainties in his mind he would dearly have loved Kershaw to volunteer it. Kershaw deliberately remained silent. Being Eurasian did not divide his allegiances. He knew too well how the missionaries had duped and ensnared thousands of Chinese into a religion totally unsuited to their culture and he knew with what rapacity every one of the Ministries on Legation Street, the American, French, German and English, were conspiring to extract the last drop of advantage from a race of people they totally despised. And when it came to the final analysis the Chinese component in his character dominated the American. He was not a man of action who talked easily, and now suppressing his response came naturally.

Picking up the paper again and staring down at it as if he were thinking aloud, Sir Archibald said: "The Ministers are pressing for guards to be sent from Taku. I do not think that is necessary yet."

Once again no question-mark appeared at the end of the sentence but somewhere it hung on the air. Kershaw again ignored it.

"Seventeen men of war of different European nationalities are now anchored off Taku as a safeguard against emergencies. Taku is close to Tientsin, and from Tientsin the railway runs eighty miles to Peking. Detachments from all ships could reach Peking within two or three days. That seems to me the perfect safeguard."

Kershaw remained silent. Sir Archibald waited a long moment and then leant forward to press the silver bell on his desk. When his secretary appeared he said, "I've run out of memo paper. Can you let me have some more? Oh — and — Mr Kershaw here would like some tea."

It was typical of him that he did not ask Kershaw what he would like but, as he would have put it, divined his need. He was constantly "divining" people's intentions, needs, motives and now, with the Chinese, divining their strategies.

As his secretary retired Sir Archibald came to his feet. He was tall, bony, and as he began pacing round his office it became clear that his strides had to be big ones because small ones cramped his style. An office seemed ill-suited to contain his big, restless frame. He paced jauntily for some minutes and as he walked he talked as if he were dictating the travesty of a memo to the Foreign Office. One key sentence came through clearly. "Although this Edict is regarded in some quarters with misgiving, in view of the divergence of opinion I do not propose pressing for guards to be sent from Taku."

He paused, turned and stared down at Kershaw. At that moment his secretary, Elizabeth Smythe, returned with a daintily set tray with two bowls and a pot of tea. She poured the very pale golden liquid into the porcelain bowls and handed one to each man. "Sugar?" she said to Kershaw. He shook his head. She knew Sir Archibald took everything unadulterated — tea, coffee, whisky and his opinions. As they sipped the tea

Sir Archibald was at last driven to be direct: "You move round the city, Kershaw. What do you find?"

"My sources of information," Kershaw said, "are no match for yours."

Sir Archibald stared uncompromisingly straight into Kershaw's eyes.

"You give me the impression, Kershaw, that you are evading my question. Why is that?"

"No evading, Sir Archibald. There is so little I have to add. And what little I have would not be palatable."

"Why must it be palatable?"

"I have the impression, Sir Archibald, that your mind is already made up, and I doubt whether anything I could say would change it."

It was absurd. In moments of embarrassment it was absurd that Sir Archibald should actually do what theatrical villains of the Victorian stage were busy doing in far off London, but now he did it without any sense of caricature. He took the fine hairs of his wide-swung moustache and twirled them.

"I did not ask whether you could change my mind. I simply asked for information. Have you ever seen a Boxer in the city itself?"

"Yes — I have. A week ago."

Sir Archibald suppressed his surprise.

"In the actual city?"

"Yes."

"Why didn't you report it?"

"Forgive me," Kershaw said softly, "but I did not regard it as part of my duties to spy on the Chinese."

"Nonsense!" Sir Archibald said with a touch of sharpness. "No one is asking you to spy. What did you see?"

Kershaw made his description of the sudden apparition as vivid as possible, and suddenly it seemed to him that the sharpened knife — which was really a sword — flashed in the room.

Sir Archibald stood up. "Indeed," he said, and again, "Indeed." He walked a full circle round his desk and then repeated the move and the word. Kershaw felt that as an exercise in fatuity it had high quality.

It was at that moment that Sir Archibald's secretary gave a knock on the door which approached the peremptory.

"Excuse me, sir — a man has broken into the Legation and he's demanding to see . . . "

"I'm seeing no one," Sir Archibald said. And then, as if he had not registered it before: "*Broken in*? What do you *mean*, broken in?"

"He pushed his way past the guards, sir — and — and — "

"Get it out, woman. What is it?"

"He terrifies me sir. He is a peasant and he smells."

"Well, have him removed at once. I am not seeing a Chinese peasant. Who the devil let him in."

"But it's Mr Kershaw he wants to see, sir, not you."

"Mr Kershaw! Good Lord, Kershaw, were you expecting a Chinese peasant?"

"Certainly not."

"Well, I don't want him smelling in this office. Perhaps you had better go out and deal with him. Have him removed as fast as you can."

Kershaw went at once, with a vague sense of alarm. Slumped in a chair in the secretary's office was a figure at first unrecognizable. The greasy pigtail, the knee-length breeches, the shabby tunic were all part of the stereotype peasant who travelled by cart. The face was haggard, sweat still gleaming on the brow, and down one cheek a red slash still gently pulsed blood. Kershaw stood astonished for a moment and then through the dirt and the sweat he recognized that this was not the face of a peasant and slowly began to give it identity.

Lu-Ching! It was Lu-Ching. He went over to the chair, half bowed and said, "Greetings, Lu-Ching. For God's sake — what's happened?"

Lu-Ching just managed to stagger to his feet, and produced a half bow.

"It is a great relief," he said in Chinese, "that you are so quick to remember."

Suddenly he collapsed into the chair again and his yellow face went white.

"What is it?" Kershaw asked. "Are there other wounds? We must get you to the dispensary. I'll call Dr Morrison."

Almost plucking the relatively frail Lu-Ching from his chair, he half carried, half escorted him out of the office, down the corridor and across the courtyard. In the dispensary Lu-Ching slumped into the single wicker chair, and Kershaw looked at the row of first aid materials. It was tempting to handle this himself but he decided to find Dr Morrison, the remarkable Australian who was at once *The Times* correspondent in Peking and a doctor. Unlocking the brandy cupboard he poured a large brandy but Lu-Ching feebly waved it aside. Kershaw insisted and finally almost forced the first gulp down his throat. It was a serious breach of etiquette for Lu-Ching and he remained silent while Kershaw called one of the Legation messengers and sent him in search of Dr Morrison.

Half an hour later, with the sword slash bandaged and the brandy releasing his frozen psyche, Lu-Ching began to tell his story.

The Boxers had come back to the yamen as he expected, but now they were carried on the flush of many new victories, and demanded to put him on trial at once. Again he rode to the temple with his secretary but now he was taken to a specially prepared apartment where a square table placed upon a platform had two empty chairs arranged as in a Chinese hall of judgment.

He knew that he must at any cost maintain his high status and dignity as a magistrate and he boldly pushed one chair aside and sat in the other at the centre of the table. The Boxers were annoyed and muttered among themselves, but then the Six Immortals sat around the table enclosing him and robbing him of his customary distinguished isolation.

The ceremony of the wicker shield and yellow banner followed. A man, even more ragged than his fellows, took the shield and banner, waving them wildly about each other. The banner was of yellow satin with red flames and the ideographs spelt out the two words "Imperial Command".

Lu-Ching knew that he must respond at once. "I am by reason of my position as magistrate in duty bound to kowtow to the Imperial Command," he said and directed his secretary to call the three kneelings and nine kowtows. No sooner had he carried out the ceremony than the man wielding the banner deliberately thrust one end into the incense burner and slowly the smell of burnt cloth and smoke increased until a flame leapt and there before Lu-Ching's eyes the most sacred symbol of Her Majesty the Empress Dowager of China was deliberately demeaned and destroyed.

Couching his protest in elaborate Chinese to emphasize the gulf between himself and these common people he raised his voice for the first time from the flat authoritative tone he normally used, and an odd thing happened.

His secretary had failed to halter Lu-Ching's horse Po-Jo properly, and suddenly the beautiful black animal appeared at the doorway, the sound of his master's voice drawing him on to try to enter the chamber itself. The proceedings came to a halt while a lithe young Boxer attempted to persuade the horse to leave, but such was the bond between man and beast that the animal dipped and dodged, evading all efforts to control it and slowly tried to force its way towards Lu-Ching. A plan formed swiftly in Lu-Ching's mind. If he stayed for the judgment, now, he knew that he was doomed. They would condemn and behead him within minutes.

"I will handle him," he said, coming to his feet, and before anyone could stop him he had leapt on Po–Jo, set him at full gallop and scattered Boxers and benches in his path. A sword slashed his cheek as he passed but he felt no pain. Every fibre of his being was concentrated on urging the horse to greater speed and once out in the open he swerved and turned as guards tried to stop him and then he was away, bending his body low on Po-Jo's, lifting and rising as if he were one with the animal.

The chase continued for half an hour until they entered the maze of lanes and side turnings which made up the meaner parts of Peking.

Once into the maze he used his intimate knowledge of the streets to twist and turn until he had thrown them completely off the scent. Next he headed for the London Mission, explained to the missionaries what had happened, said he must warn his friend Kershaw in the British Legation, disguised himself as a peasant and set out on foot.

Now he said to Kershaw, his voice hoarse with exhaustion:

"They are massing to attack the Legations. Either you must

fly — which will be very difficult — or you must ask for soldiers and barricade Legation Street."

"Why have you come to me?"

"You once saved my life Mr Kershaw. I could not forget. But I also need sanctuary — for a time."

"You have never met Sir Archibald Mainwaring?"

"No."

"He is hardly likely to take advice from you. We can try when you are rested. I'll arrange an audience with him."

The meeting, Kershaw knew, was a foregone failure. Lu-Ching repeated his story but Sir Archibald found it distasteful having anything to do with what he now regarded as the enemy and he could not believe that this small, sallow man, even when bereft of his pigtail, spotlessly clean and clothed in elegant Chinese tunics was either a distinguished magistrate or a reliable source of information. According to Sir Archibald a Chinaman of any class or kind remained loyal to the Chinese and he suspected a plot to plant this man in the Legation with false information about the steadily mounting power and horror of the Boxers. Either they wanted to create panic, or drive the Legations to make an ignominious retreat down the line to Taku. British pride, Sir Archibald believed, required that the British, if not lesser breeds like the Americans and Germans, must out-face these threats and remain calm.

It was not until the following day that he decided to call a meeting of the Corps Diplomatique and repeat once more Lu-Ching's story.

There was a small silence afterwards and then the Deputy Minister, Major Colin Fraser Shelham, said in his clipped way: "If they are murdering their own magistrates — why not murder us."

"We must not put too much store by this melodramatic account," Sir Archibald said. "And there's something else that worries me. I can't understand why he should come rushing into the Legation. Why didn't he take refuge in the Imperial Palace. Supposing for instance he is a planted spy and all this has been contrived. We have no way of checking."

"Checking!" exclaimed Monsieur Bleriot. "We don't need to check. There are scores of such stories."

"The sword slash," Major Shelham said. "He did have a sword slash."

"It could have been caused by a brawl," Sir Archibald countered. "And they are quite capable of making the story convincing by inflicting one."

The meeting rumbled on explosively for an hour but by then there was no doubt about it: the Corps had decided at last in favour of asking for troops from Taku. And then, to the anger of Sir Archibald, Monsieur Bleriot revealed that he had already sent such a request to Taku.

"You cannot speak for all of us," he protested.

"I spoke for the French."

"But you pre-empted our meeting."

"Someone had to pre-empt something — we are drifting into disaster."

"Did you notify the Tsungli yamen?"

"No."

"But that is absurd. They will close the Peking gates against them."

"We can ask the Tsungli now."

"It seems to me," Sir Archibald said icily, "that you fail completely to get your priorities right. Indeed, I begin to doubt that you know the meaning of the word."

As symbolic representative of the Empress, the Tsungli yamen controlled all movements in and out of Peking. Allowing foreign troops free passage into Peking meant a loss of Chinese face which the Tsungli yamen could not countenance. It was decided to telegraph Admiral Seymour, commander of the Allied Fleet at Taku, and request free movement from the Tsungli yamen simultaneously.

A week later, as dusk came down, Kershaw slipped away into the labyrinthine streets around the Legation and made his way to the magnificent Yung Tin Men gate by which the guards would enter. Normally closed at dusk, the gate was still open, but a sight which filled him with apprehension flowed from the gate to the railway terminus. Thousands of truculent Mohammedan soldiers were concentrated there, with the obvious intention of annihilating any intruders. Making his way swiftly back he found the streets filling with mobs, who openly threatened him, and as he passed the Curlew Mission he saw European women disguised in Chinese costumes being wheeled out in crude carts, travelling as peasant women would travel and heading fast for Legation Street.

Half an hour later he re-entered the British Legation, crossed the outer courtyard and was moving across the theatre on his way towards Sir Archibald's office when a woman's voice called softly: "Kevin."

It was Lucy Shelham. As he turned and saw her lit by the lanterns, she seemed unreal, her face fragmented by the flickering lights. It did not destroy the grace of her features or the warm glow of her eyes and chestnut hair.

"You've been avoiding me," she said. "Why?"

"For God's sake!" he cried. "You know why."

She laughed. "You're so damned conventional, Kevin. You're so afraid of what other people think."

"Of course I am. This place is a glasshouse. Do you imagine they're not already talking?"

"They never stop," she said. "So where's the point of worrying."

"What do you think would happen if Sir Archibald thought I was having an affair with you?"

"But you're not."

"So long as they believe it — " He gestured.

"I've made a decision," she said.

"Tell me some other time," he replied. "I must see Sir Archibald."

"It's important. It can't wait," she went on.

It was his turn to laugh. "We're all about to be slaughtered, and you have made a decision which can't wait."

"I'm going to ask Colin for a divorce." As she spoke she took Kevin's hand and tried to draw him into the lampless theatre. Half resisting, the touch of her hand acted like a magnet and he was in the shadows almost before he realized it.

She reached up and offered her lips to him.

"This is madness," he said. "And *I must talk to Sir Archibald.*"

"There's another stuffed dummy parading around in a fancy uniform."

"Do you know what's happening outside?"

"We're all going to be put to the sword, aren't we?" she chuckled softly.

"I shouldn't make too much of a joke of it."

"If we're going to die, we're going to die."

"It isn't death," he said. "It's the way of death."

"Are you afraid of dying?"

He hesitated before he answered. "I've faced it twice. I didn't like it either time. But I was young then. Now — " he gestured.

"You talk like an old man."

"I am."

"Nonsense."

She put her arms round him and reached up again. He pushed her away.

"Not here," he said.

"Listen — Colin is going to dinner with Bleriot. I managed to get out of it. I'll come to your room at eight o'clock."

"You certainly will not. . . . "

As they talked on, somewhere in the background a deep murmur began and slowly increased in volume. Footsteps came from the direction of Sir Archibald's office. Kevin pulled Lucy behind a fluted pillar deeper in the shadow. The tall, pale ghost of Sir Archibald went striding by with his curious stilt-like walk.

By now the murmur was increasing to a roar.

"What are they up to now? Let's get out of here. You go first. Yes — now — " he gave her a push.

"See you tonight?"

"Certainly not. I shall lock my door."

Across the courtyard he could see a group of Legation staff at one of the square windows looking out on Legation Street. He joined them. Thousands of Chinese were milling around the street and making gestures which were openly threatening.

At that moment a missionary, his hair caught in a pigtail, his tunic and cotton shoes those of a peasant, came panting along pushing a wheelbarrow holding two children. He had to force a passage through the crowd and the guard opened the main gate momentarily, quickly slamming it shut again.

A small hunched man with cadaverous features, the missionary lacked only the slant to his eyes to be completely Chinese. He nearly collapsed in the courtyard but no one hurried to help him. There was nothing the Minister hated so much as these Europeans who abandoned all class distinctions and tried to live like the natives, with coarse clothes, pigtails and a brand of broken Chinese excruciating to the ear.

At last, Kevin and two other staff members went over to help him.

The missionary stammered out his story. "They have murdered everyone in the Mission — mutilated their bodies. We disguised the women as Manchus. They were caught and raped. It's terrible — terrible."

He spoke like an automaton. Some powerful check was preventing his emotions from working.

Recoiling from the smell of the missionary, Kevin led all three to the bathrooms in the student quarter and returned rapidly to the window overlooking Legation Street. He felt someone push in behind him a moment later and there, once again, was Lucy. "Do you often play Sir Galahad?" He didn't answer but felt the pressure of her body as she leant against him.

There was a new hubbub in the distance. Presently a great howl went up from the mob and there at the end of Legation Street the guards — American, British, French, Japanese — came marching up the street in perfect order with fixed bayonets. A detachment of United States Marines, led by a huge sergeant major, headed the procession. It was an ordered piece of human machinery glittering with arms and discipline in a sea of squalor and confusion.

The crowd became even more threatening. For a moment it looked as if they would surge forward, attack and simply overwhelm by sheer numbers the small marching phalanx, but bayonets held with such rigid precision, moving relentlessly forward, dismayed even the more reckless.

The group at the Legation window cheered. The cheer was taken up in other parts of the Legation and a shiver of relief seemed to run through the whole compound. Tongue-tied people began to talk, gloomy faces relaxed and an English sergeant major came striding in asking for Sir Archibald Mainwaring.

The French were the first to break ranks and they all began brushing each other down from the terrible Peking dust, cursing the *sacrée poussière*. Other detachments headed towards their different Legations. The British — a few score pink-faced sailors, some tougher Marines and a handful of officers — went through the dust-brushing ritual and one N.C.O. said, "Where's the bloody emergency."

And then, immediately behind Kevin and Lucy, a deep voice called out, "See some action now."

Colin Fraser Shelham was a thickset, balding man whose presence emanated great physical power. Once an army major, he still spoke in clipped phrases but the apparently innocent eyes were searching Kevin's face in a way which made him uneasy — or did he imagine it?

"What d'y' think Kershaw," Shelham said, gesturing towards the troops.

"Not enough," replied Kershaw, for some reason finding it helpful to imitate Shelham's clipped manner.

Shelham gave a neighing laugh.

"Oliver Twist asks for more!" he exclaimed fatuously.

"A lot more," said Kershaw, and was aware of Lucy withdrawing her body and turning round to face her husband.

"One Englishman's worth a thousand Chinese," Shelham said.

"One million Chinese equals one thousand Englishmen. I think we've got about eighty."

"Bloody pessimistic. No call for pessimism. Everything's going to be fine. Well m'dear. Must rush. Seeing the Frogs — shan't be late. Entertain her Mr Kershaw, she needs entertaining."

As the mob outside slowly dispersed Legation Street came alive in a different sense, with people talking, drinking, walking from one Legation to another, the gaiety becoming almost obligatory.

At nine o'clock that evening Sir Archibald sent a telegraph to Admiral Seymour: "No more ships wanted at Taku unless matters become more complicated which I do not think they will."

Simultaneously, in the far left wing of the Legation Lucy Shelham knocked on the door of Kevin Kershaw's small room and as he whispered a refusal slipped swiftly in. When she put her arms round him and reached up to his lips he made no response. When she persisted he gently disengaged her and said, "I'm hopeless Lucy — you would be very disappointed."

"I don't believe you," she replied. "You're simply scared."

"Maybe I am," he said. "Doesn't that disappoint you?"

"Yes, it does." She closed her arms round him and tried to kiss him again. He picked her up then, and even before he reached the chair into which he lowered her, the sensuality of her body under its flimsy dress had stirred him.

"You can't stay long," he said. "It's too dangerous."

"What a damned coward you are."

"Yes, a devout coward."

"Why did I have to fall in love with you of all people? There isn't another man on the staff who isn't goggling to sleep with me."

He began pacing round the room. "Let's talk about something else," he began.

"Don't tell me I'm physically repulsive."

"Exactly the opposite."

"In that case — "

"I can't make love to women unless — "

"Unless what?"

He waited a long moment before he said softly, "I love them."

"And you don't love me."

He frowned. "It takes so long with me," he said. "Love grows very slowly."

"Do you want it to grow?"

He hesitated again.

"I don't know."

"Why don't you know?"

"It takes months, but then it runs so deep I'm in the power of the person I love — and I don't like being in the power of anyone."

"I'm in your power already," she said. "And I love it."

"Do you?" He stopped pacing to look down at her. "Let's be

realistic, Lucy. Nothing can come of this."

"I'll divorce him."

"Don't be crazy. I'm not in a position to marry anyone. And think of the scandal. He'd lose his job — "

"I don't mind scandal."

"You'd be ruined, too."

"If escaping from misery is ruin, then I'm all for being ruined."

"We don't know a thing about each other. I might be a madman in disguise. This is only the sixth time we've met."

"All right," she said. "Tell me about yourself."

At first he refused to talk but slowly her persistent questioning made inroads on his reserve and she pieced together something of his story. The story of his Chinese mother who owned a restaurant in New York and his father, an unsuccessful lawyer turned professional alcoholic. They had educated him at Yale University where he read law and languages like his father, but when he came to try to conduct cases in the Chinese quarter he found their minds so tortuously engaged in reading a different logic into events that he decided he could not cope. He should have understood, because he was half Chinese, but American logic was so deeply programmed into him it confused even his sense of identity. He travelled the world, then, taking odd jobs wherever he could get them and since he now spoke five languages became, wherever possible, an interpreter. Some inexorable demand of his blood drew him back to China to discover the nature of his roots and here he had remained for eight long years.

"What about you?" he said as he answered her last question.

"Nothing much about me," she said. "I've told you half of it. The stereotype story of a girl brought up to sew prettily, play the piano prettily, make love prettily and dote on her husband." She filled in the details. She told him of the intolerable snobbery of her Kensington family, the feuds and rivalries between father and mother and two sisters. She, the eldest, was left to look after herself, while Rosa and Mary, the younger sisters, were spoiled by her parents who used Lucy as a pawn in their quarrels, blackmailing her into taking sides until she could no longer bear the murderous atmosphere. It frequently led to her mother saying "I'm going to murder your father." There was sufficient venom in her mother's voice to make the phrase sound sinister. She met her husband, Colin, at a Royal Garden Party in the grounds of Buckingham Palace where peacock men preened themselves in morning coats and top hats and women concentrated considerable ingenuity in displaying parasols and hats of elaborate designs. He was a major in the Queen's Light Infantry, slim, handsome, full of conventional charm. Above all he lacked any sign of that intensity her family so deliberately cultivated and it was this, she claimed, which drew her to him. Twelve years older than she was, he became a satisfactory father figure.

"Don't let's *talk* any more," she said, cutting off her story abruptly.

He was sitting on the bed and she went straight over to him, pushed him back and began kissing his brow, nose, lips, but tenderly now without the urgent passion with which she had greeted him.

He was deeply stirred by the time she stopped, but he sat up abruptly. "There's no time," he said. "You must go."

She pushed him back again and as she lowered her breast against his chest he at last kissed her very gently on the lips.

The knock on the door made them jump apart. Kevin put his fingers on her lips, motioning her to silence.

"Mr Kershaw! Are you there Mr Kershaw?"

It was Lu-Ching speaking in Chinese. The knock came again and the door handle turned in the locked door.

"Mr Kershaw I have urgent news for you. Are you there?"

They remained frozen, silent.

Two minutes later the softest shuffle of receding footsteps from cotton soles disappeared down the corridor.

"You must go at once," Kershaw said.

But she took him into an even deeper embrace and he had to struggle physically in his insistence that she must leave, now, before Lu-Ching returned.

She reached the two rooms reserved for the Deputy Minister in the south wing of Sir Archibald's oriental house barely ten minutes before her husband came back. He was a very different person from the man she had married and as he came in he brought with him a combination of smells she found distasteful — drink, sweat and stale cigar smoke.

CHAPTER IV

CHAIO MIN HSIANG or Legation Street ran parallel to the great Tartar wall. Beginning at the Chien Men Gate, the Dutch, American, Russian, German and French Legations came first, and finally the British, which was a natural sanctuary, protected on two sides by other Legations.

At five o'clock in the morning, as the very pink Chinese dawn began to glow, a crowd of refugees, lumbered with luggage, carts and children, came pouring down Legation Street towards the British compound. They told stories of the great fires started by the Boxers which had destroyed homes and missions and were threatening to reduce the city itself to ashes. They came white and trembling into the compound, and some collapsed once they felt safe within its walls.

Kershaw had risen early, determined to go out into the city and discover which of the wild rumours had any substance. As he made his way through the refugees to the main gate he suddenly saw Lu-Ching heading fast towards the Legation with another man stumbling close behind.

"Where in God's name have you been?" Kershaw said.

"I would like to talk to Sir Archibald at once. I tried to find you yesterday. No one knew where you were."

Kershaw laughed. "Sir Archibald at this hour will be soundly asleep in bed like all the other respectable Ministers."

"They are mad!" Lu-Ching said. "At any moment now the attack may begin. This is Hai-Fung, the gate-keeper of Ha-ta Gate. Let him tell you."

A middle-aged man, Hai-Fung was weeping as only certain Chinese could weep, without tears or any movement of the features, but with a low, soft moaning. He did not pause, or vary the note, he simply maintained an anguished crying from somewhere deep inside him.

Kershaw sniffed at the man. If there was one thing which

drove Sir Archibald or the Deputy Minister to near rudeness it was a Chinese peasant who stank of sweat and soil. This man had no smell. He was a relatively well-to-do gate-keeper, but his moaning would disturb the whole Legation.

"They've prepared a communal kitchen to cope with refugees," Kershaw told them. "We'd better go there first."

As they made their way from the north-east corridor, a tall apparition suddenly appeared at the far end, and there, to Kershaw's astonishment, was Sir Archibald.

"You're up early, sir," he said as they met and Sir Archibald automatically stood back against the wall.

"Too much damned noise in the night," growled Sir Archibald. "Who is this?"

"You remember Lu-Ching."

"Oh, yes — how do you do."

"He has a report from the city. He's been out gathering information."

"Splendid!" Sir Archibald said. "But who's this? And — " dropping his voice " — can't you stop him making that din. He'll wake the whole place up."

"He's the Ha-ta Gate keeper, Hai Fung, sir."

"I don't care what he is. For God's sake stop the noise."

"Lu-Ching wants you to hear his story, sir."

"Must I?"

"Lu-Ching says it's important."

"Come to my office."

He swung on his heel, stalking back down the corridor. It was still half dark in his office as Sir Archibald lit the kerosene lamp. He pulled the blinds and said, "Let's get it over fast. I have a heavy day ahead of me."

The gate-keeper began with his usual protestations. "May my tongue be torn out if I utter falsehoods — "

"Yes, yes!" Sir Archibald said. "Get on with it."

Then came the story. His father and mother, wife and four children had all been burnt alive by the Boxers. They had set fire to a whole street of wooden houses and pushed his family into the flames with spears. As fast as they screamed and recoiled from the agony of fire, spears were thrust into their limbs and bellies and they were forced back into it again until they collapsed in agonized unconsciousness.

Translating as he went, Kershaw deliberately dwelt on each new and horrifying detail, but Sir Archibald suddenly cut him short and asked, "What's happened to the missionaries at the Catholic Cathedral?"

Lu-Ching took up the story. The Reverend Robert Childs was trapped by the Boxers, with his wife and children. They prepared a beheading block and when they were ready called him to the block. His wife clung to him screaming, but he managed to disentangle himself and walked calmly and with great dignity to the block. Instead of beheading him, they chopped off his arms and legs one by one, and left him there rolling in death agonies while three Boxers raped his wife and then beheaded her.

"Enough!" Sir Archibald interrupted. "I have heard enough."

Lu-Ching added flatly, "They have burnt the cathedral to the ground."

"My God." For the first time it seemed that the horror of the situation had broken through his defences. Sir Archibald began to question Lu-Ching about the situation in detail. No longer were Europeans mere Yang Kuec-tzu or foreign devils: they had been promoted to the proud estate of ta mao-tzu or long-haired ones of the first class. "What does mao-tzu mean?" Sir Archibald asked. Kershaw translated. "Mao-tzu is a contemptuous term referring to the hair of animals, and unshaven Europeans are now classed with the beasts, something to be destroyed without a qualm."

All converts had become mao-tzu, or second-class hairy ones. As for the third class, san mao-tzu, it consisted of all those connected in any way with the work of the foreign devils from servants to messengers, cleaners to shopkeepers.

"Are all Christians supposed to die?" Sir Archibald said despairingly.

"The religious persecution is only a façade," Lu-Ching said. "The ultimate aim is the extermination of all Europeans."

"Oh, come," Sir Archibald said. "How can they do that. We have the assurance of the Ysun-yamen that they will protect us and we have our own guards, haven't we."

That night as the gates piercing the Tartar wall were closed by the Imperial Guards a great tide of sound rose and fell in waves, beating against the wall like huge pounding fists. The Boxers were massed in their thousands, chanting in chorus "Sha-shao — sha-shao — kill and burn — " in ever-increasing crescendo.

Kershaw and Lu-Ching made their way up to the top of the wall and looked down on to the confusions of the Imperial City. The mighty ring of outer fortifications, the Yellow Lama temples in the Tartar City, the Temples of Heaven and Agriculture and many of the Manchu palaces all rang tonight with one terrible litany — "kill, kill, kill — ". Even as they watched, flames began to shoot up as the Boxers recklessly set fire to buildings in the very centre of the city, the flames leaping from one wooden construction to another with malevolent rapidity.

The great Tartar wall on which they stood was fifty feet thick and both were thinking what impenetrable protection it offered when suddenly thousands of sparks ascending from the inferno caught the pagoda tower facing the Chinese City and the ornate pile began first to smoke and then the teak rafters — brought to China six centuries before — caught fire, the foundation of the tower followed and out of the hundred small square windows — once lined by archers — flames came licking to concentrate in the funnel of brick, and shot hundreds of feet into the air, a great fountain of fire which left Kershaw awed and drove Lu-Ching to mutter, "Where, oh ancestors, are the reasons for this?"

Twenty minutes later they became aware of a change in the scene. The roar of the Boxers, "Kill — kill — kill!" diminished and died away. Far down from the top of the wall, tens of thousands of ordinary Chinese came out of hiding and began fighting the flames, trying to salvage homes, merchandise, relatives. The red sashes of the Boxers dwindled in number and dispersed. As if even they were dismayed by what seemed a whole city in flames, appalled for the first time by their own handiwork, they slid back to their haunts leaving the city to weeping, despairing citizens who had no part in their barbarities and desired only to return to the dust-laden indolence of Chinese peace.

Kershaw asked, "What are our chances, Lu-Ching?" The roar of the fire drowned his words and he had to shade his eyes against the flying sparks. He shouted a second time, "What are our chances?" Lu-Ching shook his head. "We shall both be with our ancestors before very long."

For the first time Kershaw thought what a split-second horror it must be to be beheaded. Split, yes — but was it a second? He had known the executioner driven to a second and third blow, like some ghastly butcher learning his profession. Perhaps the first appalling shock numbed the senses, perhaps the second set all the arteries pumping death, but what went on in the still-conscious brain between the second and third blow as the half-deserted body leapt like a bow from a shock which tore into every fibre of its being?

In the morning a sudden impulse drove him to climb the wall again alone. The devastation shocked him. Where there was once a mighty bustle of human beings somehow contriving to find order in disorder, now there was near silence and thousands of houses with skeleton walls, charred out of all recognition. The great tower which had blazed so wondrously the night before was only half standing, its mighty brickwork partly defeating the flames and still proclaiming the contempt of the Tartars for the pigmy barbarians, so far removed from the paladins of old. Moving his eye slowly over the panorama, it seemed to him that Peking could never be the same again.

But it was not the great fire, or the mutilated missionaries, or the slow invasion of refugees, or even the wild vacillations of the yamen who one moment promised Chinese troops to protect the Ministries and the next said there was no danger, which drove the troubled mind of the elegant Sir Archibald finally to take action.

It was an event which took place in total isolation from the general scene and involved a sacred symbol of the European civilization which the Legations had striven to create amongst Chinese barbarity.

The news reached Kershaw first from Lu-Ching. The grandstand, built by Chinese sweated labour, to give the European gentlemen a better view of the horse races which represented in their view one of the finest flowers of their culture, had deliberately been burnt to the ground by the Boxers.

"My God!" Kershaw said to Lu-Ching. "Now they've done it."

"Done it?"

Lu-Ching could understand a wide range of English without being able to speak it, but phrases like "now they've done it" were beyond his comprehension.

Kershaw spent some minutes trying to explain the colloquialism and when he failed, simply said, "The holy of holies has gone up in smoke," compounding Lu-Ching's confusion. Seeing his incomprehension, he said, "Let's simply say that now Sir Archibald will take action."

He did, the following day. The Corps Diplomatique met that afternoon and a message was telegraphed to Admiral Seymour in Taku: "Situation in Peking hourly becoming more serious. Troops should be landed and all arrangements made for an advance on Peking at once."

CHAPTER V

A STATE OF SIEGE had been declared. Barricades of up-turned carts, rubbish, bricks and stones were thrown across the streets, every able-bodied man was given a weapon of some kind and asked to take his turn in manning the defences. Water and food were to be rationed and the steady flood of refugees controlled, but neither actually happened. At first only English refugees were accepted, and even they threatened to swamp every corner and facility, but pleading mothers and Chinese converts quickly broke all regulations. Slowly chaos built up. Within a few days and nights jostling proximity became a menace to raw nerves, tiredness and anxiety made tempers short, rumour and counter rumour flew round the Legation.

The big question remained: were they going to accept the offer of safe conduct through the Chinese soldiers and Boxers, or was it all a conspiracy to lure them to the certain death predicted by the Australian Dr Morrison and Kershaw?

The diplomatic meeting was tense. Frequently called on to translate, Kershaw had hardly uttered a few sentences when one Minister or another interrupted. Eleven sorely tried and very anxious Ministers struggled to conceal their fear, behave rationally and find some wise course of action in a situation which flatly excluded anything so esoteric as wisdom. A proposal for all eleven Ministers to visit the Tsungli yamen and demand safe conduct was torn to fragments and finally defeated. The meeting became stormy. Sir Archibald and Monsieur Bleriot were at loggerheads, with Bleriot bursting into a torrent of gesticulating French and Sir Archibald going red and saying nothing. At last, Baron von Ketteler turned to Kershaw and said in German, "Tell them I have a previous appointment with the Tsungli yamen at eleven o'clock and in spite of a possible state of war I intend to keep that appointment

— come what may."

When the meeting broke up the Baron returned to his Legation and Kershaw decided to follow him. Asking for audience, Kershaw told him he was mad to venture out beyond the barricades, even with heavily armed guards.

"I have evidence that the Boxers will murder any white man who ventures out of Legation Street," he said. "I have it from a Deputy Chinese Magistrate himself."

"Nonsense," replied Baron von Ketteler. "I am going and I do not intend to take any guards — they would be sheer provocation."

Some innate sense of superiority and aristocratic disdain combined to convince him that he could, by sheer force of social distinction and personality, dominate any danger that might arise.

Kershaw's last appeals were brushed aside as he watched the Baron climb into his official red and green chair with his dragoman in a similar contrivance. Two Chinese outriders moved off with the Baron, and Kershaw stood hesitating while precious minutes slipped away. The American man of action was brought to a standstill by the phlegmatic Chinese. One side of him counselled resignation to the inevitable. That part of his character which kept him withdrawn from life and action, left him in a state so incongruous it became farcical. . . . Meditation. . . . This situation required meditation. . . .

And then for the first time in years some wildly contradictory impulse suddenly welled up from — nowhere — and he seemed to observe himself — out of control — rushing round to the stables to commandeer a pony and ride furiously after them. Loosening the massive Mauser pistol he now carried in his belt he tried to analyze as he rode what had driven him to take this course of action. He liked the Baron and admired his courage, he wanted to discover what was really going on beyond the Legation and . . . could it be that he wanted to test his own courage in physical danger? Whenever asked he always claimed to be a devout coward but he had never really been put to the test. Violence seemed to melt on his appearance and even in the worst areas of New York no one had even so much as threatened him, but given the threat he would have retreated.

Here and now, in a far worse situation, he had suddenly reacted differently. Why? The question was still echoing in his mind when he came within sight of the four men and simultaneously a shot rang out. The Baron slumped in his chair, the dragoman dashed out of his chair dripping blood and the two outriders simply turned tail and fled. Kershaw pulled his pony into the shelter of a house and hesitated. A hail of bullets continued to pour round the broken sedan chair. Charging towards it in a rescue attempt was certain death and even the new-found man of action did not contemplate it, but remaining where he was meant death too, because now the Boxers were beginning to pour up the street firing wildly in all directions.

Only one course of action seemed possible: turn back to the Legation, rally the German battalion and come in force to rescue the Baron, or recover his body.

As he rode away and bullets whistled after him the sweat of fear ran down inside his flimsy clothing. It was the first time in his life that he had been under fire and he bent low over the pony, urging it on with every fibre of his trembling body. Somewhere at a deeper level a terrible sense of inadequacy, cowardice, or was it simply guilt, caused him to redouble his efforts. And then, slowly, as he rode, at an even deeper level he felt the still pools of Chinese resignation absorbing his reactions, reducing their urgency and melting them back into a world where the transformation of physical events by action was a sadly mistaken activity because in the end nothing was changed.

His story, when at last he told it to Sir Archibald, shattered the last remnants of optimism in the Legation. Within hours a new flood of refugees poured in, with ponies and mules struggling to move between the piles of packing cases and human beings, all searching for a resting place. Missionaries who once bullied Chinese peasants into accepting Christian dogma were wandering helplessly among their flock, some cowering in the deepest corners afraid that the bloody scenes they had so vividly witnessed would soon be reproduced here. The great Director of Chinese Customs and Scholarship, Sir Robert Hart, sat on an old mattress, paralyzed by the turn of events and unable to invoke the stoicism he believed he had acquired from years of saturation in Chinese culture. Dr Morrison, *The Times* correspondent, sat gloomily contemplating the useless stacks of his books which he had rescued as they were about to be converted into barricade-fodder.

A kind of spontaneous combustion, peculiarly British, was already producing a proliferation of committees and as Kershaw moved from group to group he found at least three food committees were busy selecting members in complete ignorance of rival committees. Orders and counter orders came from every direction. A sandbag committee had more men directing operations than filling sandbags; men walked around ostentatiously bearing rifles which they could not fire; stores of ammunition were being painfully counted by women who had no idea where to find equivalent weapons; nurses and mothers battled with each other over lavatories; children sat in heaps, some howling, some fighting.

Suddenly a few stray rifle shots came from beyond the barricades and pandemonium broke loose. Fifty ponies tore away from their tethers and went tearing round the compound, scattering human beings in all directions. Men with wavering rifles peeped over the barricades at a completely invisible enemy.

Pushing through the chaos Kershaw made his way towards Sir Archibald's office. In the outer office he found Sir Archibald's secretary solemnly sitting with complete composure under a table. The man everyone required was missing.

"Sir Archibald," the secretary informed Kershaw without emerging from her shelter, "is in conference with the American Minister at the American Legation."

He stormed out of the office and as he turned towards the main gate there, coming straight towards him, was — once again — Lucy Shelham.

"What are you going to do in all this?" she asked unexpectedly. There was no sign of emotion.

He shrugged his shoulders. She seemed irritated. "Surely you're going to do something?"

"What we need at the moment," Kershaw said, "is a commander."

"What we need," Lucy replied, "is somewhere to cook for this mob."

It was a new practical Lucy. She was looking round, shrewdly measuring the chaos. "That ornamental garden," she said. "One could clear it out and sink some cooking pots. Oh, by the way, your Chinese pal was looking for you again."

"Where is he?"

"He was in the Chancery a few minutes ago." Her voice dropped. "Oh Lord — here comes Madame."

Lady Mainwaring bore down on them with a stride oddly reminiscent of Sir Archibald's. She was wearing a blue silk summer dress and a wide-brimmed straw hat more suitable for Ascot than a state of siege.

"Lucy," she said ignoring Kershaw. "We've simply got to get some sense into all this. I told Archibald this morning he must take over — but you know what he is — paralyzed by English modesty. Don't you think modesty's out of place in a situation like this?"

"Absolutely," Lucy said, thinking how immodest were her thoughts about Kershaw.

"Someone's got to keep check on the food, the water, the cooking."

"I was thinking," Lucy said, "that we could convert the ornamental garden into an open air kitchen."

Lady Mainwaring frowned. "I'd hate to disturb a beautiful garden," she said and then, stiffening, "but that's nonsense. There's no time for niceties — we shall have cholera and typhoid breaking out before we know where we are. Can I leave it to you to do something about cooking arrangements — but you will consult me first, won't you."

"Don't you think," Lucy replied, "that if we all go about consulting each other we shan't get anything done?"

"We can't have everybody going their own way," Lady Mainwaring said sharply. "Look what's happening now. All these committees all over the place — all contradicting each other. We must have leadership. I told Archibald again this morning — we must have leadership."

"Do you agree I convert the garden into a kitchen?" Lucy asked with a decisiveness which once again surprised Kershaw.

"Does it mean tearing everything up?" said Lady Mainwaring.

"I'm afraid it does."

"Oh all right — go ahead — but don't do more damage than is necessary, will you. . . . Ah, Mr Kershaw." She had deigned to notice him. "What role do you propose to play in all this?"

"My usual one of interpreter, Lady Mainwaring."

"Yes," she said. "It's going to be difficult to issue commands in six languages. We shall certainly need you. Why are you smiling? There's nothing to smile about."

Kershaw's smile expressed his amusement at the automatic assumption that the British should lead. Sir Archibald was not the senior minister in the Legation Quarter but his wife had swiftly readjusted diplomatic ranking.

"To be quite frank, Lady Mainwaring," he said, "I don't know why I was smiling. It's a habit I have in certain situations."

Lady Mainwaring never knew quite what to make of Kershaw. She suspected that under his retiring appearance he concealed a mind capable of insights far beyond the endless parrotting required by his profession. "If you'll excuse me Lady Mainwaring," he said, "I have to see Lu-Ching."

"Lu-Ching? Who on earth is Lu-Ching?"

"Don't you remember the Chinese magistrate who sought sanctuary in the Legation?"

"Extraordinary thing for a Chinese magistrate to do — I don't understand." Ignoring Kershaw once more Lady Mainwaring continued, "What are we going to do with all these converts Lucy — we can't feed everybody — Archie tells me Colin has been deputized to find somewhere to put them. Frankly I think they should go back to their own people."

In the course of the next five minutes of conversation Kershaw was glad to be ignored and he slipped away almost unnoticed. He found Lu-Ching sitting in the courtyard beside the theatre, oblivious of the sun now beating down with fierce intensity.

"I'm waiting to see Sir Archibald," Lu-Ching said.

"He's with the American Minister," Kershaw told him. "What's the news?"

"The Empress summoned an Imperial Council two days ago. She was shown a document which was really an ultimatum. It came from the Governments of the Legations. It demanded that the collection of revenues and the conduct of military affairs throughout the Chinese Empire should be placed in the hands of the Foreign Ministers."

"I don't believe it," Kershaw said. "They're crazy, but not that crazy."

"Wait." said Lu-Ching. "Something far more serious also appeared in the document. It demanded that the throne should be restored to the Emperor."

"And your source for all this?"

"That is why I wanted to see Sir Archibald. My position here has become very complicated. There is a spy in the Legation who thinks I, too, am an agent for the Empress. He comes and goes easily through the Water gate at night. He tells me that this document containing the ultimatum is not a true document — it was forged by Prince Tuan."

"Who is this spy?"

"He worked in the grain shop in Legation Street before it was sacked."

"We must arrest him at once."

"It would be wiser not. He can come and go with much freedom. He is a good source of information, of what your people call intelligence and he thinks I also am a man of concealment."

"What will the Empress do now?"

"She will issue her own ultimatum in reply."

"We must see Sir Archibald at once."

It was one hour later when Sir Archibald at last returned and received them in his office. The Minister's Office was a square room with an oval table, set under one of the windows, flanked by two elaborately carved filing cabinets. The room reflected three of his deepest devotions — the swivel chair, to his job; the books, to Rudyard Kipling; and the portrait of Queen Victoria, to monarchy.

An ironic smile deepened on Sir Archibald's face as he listened to Lu-Ching's report. At last he said:

"I'm afraid, Lu-Ching, your information is out of date. I

knew about the forged ultimatum. Before the death of von Ketteler, in fact. You must realize we still have the right of direct communication with the yamen. At least six of these fancy scarlet envelopes have landed on my desk. One of them contained another ultimatum — from the Empress to us. Here — read it." He thrust an enormous piece of heavy parchment at Lu-Ching. "The ultimatum expires at four o'clock today. Either we allow ourselves to be escorted to safety or the yamen will not be responsible for what happens. There will be a meeting on the lawn outside my residence at three-thirty. I do not trust the yamen's escort. I have no intention of moving a yard. Come to the meeting at three-thirty. . . . "

The news of the ultimatum spread through the Legation and more than a hundred people gathered on the lawn that afternoon, among them Captain Strouts, commander of the Royal Marine Light Infantry. At first the meeting had the air of a casual social gathering, with women in summer frocks and cartwheel hats. While they waited two student interpreters laid out a clock golf course on the lawn in preparation for what Sir Archibald referred to as "a possible period of enforced confinement."

As the deadline of the ultimatum approached, people ceased to stroll and gossip and gathered in groups which one by one fell almost silent. At three-fifty Sir Archibald looked at his watch and said, "Ten more minutes and we will know."

His wife standing beside him said, "Do you really expect the Chinese to start a war punctually?"

"It's not exactly a war," he replied tetchily. A hush descended on the company as the minutes ticked away and presently one student interpreter began counting down the time. The sky was brilliant blue, the sun burnishing the scalloped tiles and upswung eaves of Sir Archibald's residence. The Union Jack lay inert against its flagpole in the heat. The scene became as immobilized as a tableau.

Four minutes . . . three . . . two . . .

Suddenly heavy firing broke out in the east which was the location of the Austrian Legation. A sergeant marched up to Captain Strouts and saluted. "Firing," he raised his voice to make himself heard above the musketry, "has commenced." Captain Strouts saluted in return. "Thank you, Sergeant Murphy."

The siege had officially begun.

As the small group dispersed Sir Archibald turned to Captain Strouts and said, "There is a spy in the Legation. Mr Kershaw will take you to him. Have him arrested."

CHAPTER VI

A TERRIBLE SENSE of inadequacy overtook Kershaw as he watched Sir Archibald, Colin Shelham and Captain Strouts turn swiftly away from the group and move purposefully in different directions. It was as if they were fulfilling some prearranged plan in which he had no part. He stood there hesitating in the burning sun. The urge to withdraw to his room, take up his copy of the *I Ching* and bury himself in its pages was strong. Among the six books which followed him on his travels two contradictory volumes provided frequent solace. One, *The Origin of Species*, flatly contradicted the mode of thinking of the other, the *I Ching*. He chose according to mood, and the urge was now towards the *I Ching*. As he was about to turn away he suddenly realized that Lu-Ching was still standing beside him, and he said, inconsequentially —

"What do you think of the *I Ching*?"

"Forgive me," Lu-Ching replied, "but the matter of the spy is in my mind. If my counsels have any meaning, and I know they do not contain much, it is very unwise to arrest him. It will bring to an end one of my most important means of communication."

"I don't think you'll change Sir Archibald's mind," suggested Kershaw. "Spies to him are something you shoot."

"Surely they will not shoot him!"

"Not without some sort of trial."

As he spoke he thought — was there ever a man less suited to the requirements of a siege than a Chinese-American interpreter born uncomfortably close to the Bronx in New York City, hating manual labour, knowing nothing of guns or military strategy and divided in his allegiances. He was likely to become more help to the Chinese than the English. Of course he could always retire into his books or his fantasy world which was rich, but what would Sir Archibald say if he ever discovered the nature of those fantasies. . . .

"You are listening to the wind Mr Kershaw. It is important to be present on certain occasions."

They went off in search of Sir Archibald to protest at the imminent arrest of the spy but when they found him he was too busy to see them.

"Nobody seems to want us," Kershaw said. "Let's go to my room and talk." His room, which was a very minor affair in a tight corner of the left wing of the Residence, had once belonged to Pretty Poo, Lady Mainwaring's maid. It contained a table, chair, bed and a finely carved Chinese chest, with rush matting on the floor. Two hours later they were still undisturbed and deep in conversation about the *I Ching* when there was a commotion in the distance.

Shouts, cries and pounding feet suddenly broke in upon them.

"It can't be the Boxers already?" exclaimed Kershaw.

Lu-Ching shook his head. "Those are not Boxers."

Kershaw hurried down the corridor, out into the compound and made for the main gate with Lu-Ching following at a dignified pace. There they witnessed an astonishing sight.

Captain Wiedmann, who commanded the forces protecting the Austrian Legation, came pounding in followed by his men. "Savage attacks — overwhelming numbers — taken by surprise — no guns. . . ."

Within minutes another rush of men brought the French and Italians back from their barricades, all talking volubly.

Captain Strouts hurried up with Sir Archibald, both demanding explanations as the compound quickly filled with a mass of armed men, all jabbering in many languages. They pushed and jostled, stumbled over each other's weapons, cursing and fuming in complete confusion. It looked as though the whole of the semi-circle of armed forces protecting Legations to the north and south had simply abandoned their posts and retreated into the British Legation in one appalling rout.

Sir Archibald was dumbfounded and furious. Momentarily he could get no sense out of anybody. "Silence!" he shouted — "Kershaw, ask that damned Austrian what this means."

Captain Wiedmann explained that the Austrian position

was a very exposed one, which took the brunt of the first Chinese assault, and when they retreated towards the French barricades, the French had turned and fled to the Italians and the Italians led a further retreat into the only safe place — the British Legation. This was palpably untrue since the Austrians had arrived first.

Sir Archibald exploded. Courage, organization, morale — all had gone up in smoke at the first burst of gunfire. They must get back to their posts at once. At any moment the Boxers could simply come pouring into — he paused and literally shouted — "The British Legation" as if the holy of holies was about to be violated.

And then to compound burlesque into terrible farce, the Americans manning the Tartar wall — the main point in the Western defences — also came pouring into the British Legation, leaving yet another appalling gap and openly cursing their officers as they did so.

By now the French, German and Italian Ministers had joined the throng in the courtyard. The missionaries and their lamb-faced converts added further confusions. Yet another incident now occurred. A large part of the armed forces intended to protect the Legations were falling into line and standing very much at ease awaiting the next move as if all threat to their safety had been removed and they were merely on parade.

Slowly a crowd of civilians concentrated around Sir Archibald's tall bony figure. Kershaw felt that Sir Archibald sensed his moment had come. He waited while the shouts, arguments and jostling subsided and then Bleriot called for silence. A rifle slung over his shoulder, his slouched hat at an angle, his manner ingratiating, he appealed to Sir Archibald to take supreme command before they were all slaughtered. He spoke in rapid French, and Sir Archibald signalled to Kershaw who pushed his way through towards him.

He wanted the whole assembly to understand what Bleriot had said. "Translate." Sir Archibald snapped. "But hurry." Afterwards there was applause and cheering, with a number of the missionaries chanting, "We want Sir Archibald! We want Sir Archibald!"

He smiled, saying simply, "You honour me — and I accept. But we are in an emergency. Everyone must move fast. I will prepare the first Order of the Day."

It would have seemed impossible that any further absurdity could add to the comic-opera nature of these events but before he had a chance to announce his first Order of the Day the plenipotentiary Ministers struck from him the very authority with which they had just invested him. Kershaw laughed silently to see the French, German and Italian Ministers moving among their troops and simply ordering them back to their respective Legations with a total disregard for the fact that such orders should now come from Sir Archibald.

He also admired the iron control with which Sir Archibald checked his fury and pushed his way towards his office, gesturing for Kershaw and Major Colin Shelham to follow him. Once inside, he at once appointed Shelham as his Chief Staff Officer and told Kershaw to stand by for translating orders.

It was a different Sir Archibald who now emerged. Indecision vanished, relaxation gave place to alertness and his long-winded sentences were cut short. Kershaw found a kind of theatricality in the transformation. It was as if Sir Archibald modelled his behaviour on a preconceived stereotype he had read about in some military biography, but it was soon evident that, stereotype or not, the new impersonation removed the old ineffectuality.

"I want you, Colin, to make a survey of our defences right away," Sir Archibald said. "Take Captain Strouts and Kershaw with you."

"My wife would like to take over the cooking," offered Shelham.

"I think she should organize the domestic side generally. My wife's planning a hospital in the Chancery. We must get that food committee working at once. How many wells are there in the Legation?"

"Five," said Kershaw. "Two fresh water — the rest dubious."

As they talked on he thought — I'm going to spend the rest of the day with Shelham.

"Take a look at this rough map." To Kershaw's surprise Sir Archibald had already sketched in a crude outline of their defence system, if any such haphazard accumulation of upturned carts and sandbags qualified as a system. He pointed with a ruler. "The Americans on the Tartar wall here, and the Russian Legation there, effectively protect the British Legation from the West. The French, German, Austrian lines and the Japanese in the Su Wang-fu mask the East, and the Imperial Carriage Park — big open space easily covered by rifle fire — makes attack from that quarter difficult. North is covered with buildings belonging to Chinese government — they won't want to destroy them. Only real dangers to British Legation are these two corners — " he pointed " — to the north and south-west. I want you to go out and check on the accuracy of all this."

It did not occur to Sir Archibald, Kershaw reflected, that he was giving top priority to the British Legation as the kernel of defence and was clearly prepared to relegate the other Legations to the role of sacrificial outposts. But since popular consent had made him Commander in Chief, and the British Legation naturally fell into the best defensive position, perhaps he was right.

Ten minutes later the three men set off, Captain Strouts proceeding with short quick military steps, Shelham stalking beside him and Kershaw loping uneasily in the rear.

"Seen any fighting before?" Shelham asked over his shoulder to Kershaw.

"Not fighting," Kershaw said. "I saw von Kettler killed."

"Did you, by Jove. Nasty business. You're going to enjoy this, Strouts."

Captain Strouts was a taciturn person whose countenance had long learnt to iron out any unnecessary expression.

"I wouldn't say enjoy."

"What are our chances?" asked Shelham.

"Fifty-fifty. If they've got any artillery they can simply blow our barricades to hell."

"You married man?"

"Yes."

"You, Kershaw?"

"No."

"Nearly said lucky man. Damned impertinence to my wife. Wonderful woman. Which way we heading, Strouts?"

"Prince Su's ornamental garden, sir . . . we're almost into it."

A rattle of fire sent a series of bullets hissing dangerously close, and Strouts and Shelham automatically flattened themselves on the ground. Kershaw ducked his head and stood there, a swaying frightened figure.

The fusillade stopped as suddenly as it had come. "Have to learn to take cover, Kershaw. Mustn't be sitting duck."

As they entered the great outer wall of the Su wang-fu — eighteen feet high and three feet thick — they were greeted by a dapper Japanese Colonel. "This position's hopeless," he said. "Too many walls — too many buildings — too much cover for enemy."

He had fifty men on a fortified hillock in the ornamental garden, the post commanding a great stretch of territory which was split by endless interlocking walls and dragon-adorned roofs.

They approached a barricade. Kershaw exercised the whole of his considerable reserves of self-control to conceal his fear, but his hands were sweating as he bent low to peer through a loophole. One bullet penetrating some small and equivalent aperture seemed destined to find him, he felt, and he swiftly shuddered aside as a shower of brick dust fell from the parapet.

Shelham laughed. "Rough stuff, Kershaw, you'll get used to it."

Strouts was peering through another loophole. "They're building brick barricades — many barricades. Sheltered by one, they move forward another. Someone's directing them. That's not just the Boxers. It's the Chinese army."

A single shot rang out and they all ducked. "Snipers," observed the Japanese Colonel: "Plenty snipers." They moved on the centre of the Fu which held Prince Su's Palace and his retainers' quarters. On the southern side they came upon droves of Chinese refugees. Entering the first building, they found scores of native schoolgirls, all wearing sober blue coats and trousers, sitting in row after row on the ground. Some were combing their hair, some working on sandbags, some simply staring into space but all were quiet with that ultimate imperturbability of the Easterner who has passed through unease and fear to the final stage of resignation. Three generations sometimes crowded for reassurance on big straw mats, others gathered in family groups on the hard earth.

Kershaw spoke to a mother trying to feed a child with half dry breasts. She said that they had been besieged in the French Mission for days without food. Now there was so little to spare she was already near to starving, and how could she be expected to feed her daughter.

"We have organization," commented the Japanese Colonel, "but food for soldiers only."

Organization, yes. The Colonel had drafted every able bodied man and woman into barricade or sandbag work directed by Boss Men with white labels written in square Chinese characters. At a small table two writers with brushes and ink were keeping records of everything that happened. Organization — yes. The Colonel said he knew the state of his barricades and the disposition of his men at any hour of the day or night. The refugees — did he worry about the refugees? No — he did not keep reports on refugees.

Following a network of alleys and barricades they moved on to the Italian position. There, Lieutenant Pinoni was sitting far in the rear of his troops, stripping a Bologna sausage with a knife which he used to eat and punctuate his words almost simultaneously. "Our Legation burnt down so we retreated here." Excitedly he added, with dangerous gestures, that no one — but no one — would pass through his barricades. "Do you always lead your men from the rear?" Captain Strouts asked sarcastically. "But always — always," Pinoni assured him, almost stabbing him with the knife.

They watched a sharpshooter place his sailor cap in front of an empty loophole and leap swiftly to the left. The Chinese poured half a dozen bullets around the hat and, immediately the fury ceased, the sailor leapt up and fired back, disappearing at once behind the barricades again. Other Italians manning the post simply lay protected on their stomachs, firing off wildly with an appalling waste of ammunition. Captain Strout's protests were met with a torrent of Italian patois which

Kershaw found difficult to interpret. "Must let them know we are here" was the best he could manage.

The French post next, and there the first serious shock. A man had been hit and lay groaning, his stomach pouring blood. It needed a tremendous effort of will to stop Kershaw's medical reflexes taking over. That was something he had never told Lucy. Amongst his other failures was eighteen months as a medical student, ending disastrously when he performed an amateur abortion on a woman student. They had fired him for that, and afterwards he turned to the law because he felt that not only had justice to be seen to be done — it had to be seen to be believed. The thought of becoming an amateur doctor in an improvised hospital with no antiseptics, anaesthetics or instruments appalled him as he watched the wounded man. At any cost he must conceal his unfinished medical training, but it was hard to resist the impulse to go to the aid of a man who could be bleeding to death. As he watched he hesitated, as he hesitated his resistance weakened and then out of nowhere came two Frenchmen with a plank of wood they were using as a stretcher. The man slumped into unconsciousness as they strapped him to the plank and carried him away.

Shelham said, "Get used to it Kershaw — all do."

Captain Strouts made a few careful notes on his map, and they moved on again. Across Legation Street the link with the Germans was by loopholed barricades connecting the Germans with the French, the French with the Austrians and the Austrians with the Japanese.

"What about Tartar wall?" Shelham asked.

"Americans and Germans," replied Strouts. "Look, you can see them." They were lying flat on their faces, in their slouch hats and khaki suits, already under heavy fire.

"We'd better check," Shelham said.

"Wait until the firing eases up," advised Strouts. Kershaw's relief was immense. Within a few minutes the firing faltered and fell silent. They made their way, sweating, up the long ramp of the Tartar wall.

On the wall, behind their sandbags, the Americans were mutinously silent. They refused to talk. They had been browbeaten by Sergeant Jenkins into holding their positions, the most exposed and vulnerable of any. At last, when Strouts insisted, Sergeant Jenkins told him, "Listen, buddy, I'm running this show — not you."

"I represent the Commander in Chief," maintained Strouts, coming to attention.

"Commander in goddam chief, eh?" Jenkins spat noisily. "Okay buddy — just tell him he can do a spell on this wall any time he likes."

Shelham intervened. "Realize great danger. Send relief soon."

"Soon is too late. Make it right now." A huge round-shouldered bear of a man, Sergeant Jenkins seemed to dwarf Strouts and Shelham and did not trouble to conceal his contempt. Strouts remained unmoved. By sheer military personality he matched up to the challenge Jenkins represented.

"You'll be hearing from us," he said and headed once more for the ramp.

They now re-approached the British Legation from the rear and as they made their way through the empty courtyards and houses Shelham exclaimed: "My God! Look! Nobody here!"

"Yes," Strouts said. "It's a weak spot. A very weak spot."

As if aware of their words an enfilading fire began and made further approach almost impossible. Every kind of bullet from iron ones with a deep mutter, to nickel-headed moderns spitting treble notes filled the air with a horrible music.

Kershaw shrank into himself. However were they going to make it back into what suddenly seemed the illusory safety of the British Legation?

The fusillade increased with hundreds of bullets ricochetting from walls, trees, roofs, sliding from one surface to the next, thereby setting up a humming which was to become a familiar background sound.

"Double down and run," Strouts shouted, upon which he hunched himself and ran with an agility which surprised Kershaw. Shelham followed him. From the protection of the further wall both men looked back. A surge of conflicting emotions held Kershaw rooted to the spot. Fear of mutilation, humiliation, anger that his weakness should be revealed by a man like Shelham, and a sense of misplaced destiny — what was he doing in a situation like this? — all combined to paralyze him. Distantly he heard Strouts say to Shelham, "Let's leave him. He'll follow."

"Come on, Kershaw," Shelham shouted. "God's on our side!" He let out his snorting laugh.

Kershaw closed his eyes, drew a deep breath and stumbled rather than ran the length of the wall. He was white and sweating when he joined the others.

"Good chap." Shelham patted him on the back. As they entered the rear of the British Legation Kershaw couldn't make out what had happened to the old Shelham. As Deputy Minister he should have sneered at Kershaw's cowardice. A completely new tolerance appeared in his character.

Walking back through the compound Kershaw felt he was in a different world. No sign of the enemy, no bullets, unmarked sandbags and scores of healthy young men from the junior ranks of the Legation Staffs, all quite capable of playing an active role, simply idling in the background or desperately displaying a zeal for committee work. They matched his own deepest desire to escape any real involvement in the horror which had come upon them.

Sir Archibald received their report with reassuring noises. "Good — good — " he kept interjecting, and then suddenly he seemed to change his point of view. "I've received a report on our so-called guns. The Italian one-pounder is more or less useless — the Austrian machine-gun should throw 200 bullets a minute but doesn't — the Nordenfeld refuses to work. We have just one efficient gun — the single-barrelled Colt." He laughed. "Imagine that — a single-barrelled Colt against batteries of heavy artillery!"

"There are rifles, sir," Strouts said.

"Oh yes — I'd forgotten the rifles." Momentarily they were all deadpan and then everyone laughed.

CHAPTER VII

LADY MAINWARING'S BEAUTIFUL bedroom was in chaos. Her silk curtains had been torn down to join the exquisite satins of Prince Su's concubines as material for sandbags. Some of her sheets were ripped and rolled for bandages, her spare children's cot occupied by a sick child, her own two children, Andrew aged six and Vanessa, nine, playing cowboys and Indians among the piles of clothing. Two sewing machines whirred ceaselessly in one corner, one driven by her maid, Pretty Poo, and another by a girl from the customs service.

At her dressing tablc, converted into a desk, she sat cheek by jowl with Lucy Shelham surveying the domestic dispositions. Lucy filled in the details on a map as Lady Mainwaring read them out. This building had gone to the Russian staff, that to the French, a third to Imperial Customs. The stable house was full of Norwegians, the rear pavilion divided into eating messes, the Legation chapel turned over — in part — to American missionaries. As they worked, Lucy Shelham was thinking — and what purpose will all this map-making serve except to fill in time and make us think we are doing something important. Lady Mainwaring seemed to hear her thought.

"At least we know where everybody is — and the men won't get mixed up with the women," she said.

Dire threat, Lucy reflected. In the middle of a death-dealing siege the men might get mixed up with the women.

"What would you do if a Boxer came bursting in at that door this very moment?" asked Lady Mainwaring.

"I should shoot myself," replied Lucy.

"Shoot yourself — whatever with?"

"I've a gun."

"You have a gun?"

"Colin gave it me — in case of trouble."

"Do you mean to say you carry it with you?"

"No — not at the moment." What a shock Lady Mainwaring would have if she knew that she had given it to Kershaw with instructions to shoot her if the Boxers — the word she had used was "arrived".

"That's not very efficient, is it. You intend to kill yourself, but you've mislaid the gun."

"I haven't exactly mislaid it."

"Do you believe in God?" Lady Mainwaring asked irrelevantly.

"I'm not sure."

"Not sure? I can't stand agnostics."

"Sorry," Lucy said firmly. "I am one."

"I like people to be one thing or the other."

"Does that mean you'd prefer me to be an atheist?"

"Yes."

Lucy felt like saying, you've hit the nail on the head. I am in fact an atheist but I daren't admit it. She changed the subject hurriedly. "Don't you think you should draw up menus?"

"Yes — it would help to save food. We've got the ponies — they'll have to go for meat. We have rice and flour — the water's all right — and loads of wine."

"How about making a siege pancake out of bits of cereal, rice, stale bread and baking powder to make it rise."

Lady Mainwaring's laugh surprised Lucy. Until now a machine-like efficiency had brooked no relaxation. Now her laugh was warm and spontaneous and the strong lines of her face softened.

"Let's work out a day's menu — and get everyone to stick to it."

"It's my children I worry about." Lady Mainwaring surveyed their finished list. "We must have it posted on the bell tower."

"I suppose I'm lucky, not having children," said Lucy.

Lady Mainwaring looked at her, amazed.

"Lucky," she said. "You really mustn't say that. I mean what's the point of marriage if you don't have any children."

If only she knew, Lucy thought, about my small brown sponge and its soap-saturated pores; if only she realized what risks I took in that first year of marriage and how disastrous it would be now if I did have children.

"Perhaps I shouldn't probe," Lady Mainwaring said. "People don't like talking about such things."

"Oh, I don't mind," Lucy replied. "We just seemed unlucky, that's all." As she said it she thought — hypocrisy comes naturally and unquestioned in my relations with Lady Mainwaring. It not only makes life easier to let her think you agree with her but in this situation is absolutely essential.

Suddenly the sound of the bell on the central bell-tower began to peal.

"I wonder if we're under attack," Lady Mainwaring said with matter-of-fact calm. Lucy was astonished. She felt her own heart beat faster. The rapid ringing of the bell on the tower was the agreed signal for everybody to rally for an emergency.

"We'd better go," said Lady Mainwaring, throwing down her pen.

Outside in the compound the nature of the trouble quickly became evident. The narrow northern end of the Legation was surrounded by a rabbit-warren of Chinese houses which pushed right up to the Legation walls. Creeping stealthily in, the Chinese had thrown incendiary torches with such skill that half the houses were blazing before anyone realized what had happened. People were pouring out of the Legation buildings, with pots and cans of water, as Lady Mainwaring and Lucy arrived.

A long, lean Yankee missionary seemed to be directing operations. Lady Mainwaring strode over to him. "Who put you in charge?" she demanded.

"Your husband, I guess," the Yankee drawled. "We need everybody — you prepared to help?"

"Well. . . . " Lady Mainwaring said and looked sharply at Lucy.

"My God!" Lucy exclaimed. "Look at that!" Behind them, on the south-western corner, a flurry of flames had suddenly leapt fifteen feet into the air and a great black cloud alive with sparks began to drift over the Legation. "They're trying to burn us out." Lucy's voice trembled.

Ignoring Lady Mainwaring the Yankee missionary bawled, "Make a double line from the wells — use anything — " A ragged line of men and women began moving to and from the wells. Lady Mainwaring hesitated again, then she rolled up her sleeves, said "Come on Lucy", hurried over and grabbed a bucket. The only empty pot left beside the well was a *pot de chambre.* Momentarily Lucy quailed at the idea of publicly carrying such an object, but then she muttered, "No time for niceties", filled it from the well and ran, spilling half the contents, across the compound. Lady Mainwaring repressed her laughter simply to maintain Lucy's dignity. "I wonder what next," she said as they struggled along side by side. Already social distinctions were diminishing, human responses breaking through. It was Lady Mainwaring's lack of fear which most worried Lucy. As she hurried to and fro carrying her minimal contributions she wondered whether Lady Mainwaring simply lacked enough imagination to realize that her life was in danger. No — she wasn't highly gifted imaginatively, but she wasn't a fool either. It was sheer upper-class English control which kept the efficient Lady Mainwaring in the ascendant, and that worried Lucy because she knew her own control was slender. As she paused and looked at the leaping flames her heart began pounding, and her body poured with sweat. Ever since, as a child, she had fallen into the fire, uncontrolled flames represented to her a hell which could disfigure her for life one day, just as that early fall had left its scar on her left breast and hip. Death by burning . . . she redoubled her pace, spilling half the contents of the *pot de chambre* before she reached the fire.

Lady Mainwaring materialized beside her. "Do you know what they've done?" she hissed, unaware of the black smudges on her cheeks and her hair beginning to fall about her face. Without waiting for an answer she rushed on, "They've set fire to the Hanlin. Think of it, the Hanlin! It's too horrifying. . . . "

Lucy had heard about the Hanlin, first from her husband and then from Kershaw. He had talked for a whole hour, comparing respect for scholarship in East and West. In the West it was acquired and in the East in the blood, and the Hanlin had become the temple where the holiest tablets were laid, a sumptuous feast of learning, centuries of accumulated labour by the leading scholars of the Celestial Empire.

Thousands of volumes, some clad in silk covers, some heavily embossed, some in tooled leather crowded the endless unvarnished shelves. In a country where a knowledge of classics was respected by prince and beggar, the Hanlin enshrined untrammelled pedantry and brilliant scholarship in volumes whose worth was beyond measurement.

These sentiments had seemed to Lucy grossly exaggerated. She hesitated to hit back at a "lot of old books full of out-dated ideas", but she could not see why they seemed to be worth more than an equivalent number of human beings. Now, pre occupied with her spilling pot, she said, "Oh yes, the Hanlin."

"You speak as if— " Lady Mainwaring began but her words were overwhelmed by the Yankee missionary moving down the line and bawling, "Keep moving — keep moving!"

Lucy hurried towards the fire. As she threw her water into the leaping flames it seemed absurd. Nothing short of an ocean would quell them, and then she saw, through a gap in the flames, a group of marines smashing a hole in the wall to gain entrance to some rooms which they wanted to convert into a firebreak. A rattle of rifle fire from the Chinese, and the marines threw themselves to the ground. A moment later some were up again, working under covering fire from the others. At last they broke in, firing at close range and the Chinese retreated.

Now the cry went out for every able-bodied person to fight the fire. It must be stopped at any cost because the whole Legation was at risk. Lady Mainwaring became a fury of energy, filling, carrying, emptying with a total disregard for rank, her dress torn, her hair dishevelled, her cartwheel hat split and abandoned; and Lucy marvelled at the sheer concentration she brought to the work.

Priceless books were thrown and tossed about like rubbish, water poured on to silk-covered volumes, heaps of smouldering pages written by masters of the Chinese brush dashed into dragon-adorned pools. Suddenly a gaunt figure gathered up an armful of the books and was making back into the Legation when Lucy challenged him. "Put those down — they don't belong to you," she shouted.

"They don't belong to anybody," he replied. "They've got to be saved."

"Who are you?"

"Mind your own business."

Lady Mainwaring came up alongside Lucy. "Don't worry," she shouted above the roar of the flames. "He's one of those crazy old Sinologues. I forget his name."

"But he may be pinching the books."

A rattle of fire drowned out the words and everybody went flat except Lady Mainwaring and Lucy, who stood there swaying slightly, feeling frightened and absurd. Two minutes later everyone was at work again. Slowly the flames began to subside. Gradually the extent of the cultural destruction revealed itself as the smoke cleared and the gunfire ceased. The centuries-old rafters had collapsed on the half-burnt books and the scene, with water flooding everywhere and the acrid smell heavy on the air, was desolate.

"I think we've done enough," Lady Mainwaring said. "Let's go back to the house and clean up."

CHAPTER VIII

When Kershaw was appointed one of Sir Archibald's personal runners he received the news with dismay. It meant that he must make several forays carrying messages to hard pressed points under constant fire. In the British Legation he was relatively safe. The bullets flew high overhead but the enemy remained invisible, and no threat of frontal assault troubled the English marines. Kershaw found himself about to sally forth to the French, Austrian and American defences, and no activity was more dangerous than moving in the open between one barricadc and another.

Sir Archibald had no direct communication with outlying defences. Messages, orders, instructions — all had to be written by hand on scraps of paper, and long intervals elapsed before incoming messages could be answered.

At three o'clock in the afternoon, a message written on a grimy scrap of paper came from the Russian defences: "Please remove sandbag barricade blocking our withdrawal route to British Legation." The message ended with a graceful flourish in French. "*Veuillez agréer, Monsieur le Ministre, l'assurance de ma très-haute considération.*"

Sir Archibald wrote a reply on the splendid parchment paper of the Legation and passed it over to Kershaw for delivery. "Under heavy attack from the North. Can spare no men for this duty. May have to call upon you and Americans to help repulse attacks, so please have some men ready."

The message was no exaggeration. Attack by fire had quickly revealed the Legation's weaknesses. As the flames laid waste one section after another they cleared an area round the Legation which was useless to the incendiarists. Now, instead, they were concentrating on the northern defences, and ominously two nine-pounder Krupp's guns were beginning to play on these defences from the burnt-out tower over the Chien

Men. If the enemy concentrated their artillery fire and made it accurate the barricades must slowly crumble under the attack.

Kershaw put the message in an absurd pouch ceremoniously provided for him by Sir Archibald and moved cautiously across the compound to the first barricade. Already his mind was working fast to find a means of escape. If he managed to make it safely between the first barricade and the second, he could disappear in a rabbit-warren of ruined houses, sit smoking for half an hour, burn the message and return with a garbled reply.

For a long time he simply crouched beside the sandbags talking to a marine.

"The Chinks have got our number," the marine said. "They only have to rush us — chop chop — and it's all over."

Kershaw didn't reply. The marine went on talking. "Cut your balls off mate — that's the first bit — then they go for the cock — slowly do you bit by bit. Death by a thousand cuts — ever heard of it? Great choppers the Chinks . . . Sssh. . . . "

In the orchestra of noise Kershaw hadn't yet said a word. He buried his back flat against the sandbags with his arms spread-eagled as if he were trying to become part of the barricades.

The marine peered through a loophole, took careful aim and fired; the noise of the old fashioned rifle made Kershaw jump.

"Got 'im," the marine exclaimed jubilantly. "Got the bugger." He began reloading. Suddenly he remarked, "'Ere mate what's the matter — you're shivering."

"Am I?" Kershaw said, and bit off his words in an effort to stop shivering.

"And why don't you have a gun?"

"I'm a messenger, not a fighter."

"We're all bloody fighters in this," the marine said.

"Where do you c-come f-from?" Kershaw asked. He wanted to keep the conversation going but his teeth were chattering now and he felt completely humiliated. The marine did not stop talking for the next few minutes. He came from London — down by the docks — the old Dog and Puddle — on a Saturday night — with as many pints on board as you could take — and the old woman waiting to knock hell out of you because you'd spent half the rent — and the bloody factory siren in the fucking dawn, just when you wanted to sleep — it was worse than being behind these sandbags — hold it mate — listen to that . . . cheeky bugger, there he is — the moon-faced bastard — dead between the sights. Now . . .

The roar of the rifle made Kershaw jump again. A quite different voice with a different accent broke in. "Good show Johnson — damn good show — got him fair and square. I say, who the hell are you and what are you doing here?"

It was a young naval lieutenant standing half exposed beside the barricade with a nonchalance which Kershaw found offensive. "I'm a m-messenger," Kershaw repeated foolishly.

"Messenger — messenger?" scoffed the lieutenant, "then why aren't you messenging?" He waved a huge revolver dangerously and after a couple of flourishes brought it into direct line with Kershaw's head. "Don't want any shirkers at a time like this, do we — "

"He needs covering fire, sir," the marine said.

"Covering fire? Waste our ammunition covering a messenger — nonsense. The Russians are just over there — short sprint and you're across — no trouble at all."

"But," Kershaw began.

"No buts," said the lieutenant. "Get going."

"Don't you think, sir — " the marine said.

Kershaw straightened himself suddenly and interrupted:

"I'm the Commander-in-Chief's personal messenger. I have a vital message for the Russians. I must have covering fire. Sir Archibald authorized me to demand it."

"Demand — demand. I haven't heard a word from Archie. Ammunition worth more than gold — why should we — "

There was a sudden withering burst of fire which tore the tops off the sandbags and thudded into the brickwork. Where before an elegant lieutenant stood, now a convulsed mess of flesh and blood, broken apart and screaming, lay on the ground. Kershaw's heart stopped beating and a sickness assailed him. The marine had dropped his gun and bent over to the lieutenant. "Help!" he shouted over his shoulder. "Help — man hit."

The lieutenant lay still, now, muttering something. Standing there in twisted, useless silence Kershaw heard him say "Don't waste ammunition," and then the whole of his body went limp and his eyes ceased to roll in agony.

"Christ!" the marine exclaimed. "I do believe the bugger's dead."

He sat back on his haunches staring at his blood-soaked hands. "Christ!" he repeated, looking down as the ganglia slowly uncoiled itself from the lieutenant's stomach and flopped out on the hard earth, pouring crimson blood. The smell of blood reached Kershaw's nostrils and at last he could not stop himself— he turned away and was violently sick.

"You're a great help," said the marine.

Kershaw stood with his face pressed against the rough sandbags, his mind racing. A wonderful encasement of flesh and blood possessed of a miracle called a brain with a lifetime's accumulated skills had been wiped off the face of the earth by a stray piece of clumsy metal and an unknown assailant who had never met or even seen the object it destroyed.

And then a strange and horrifying metamorphosis took place. The broken body on the ground merged into another person, and there was a disarray of female clothing stained crimson and a neck contorted at an impossible angle. . . . His wife . . . as she lay after the suicide . . . the way he found her . . . the picture indelibly printed on his unconscious but religiously repressed for years. It came up out of nowhere so vividly, he felt the nausea about to repeat itself and knew that he must obliterate it or be paralyzed here against these crazy sandbags. But, as he shut his eyes and blotted out both visions, guilt took the place of fear and swept through him with a power which made him shiver as fear had made him shiver a few minutes before.

When he opened his eyes again the lieutenant's body had gone and the marine was saying: "You heard what he said — covering fire — here it comes, mate — get going. . . ."

A crackle of rifle fire all along the sandbags and, in the lull which followed, he raced out across the compound, trying to run sideways like a one-dimensional man because silhouettes were more difficult to hit. And then there was only one way to face the fear which paralyzed him — to challenge it, to expose himself, to extend his arms and embrace the bullets zipping round him and he was running with his arms outstretched knowing that if he was hit it would end the nightmare and he need never face it again. But he wasn't hit and as he flung himself down behind the Russian barricades he heard a deep voice say in Russian, "This fellow is mad!"

Twice that day Kershaw travelled from the British to the Russian Legation. At five-thirty in the afternoon the message he carried from Sir Archibald read: "It is absolutely essential that the Fu should be held at all hazards. I hope therefore you will order over as many of your men as possible."

The message he brought back read: "I am sending you my last ten men but I must have them back as soon as possible."

Kershaw read the message while he took cover from a burst of fire and somewhere behind his fear, at the back of his mind he reacted to these leisurely exchanges with sardonic amusement. They seemed so bizarre in the middle of a life-and-death battle. Since the outlying perimeters had no civilized resources the messages were written on grimy scraps of paper in uncertain handwriting. He almost waited for one to end, "I hope this finds you as well as it leaves me."

The following day he carried back to Sir Archibald a note — almost a letter — from Monsieur de Giers, the Russian Minister, which read:

> M. le Ministre,
>
> I regret that I am unable to share your view that by giving a nursing orderly a rifle you transform him into a soldier, or that a cavalryman with a cavalry carbine is worth two sailors with bayonets who have been trained in infantry fighting. Be that as it may I shall be most obliged if you will send me the fifteen men whom you were kind enough to promise me, together with coolies and whatever is necessary for burning down the Chinese houses. . . . They have just brought in a sailor wounded in the head; this leaves me with 57.
>
> With best wishes,
>
> Giers
>
> P.S. Another man has been wounded: This leaves 56.

Kershaw laughed as he read it. Any moment now they would be exchanging *billets doux*.

It was on the way back to the Legation that a bullet ripped open the arm of his jacket and sent a tiny red rivulet up his forearm which streamed so much blood it was dripping as he entered Sir Archibald's office.

"You've been hit," Sir Archibald said and automatically guided Kershaw away from the Oriental rug in front of his desk. Kershaw had not noticed the wound or the blood until Sir Archibald drew his attention to it. His eyes then followed the trail of blood crossing the floor and he was apologetic.

"You must go to the hospital," continued Sir Archibald. "Can you make it under your own steam?"

"I'm all right," Kershaw told him and began walking away.

"Can I have the dispatch?" Sir Archibald said.

"Oh, yes."

He tried to open the pouch but his fingers were sticky with blood. Sir Archibald opened it with fastidious fingers and took the message. "You know where the hospital is?" he asked as he read the message. "It's in the Chancery. They'll fix you up."

He turned back to a desk covered with maps and papers. He looked pale and tired and as Kershaw left the room he sank back in his chair, closed his eyes and for a few moments seemed fast asleep. Suddenly starting up again, he shook himself and took up the message.

As Kershaw approached the Chancery he was aware of stertorous breathing and someone moaning rhythmically. Inside he saw that the diplomatic dispatch tables had been washed and covered with surgical cloth which gave off a strong smell of carbolic and sweat. The verandahs had been walled up with sandbags to the tops of the windows and the heat — despite the fans — was intense with flies buzzing everywhere. It was a single-storey house with six rooms and there were mattresses and cots on the floor in the first two rooms. A group gathered round one bloodstained mattress. On it lay the moaning man. With a shock Kershaw realized that it was Major Shelham, and there, bending over him, was Lucy. Kershaw turned away and was about to retreat when she called him:

"Mr Kershaw — you're hurt — come back at once."

"It's nothing." He continued walking away. She hurried

after him, caught him firmly by the arm and said, "Don't be a fool."

He drew breath sharply as pain stabbed through his arm. "Where is it?" she asked. He showed her and she examined his arm. She dropped her voice. "Thank goodness it's nothing serious." Her voice became a whisper. "We're just trying to get a bullet out of Colin's leg. Come back and wait." She dropped her voice even more. "I love you." Kershaw was amazed at her matter of fact manner.

He wandered about the improvised hospital while he waited. A sick-berth steward from an English gunboat was preparing absorbent dressings from cotton wool and torn underwear. Two medical missionaries bandaging a sailor's arm were suitably shocked by his curses and blasphemous appeals to a god in which he clearly did not believe.

"You must keep still — you must keep still," a haggard-faced missionary repeated monotonously and was — as monotonously — ignored.

Odd trunks and boxes had been drawn together in one corner to form a bed. Sprawled on it was a soldier still wearing his Royal Fusiliers jacket but with a foot swathed in bandages and three times its normal size.

"What d'you think of this, mate," he called to Kershaw, and began singing in a tuneless voice:

"If I were a cassowary
On the shores of Timbuctoo
I would eat a missionary
Hat and coat and hymnbook too."

Kershaw grinned a suitable response.

"Took all day to make that up," the man said. "What they done to you? . . . if I get out of here alive I'm going to — " he gestured dramatically — "to every Chink I meet. Hey, that's bleeding bad — if I were you I'd get something done about it fast."

Again the matter-of-fact acceptance of the situation surprised Kershaw. If survival depended upon rapid adaptation these people were destined to live long.

"Mr Kershaw! Mr Kershaw!" It was Lucy calling him. He walked back to find Major Shelham already on his feet holding a piece of metal in his hand. His face was white and tense. Suddenly he saw Kershaw.

"Dammit man — we should know better. Never get hit first stages. Nothing serious?"

Kershaw shook his head. "A scratch."

A German doctor said in German, "Major Shelham — you must rest. It is dangerous . . . you may have a haemorrhage." Kershaw automatically translated.

Shelham nodded and Lucy begged, "For Heaven's sake be sensible."

"Misunderstanding," Shelham said. "Don't like the place. Rest elsewhere."

He was limping towards the door when suddenly he stopped, gasped and his hand went down to his heavily bandaged thigh. Lucy was instantly beside him, holding his arm. A Chinese orderly joined her and between them they manipulated him back to a second mattress and he sank down, wordless, his face set in an effort to control the pain.

A tall slim man appeared from the deeper recesses of the hospital, strode up to the group and asked, "Who's next?"

"He is," said Lucy, indicating Kershaw.

"Another damned Englishman. They've really got it in for us. My name's Roberts — Francis Kingsley Roberts — what's yours?"

As he spoke he was cutting away the arm of Kershaw's jacket and sensitive fingers lightly explored the gory furrow.

"Superficial," he commented. "Just needs a bit of antiseptic. You didn't tell me your name."

"Kershaw — Kevin Kershaw."

"You're the interpreter bloke, aren't you. They say you speak ten languages."

"Five."

"Great. We're going to need you here. In a terrible mess with a young Russian this morning." He turned away and called, "Mrs Shelham, can you spare a moment?"

Lucy walked swiftly over. "I've cleaned it up — you know more about bandaging than I do — can you deal with that?"

As Lucy went to work she said, "You'd think you were the only interpreter in the place. How many are there?"

"Five or six."

"I'm going to have to pull it tight. Tell me if I hurt you."

Kershaw said nothing but she watched his face as she tightened the bandage.

"How do you know about this?" Kershaw asked.

"I don't really know. I got bored — hopelessly bored — in India — that was his last posting — I took a course in first aid." She whispered: "We must meet soon."

Somewhere in a far corner a tiny voice began to alternate sobbing with the cry, "Baby hurt! Baby hurt!"

"It's a child. I must go. When can we meet?"

"I don't know."

"You look ill."

"I'm all right."

The sporadic rifle fire which had become the normal background to their lives suddenly caught Lucy in mid-sentence. She had begun to say, "I'm supposed to be off duty —" when a pandemonium of sound broke loose. The firing rose to a crescendo, exploding bullets crashed into and around the Legation, yellow tiles went flying to smash on the ground and the roar of return fire re-doubled. The deeper note of artillery added a menacing diapason.

Everyone had stopped to listen. As the muffled explosion of shells added a fearful counterpoint Kershaw muttered, pulling his arm away, "Must get back to Sir Archie."

At that moment the alarm from the bell-tower began to peal the slow note which meant a general attack. The instructions for such an attack were, "Every man to his post and those who have none stand by their doors." The whole Legation was suddenly alive with people moving into position and taking shelter, with some scuttling in near panic. As he hurried away Kershaw carried with him a vivid picture of Lucy, her chestnut hair coiled high on her head, her spotless white blouse swelling out to end in a ruff round her neck, her long skirts provocatively hitched for freedom of movement. The urgency of the moment did not subdue a brief sexual arousal in which his mind ran free in the wildest fantasy. He saw it later as a partial protection against the realities he was now about to face again.

"Where have you been?" Sir Archie began as he entered his office, and then he apologized, "I'm sorry. I'd forgotten." Several messengers were crowding the room and Sir Archie was in process of distributing farcical scraps of paper which allegedly controlled the battle order. Kershaw already knew too well what happened to some of those scraps. Many were read, scrupulously replied to — even under heavy fire — and then contemptuously tossed away. Autonomy was the preferred battle order. Only in the worst emergencies did central control sometimes assert itself. Whether such control paid off had yet to be seen.

Sir Archibald was trying to make himself heard above the roar of gunfire when a great echoing horn sounded from the direction of the Imperial City, and in a second was followed by answering horns and bugles in all directions. An abrupt silence, as sudden and menacing as the previous roar, brought all activity to a standstill. The whole Legation seemed to stand a tip-toe immobilized, apprehensive, hanging in the silence.

Within minutes speculation broke out all over the Legation. Sir Archibald hurried from his office with the words "What are they up to now? . . . Follow me, Kershaw." People were pouring out of shelters into the compound, talking excitedly. They crowded round Sir Archibald but he brushed them aside saying, "Later — later."

Sir Archibald knew that one factor remained constant to boost the morale of the besieged. He knew and they knew that Allied forces had stormed the forts near Tietsin and that Admiral Seymour had set out from Taku with two thousand men to relieve the Legation. As the fierce music of the long Chinese trumpets crescendoed again, sobbing on a high note and then suddenly dropping to a basso profundo, hopes were suddenly high that Seymour's approach had driven the Empress to call off the attacks.

Presently word ran around that a board with huge Chinese characters had been placed by a Chinese soldier on the parapet of the North Bridge. Sir Archibald and Kershaw hurried to an improvised scaffolding from which they could see the message.

"Can you read it?" Sir Archibald said. Someone handed Kershaw a pair of binoculars and he began translating as Sir Robert Hart — panting — arrived at the scaffolding.

There were eighteen black characters on the huge white board and as Kershaw began reading — slowly at first — Sir Robert Hart joined him and interjected alternative interpretations.

Sir Archibald said irritably, "I did ask Kershaw to do the job, Sir Robert."

"He's not a sinologue," Sir Robert said.

"Let him get on with it — and check later."

It was some minutes before the Imperial Edict was clearly understood. It read:

"In accordance with the Imperial Commands to protect the Ministers firing will cease immediately. A dispatch will be delivered at the Imperial Canal Bridge."

Sir Robert Hart raised some fine points of interpretation which Sir Archibald dismissed summarily. "The message is clear enough. Perhaps you'd like to write the reply. Will someone get a board and some brushes." Sir Archibald said tetchily.

Kershaw found his momentary triumph undermined. He could read and speak Chinese but he could not write it. Sir Robert's hurt pride prevented him from offering any help until Sir Archibald said, "Oh, come on, Sir Robert — this is life and death. We need a reply fast." At last the message was concocted and painted with care on a piece of board. "Your Edict received and understood. The despatch will be received from the Imperial Canal Bridge."

A large crowd had by now gathered round the platform and several Ministers from the Legations were talking together in an exclusive group. Suddenly the cry went up, "We need a messenger — any volunteers?"

There was a momentary silence. Kershaw froze in the silence. Would they ask him? If the whole episode was a trap, the first man to be shot down in a renewed attack would be the messenger, and no one came forward eagerly. And then at last a Chinese convert — a small man, all skin and bone — volunteered and was invested with the traditional long coat and hat. Kershaw breathed again. When the moment came to advance on the enemy's lines the messenger's courage suddenly failed, and he begged to be excused. Everybody gave him encouragement. Sir Archibald grew impatient, a marine sergeant offered him covering fire, and at last, with the big board waving uncertainly above his head, and decorated by a white flag, he moved out of the Legation. Twice he wavered and showed signs of fleeing back but urged on by cries and frantic wavings he persisted and at last reached the parapet of the bridge. After propping up the reply board, all pretence to courage or dignity vanished and he simply scrambled ignominiously back towards the Legation. Through his binoculars Sir Archibald could see that the board had been set askew on the bridge and was probably unreadable by the enemy. He remonstrated with the Chinese messenger but he flatly refused to return to set it straight.

Pouring out a flood of Chinese he said that a thousand rifles — which they could not see in the Legation — had been trained on him from positions just beneath the Imperial City wall. He would be shot to pieces if he returned. Sir Archibald went into consultation with Sir Robert but neither was sure whether the message could be read.

It was at this point that — mysteriously — out of nowhere Lu-Ching appeared on the scaffolding and said to Kershaw, "They will find a means of reading it — do not worry." Kershaw passed on the message to Sir Archibald.

"Where is Lu-Ching?"

"Here, beside you."

"Ah — yes. What do you make of all this, Lu-Ching?" Kershaw translated the conversation which followed.

"I make very little," Lu-Ching said. "The message must come from Jung Lu, the Generalissimo of the field forces — directed by the Empress. She is afraid that Admiral Seymour may reach Peking before she has won the battle against the Legations."

"So it's not only the Boxers now — it's the Chinese army?"

"Yes — but I am told that Admiral Seymour is having great difficulties."

"What does that mean?"

"He is making bad mistakes and very little progress."

Sir Archibald looked astonished. "Is this pure speculation on your part?"

"No. I have been talking to the spy you had arrested."

"But he is not a reliable source."

"He acted for me as an agent. I have come to ask you to release him. He will go into the lines and return once more with much valuable information. It is written in the nature of events as they begin to unfold according to a pattern many dynasties old."

"We may not need him if this works."

"I respectfully tell you that it will not work."

"I don't think we want depressing talk like that, Lu-Ching. Let's wait and see. Kershaw, go down to the barricades and see what you can find out."

Relieved to escape the continuous attentions of Sir Archibald, Kershaw threaded his way through the ruins to the front-line barricades and was astonished to find them empty. The English marines had clambered over the bricks and carts and made their way through the courtyards of the Hanlin, to enter the mass of ruins, equally deserted by the enemy and silent as a graveyard. Escalading several walls and hurrying down narrow alleyways he at last reached the unbroken wall-line surrounding the Legation. There, a group of English marines was standing fully exposed looking at the mysterious pink walls of the Imperial Palace not more than two hundred yards away.

Crowding outside the palace gates a vast array of soldiers, whose rich uniforms made a brilliant blaze in barbaric surroundings, held Kershaw's fascinated gaze. Black, gold, green, yellow jackets were matched by every variety of trousers, some with blood red streaks, some with black dragons; and the men who wore them tanned to chocolate by campaigning in the sun — carried great two-handed swords, bows and arrows, modern carbines, every variety of weapon, while above them fluttered blue, yellow, red flags and every variety of banner. The Kansu soldiery of Tung Fu-Tsiang's command were there, alongside the Peking Banner troops, and Jung Lu's special horsemen wheeling and turning in the slanting sun with the grace and ease of a disordered ballet. Infantry, gunners, cavalry, all intermingled in one vast kaleidoscope of colour caught and vivified by the fierce rays of the dying sun. But the Boxers, thought Kershaw at once. Where were the Boxers? Suddenly he found Lu-Ching standing beside him. "You followed me," he said. "Yes," Lu-Ching replied, "and absence of the Boxers would be inevitable once the Empress asked the army to take command. The army does not like the Boxers. They are a disturbing element to an ordered people."

"Do you believe in telepathy?" Kershaw said.

"What is telepathy?"

"Never mind. Tell me. Like Sir Archibald, I am puzzled. Why do you remain with us?"

Lu-Ching folded his hands deeply in his sleeves and remained quiet for a long minute. Then he said very simply,

"I am afraid."

"But the Boxers seem to have gone."

"Any Chinese sheltering in the Legation will be considered to be a Christian convert. The army dislikes converts almost as much as the Boxers do."

"But you are not a convert."

"No, I am not."

They stood in silence for several minutes and Kershaw reflected how little he really knew about a man like Lu-Ching, born in a different culture to a completely different way of life. Slowly his attention came back to the panorama spread out before him. The multitude milling round the palace walls came from another century, from a time when savage hordes were overrunning the world, and the isolated splendour of the pink palace walls, its scented eunuchs and despotic powers belonged to that barbaric past just as cruelly alive and vital now as it had been then. For ten minutes he observed the scene, comparing notes with Lu-Ching.

Kershaw then decided to send back word to Sir Archibald that he thought it possible to make open parley with the enemy, and they waited patiently while a Chinese convert set out to deliver the message. Twenty minutes passed before the man returned to say Sir Archibald was sending two members of the General Committee to enter into parley, and Kershaw groaned

— "The General Committee! Pompous asses who understand nothing." When the two men arrived he recognized them at once. One was a customs officer, still wearing his braided uniform, and the other Dr Morrison, *The Times* correspondent. That was a relief.

As a first step they moved to the verge of the defences and stood waving white handkerchiefs. The enemy was much too occupied with preening itself in gaudy uniforms to take much notice. Dr Morrison decided to force his presence on their attention. He would move forward, he said, with his hands high in the air. "Don't risk it," Kershaw begged, but to his surprise Lu-Ching said that the Chinese would respect neutrality. As the doctor moved towards a number of Kansa soldiers, they watched his approach with the highest suspicion.

At last a thin, sallow Chinese deliberately removed his sword, threw it on the ground and advanced from the Palace Walls. Approaching to within forty yards, they stopped and began hailing each other, Dr Morrison using his relatively limited Chinese. When that led nowhere Kershaw advanced to join him and began translating.

The officer first repeated what they already knew — that the message displayed on the board came from Jung Lu, the Generalissimo of the Peking forces. Yes, a new despatch, he said, would follow after a meeting at the palace presided over by the Empress Dowager. She was very distressed at what had happened, she had given the order to stop the fighting and now regarded the Boxers as fools. Morrison pressed him with further questions which he said he had no authority to answer. Finally he gave a farewell wave of the hand, turned and retreated cautiously. As he went he paused now and then to raise the head of some dead man, perhaps in the hopes of recognizing someone.

It was five days since the siege had begun and the garrison had killed scores of Chinese and injured hundreds more. Inside the British Legation there were two dead and six wounded. As Morrison, Kershaw and Lu-Ching turned to walk back into the inner Legation Morrison said,

"Let's hope it works."

"What works?"

"The cease-fire."

Lu-Ching said nothing, but shook his head. "Why are you so gloomy?" said Kershaw.

"Once they realize that Admiral Seymour has been delayed and possibly even turned back . . . " Lu-Ching gestured gracefully.

As they walked, the shadows lengthened, dusk came down and now they were surrounded by nothing but silent ruins, empty barricades, and every so often a Chinese corpse beginning to rot in the heat.

"Phew!" Morrison said as they passed one already decomposing. "We're going to need some protection against typhoid." Kershaw held his nostrils until they were well past the corpse.

The line of the North Bridge behind them became indistinct and disappeared, the roar of sound from the massed troops outside the Palace diminished to a murmur. As they reached the inner compound again, a messenger from the Japanese position in the Fu excitedly explained that they had seen rockets in the distance — could it be Admiral Seymour's force? Reporting back to Sir Archibald in his office, Kershaw found him quietly optimistic. His wife had acute hearing and in the echoing silence of the lull, as the dusk came down, she had sworn to hearing the sound of distant artillery of a different calibre from the Chinese.

Throughout the Legation, groups of people remained arguing and speculating as the stars came out, and the velvety darkness descended on everything. The heat that day had been tremendous with the thermometer sometimes touching 110 degrees. Now, as the cool night air flowed in, a blessed quiet held the world in near sleep, and nature and man combined to sustain the hopes of so many who so short a time ago had lived in fear.

Kershaw invited Lu-Ching to his room. He lit the kerosene lamp and poured two glasses of wine from a half empty bottle. The stocks of wine commandeered from a deserted food store within the Legation boundaries were still plentiful and drunkenness a danger.

Staring at him in the dim light, Lu-Ching said, "You must

have roots in our ancestors — your face speaks of a China older than the one we know, and your Chinese is — how can I say it? — old-fashioned."

"My mother claimed to have roots going back a thousand years," said Kershaw. "Tell me. Why has it come to this — that our people have abandoned Confucius and turned their faces to brutality and destruction?"

"You regard yourself as Chinese?" Lu-Ching asked.

"Primarily, yes."

"Then we are both in the wrong positions here in the Legation."

"Yes."

"But you do not approve of what is happening."

"How could I?"

"Perhaps with our history it is understandable."

"Yes, perhaps with our history."

"I have to remember that it was Western medicine that saved my life."

"Yes."

"And you, Mr Kershaw, were its instrument."

"Any diagnostician in the West could have seen what was wrong — appendicitis. It needed surgery or it would burst."

"It did burst — and your instructions saved me."

"They never forgave me for intruding."

"We none of us like to be shown at fault. I insisted that our doctors listened to you."

"Yes — why did you do that? Why did you trust me rather than your own people?"

"I have learnt not to be a narrow man. We have matters which can instruct us from the West, and we ourselves have matters to interest the West. The two cultures will always be in conflict but there are details we can learn from one another and it would seem wise that some accommodation should be found."

"Well spoken, Lu-Ching."

"I never understood, Mr Kershaw — what was the purpose of your visit to that Peking hospital."

"I had gone to visit a Chinese friend who was ill, a man who worked in the Customs Office. We were old friends. We even smuggled some opium together. You were in the bed next to his."

"Yes — now I remember — you said you were a doctor. You did know of medical matters. How did this come to pass?"

"I had eighteen months' medical training and then I was hounded out because I performed an abortion on a fellow student."

"That is sad. Abortions here are illegal but common."

There was a knock on the door. "Come in." Lucy Shelham entered. "Oh!" she said, surprised at finding Lu-Ching. "It's very convenient to get you both together. Sir Archie wants to see you both. I warn you, he's in an odd mood. He's gone all broody and philosophic."

Kershaw blew out the kerosene lamp and they fumbled their way down the corridor in the darkness. As they walked he became aware that Lucy smelt, an unpleasant combination of sweat, dirt and some powerful musky scent. All baths were taboo until the rains came. Water was too precious. Did it mean that he too smelt? It must. As they walked in the darkness Lucy's arm slipped around Kershaw and she kissed his cheek. He drew away sharply.

"Damn you!" she whispered. "I want to talk. What about tomorrow night? At the northern trench."

Sir Archie's office had become a field headquarters with people coming and going, maps adorning the wall, orders waiting to be signed and countersigned, and as they entered he was saying,

"Yes Mr Gamewell, we must take advantage of the lull. Build up every wall, every barricade, every defence. If it starts again we won't get another chance. . . . Yes, certainly you must rope in the Chinese converts — they've got to do something, not just sit about. Ah — hello, Kershaw — I won't be a minute. Must just sign these — you can take them when you leave."

While the nib of his pen scratched across the paper, Kershaw reflected how marvellous it was to be able to hear small sounds again in a pool of silence, as if nature had suddenly re-asserted its own harmonies.

Lady Mainwaring performed a remarkable feat while they

were waiting for news of Admiral Seymour's breakthrough. She swept away the sewing machines, the beds and the half-made sandbag covers from her dining room, resurrected its original elegance, covered the dining table with the carefully preserved damask cloth and served a composite meal for ten people which held hints of the luxurious past. Three Ministers, three wives, Major Shelham and Lucy, Sir Robert Hart, Lu-Ching and Kershaw were the chosen guests.

A pale-faced, lame Major Shelham walked with a stick and spoke in a manner even more clipped than usual. Monsieur Bleriot arrived with his rifle still slung across his shoulder and placed it ready to hand in a corner of the room. Lucy had selected a daring blue silk gown which fell so far from her shoulders without shoulder straps that only willpower could have maintained the decencies. Lu-Ching, rising to the occasion, arrived last and caused a stir. For the first time he wore his full ceremonial jacket, trousers and shoes, the gorgeous silks in flaming colours, the blue and gold dragons emblazoned on his sleeves resplendent in the candlelight. The windows were sandbagged, the room stripped of its finery like a bald man, but the silver candlesticks, the napery, the glittering cutlery and Lu-Ching's gorgeous presence created an impression of rich and civilized living. One other figure dominated the scene — Sir Archibald himself. He wore his full-dress uniform with its embroidered collar, its gold buttons and his many coloured decorations. From the moment the improvised cold consommé arrived Sir Archibald played to the full the elegant diplomat.

The main course, a miraculous concoction of rice and pony meat, entitled on the menu kedgeree, had subtle sauces intermingled to camouflage its raw materials. Lavishly interlaced with glasses of champagne the proceedings began to take on a feeling of optimism and a return to normality seemed an indisputable conclusion, which not even the Chinese dare ignore.

Lu-Ching had been placed at one end of the table with Sir Archibald at the other, a remarkable *volte face* for the magistrate. Next to Lu-Ching, Kershaw faced — as if maliciously arranged — Lucy Shelham, and Monsieur Bleriot adjoined Sir Archibald, confronting Sir Robert Hart.

Sir Archibald took advantage of a lull in the conversation to address Lu-Ching.

"I think," he said, "that if we are not relieved we shall get another offer from the yamen of safe conduct through the Chinese lines. Would you accept that if it does come through?"

Lu-Ching simply shook his head and used one of the few English words he ever risked uttering. "No," he said.

"What do you think will happen next?"

Lu-Ching was silent for a long minute, then he turned to Kershaw and put a question in Chinese. Kershaw translated "Lu-Ching would like to know, Sir Archibald, whether you want a short or full answer. There is a good deal that needs saying."

"Preferably short."

Despite the request the reply seemed long. Free from the European sense of time or the urgency of the situation, with great dignity, Lu-Ching outlined the events he understood to have taken place, his high undulating voice pausing at the right moments to allow Kershaw to translate. Slowly he reached the core of his message. Prince Tuan and other Chinese notables, he said, had burst into the Palace of Peaceful Longevity, one day, and more or less denounced the Emperor as a friend of the Secondary Hairy Ones — the foreigners. Infuriated, the Empress had intervened, and glaring down at the mob from a flight of steps she scathingly denounced Prince Tuan's conduct. She then stopped for a year the Prince's allowance and ordered his Boxer associates to be decapitated on the spot. Carried on a wave of revulsion for the rebels, she next authorized Jung Lu, the commander in chief, to order a cease-fire and to open parleys with the besieged. Once determined to "eat the flesh and sleep on the skins" of the foreigners, she now was ready for compromise.

Amazed at the detailed information, Sir Archibald asked for its source.

"I had two sources," said Lu-Ching. "One was the man you arrested as a spy. The other is a Chinese convert — once a cook — he goes in and out of the Water Gate disguised as a peasant. He brought this latest information." They talked on for some minutes and then Lu-Ching said, "I would like to request that my Chinese friend you think is a spy be released, because he is not a spy and the well of my information may run dry."

"I'll order it tomorrow," agreed Sir Archibald.

Half an hour later the ladies and gentlemen split into two groups, the ladies using the sandbagged corner adjoining the theatre, the men grouping together around the dining table. Sir Archibald circulated cigars which Lu-Ching refused and Kershaw accepted. Uneasy throughout the whole meal, because he had never before penetrated the home life of the Mainwarings so intimately, Kershaw smoked his cigar with diffidence. Symbolic of money, security and rank the cigar seemed ill-suited to his position and outlook.

It was Sir Robert Hart who set the conversation on a course which nearly proved disastrous. "Tell me, Lu-Ching," he began, "how do you scholars manage to reconcile Confucianism with Buddhism and Taoism? They all seem to me flatly contradictory in so many ways."

Lu-Ching asked Sir Robert where he found the contradictions.

"Well, put it this way," Sir Robert said. "The Buddhists advocate withdrawal from family and materialism: Confucius believes in active participation in society and praises material efforts to look after the family: Taoism encourages the spontaneous expression of the instincts — all very different and contradictory, aren't they?"

Expressionlessly Lu-Ching replied directly to Sir Robert's fluent Chinese. Puffing a great cloud of smoke Sir Archibald remarked, "Oh come, Sir Robert, you mustn't exclude the rest of the company. My Chinese isn't up to yours." He turned to Kershaw. "It's your ball, Kershaw."

"Would you mind repeating what you said?" Kershaw asked Lu-Ching. When he had done so Kershaw commented, "Ah, yes — well — I find this rather difficult. It runs something like: 'All three philosophies pursue an ideal harmony between man and the forces of nature — that's where they meet'."

"And which of the three is yours, Lu-Ching?" asked Sir Archibald.

"I am Confucian," said Lu-Ching, addressing himself now to Kershaw.

"But hasn't the Confucian vision become a bit muddied by recent Chinese history?" Sir Archibald said.

"I would like to know the episodes of our history you wish me to consider muddied," Lu-Ching said.

"We were discussing this the other night, weren't we?" Sir Archibald said to Sir Robert.

"Yes, we were — surely you would agree, Lu-Ching, that corruption has been rife in the immediate past?"

Lu-Ching waited a long moment, gathering his thoughts and words, and then he spoke at some length, once more in beautiful Chinese, and Kershaw found himself troubled by the complexity of the thought and language.

"I have witnessed in the past my ancestors selling rank for money, making nonsense of the intellectual hierarchy in which they were supposed to believe. Also in the past the rule of the literate sometimes became an excuse for appointing classics professors — hopelessly incompetent professors — because they were friends or members of the family. There were also benevolent despots who drove their officials to extort the last drop of money from the Chinese people. But all these things are misunderstood by the Western world. They are one corrupt aspect, yes — but one aspect of the harmonious whole. Corruption is necessary in order to distinguish good. Out of the corruption has come a great culture with thousands of scholars and books, beautiful paintings and marvellous architecture. Out of that again has come the true message of Confucianism. The three great joys in the Confucian canon are realized in the lives of millions of people — fatherhood, office and longevity. These, in combination with the worship of the ancestral tablets, makes a life of balance and harmony which brings as much happiness as any man can expect in this life. But without the corruption, the good and evil aspects would not balance and make of them a harmony."

Monsieur Bleriot only half repressed the French equivalent of the word "rubbish". Throughout the conversation he had not actually spoken before, but his gestures made an elaborate vocabulary of disagreement.

Sir Robert Hart looked sharply at Sir Archibald and Sir Archibald began, "That's all very well, Lu-Ching, but how do you reconcile all that with what's going on outside here at this very moment?"

"Let me first of all say," Lu-Ching continued, "that the Commander of the Chinese forces strongly disapproves of the Boxers and all their actions."

"How can you know that?"

"I knew Jung Lu before he became a general — he disapproved of all secret societies and, as you know, in China we have many. They were a threat to central authority. But he also openly favoured the suppression of the Boxers from the beginning. He is a man who knows that if one weak country fights more than ten powerful countries danger and ruin will follow. Moreover when two countries are at war it has been customary from far antiquity in Chinese culture not to injure the envoys of those countries. The founding of the Dynasty by our forefathers was an arduous task; how can it now be lightly thrown away by believing in brigands and brutal assaults on foreign envoys? In the past Jung Lu has submitted several memorials embodying these opinions to the Empress. Unfortunately he has been told by the Empress, 'Your tail is becoming too heavy to wag'."

Major Shelham had sat white and silent throughout the conversation and now when he spoke his voice was hoarse with tiredness. "Haven't answered question," he said.

"Yes." Sir Robert Hart took up the challenge. "Respecting your views and your culture as I do, how do you reconcile what is happening here with your ancient respect of envoys?"

Monsieur Bleriot broke in again with a flow of flowery phrases. It was ridiculous to talk of respect — the Boxers were barbarians — all this high-flown philosophy was misplaced. While he talked on Lu-Ching stared unseeing at the sandbagged window. At last the ghost of a smile seemed to move across his impassive features. He murmured something which Kershaw could not hear. "Would you repeat?" Kershaw asked and Lu-Ching spoke more clearly in a Chinese which was far removed from his usual flowing mandarin style. Kershaw said, "It is difficult to translate. Lu-Ching thinks that what is happening now is the result of the clash between two philosophies — they believe that Confucianism is the true basis to civilization and we — we believe that free trade plus Christianity plus the English language equals civilization."

Major Shelham gave a snort of disapproval. "Damn silly . . . not true."

Sir Archibald came to his feet and strode round the table. "Kershaw, tell him this. Tell him that I know we have sometimes behaved outrageously towards the Chinese." As he spoke he gave long pauses for Kershaw to translate. "I am a soldier and a diplomat. I do not share the avaricious vision which British traders have forced upon the Foreign Office. . . .

"These traders saw four hundred million Chinese as just one vast market to buy wool and cotton piece-goods — worse still, as four hundred million potential opium addicts whom they deliberately encouraged in the habit. We bear a heavy responsibility for all that.

"But we have also brought the elements of a superior civilization into this country — and above all a religion which is I regret to say based on indisputable authority as the one true religion. . . ."

There was a long uneasy silence. Sir Archibald went on striding round the dining room. In the sandbagged corner the women had fallen silent, listening. Due respect had to be shown when Sir Archibald was making something close to a public speech. It rolled on for some minutes and then Lu-Ching answered, "But the four hundred million were also four hundred million souls to be saved — in the eyes of the foreigners. That we did not want. Because we do not believe in any religion as the one true religion."

Kershaw reflected once more what surprises Sir Archibald concealed behind that long, lean face with its simplistic stare and Foreign Office façade.

Now it was as if some internally programmed speech, the result of years of saturation in Chinese thinking and values, began to gather force and eloquence and poured from Lu-Ching's lips in long rolling sentences which brooked no interruption. Everyone listened politely in silence except for Major Shelham who fidgeted and coughed and several times seemed on the point of bursting in because he could no longer contain himself. Kershaw knew that he was failing in his duty, knew that he should interrupt and insist on translating but as he listened to the marvellous use of the Chinese language, its beauty and power held him in silent respect. He himself could never speak it as Lu-Ching now spoke it. Sir Archibald, he knew, could pick up a phrase or two, Major Shelham seemed to understand odd sentences and Sir Robert Hart certainly followed, but none interrupted the mandarin flow in the curiously high monotonous voice.

Confucianism, Lu-Ching explained, did not think men were victims of original sin, or fallen creatures. Human nature was naturally good, and evil the result of an imbalance in the endowment of physical nature. Through moral efforts man could transform his physical nature and restore its balance. There was a perfect world — not in Heaven — but on this earth, waiting on the acceptance of wise men's thinking, and that thinking reached into the secret wells of human nature, finding and fulfilling the noble attributes which so easily surrendered to shoddy societies with shoddy values. Such values Confucianism wished to eradicate.

A silence followed. It was because of the silence that Lady Mainwaring and Lucy, completely misunderstanding, came bustling over with a coffee tray and four cups.

"I think you gentlemen have had long enough to settle your differences," Lady Mainwaring said. "Now — who takes sugar? — there's still some left, but no milk I'm afraid. The one cow we have on the premises has gone into shock from all the noise. . . ."

She expected some badinage, at least a reply of some kind, but they all sat uneasily silent, still immersed in the mood created by Lu-Ching. The women looked slightly embarrassed. "I'm sorry," continued Lady Mainwaring. "Are we intruding? . . ."

It was Sir Archibald who suddenly broke out of it. "Well, now, my dear, we must pay attention. It's really too hot for coffee." He ran his finger round the neck of his uniform. "Will you have coffee, Lu-Ching?"

Lu-Ching shook his head.

"Tea, my dear. Our guest doesn't drink barbaric coffee. Isn't there any tea?"

"Pretty Poo shall make it at once." Lady Mainwaring left Lucy to serve the coffee, and as she poured it, she became very aware of the damp patches widening at her armpits. The atmosphere, with so many air vents closed, had become putrid. Outside the night was heavy, sultry, with every small sound exaggerated after the continuous roar of gunfire.

At nine o'clock Sir Archibald sent one of the convert servants to check on what was happening.

At ten o'clock he led his guests into the compound where champagne was served in the open air. Monsieur Bleriot managed to slip his rifle over his shoulder before he emerged.

At eleven o'clock they began fresh speculation about the motives behind the ceasefire.

As if timed for dramatic effect, as the dining room clock struck twelve the first bursts of gunfire made Monsieur Bleriot jump and everyone else froze in mid-sentence, mid-gesture.

Was the ceasefire over so quickly?

CHAPTER IX

Life became an appalling mechanical routine. The unending roar of rifles and crash of shells, the repeated sentry-go, the bouts of brutal fighting, the waking at the appointed hour and automatic falling asleep again. Eight pieces of Chinese artillery were threatening to grind the barricades to pieces and as the outworks crumbled under the shells one flight of bullets was followed by another in such quick succession it created a continuous humming background.

At six o'clock on the morning following the dinner, Kershaw made his way stealthily to the disused trench at the far northern boundary, well away from normal traffic in the Legation. Dug as a shelter from shells, it had quickly filled with water and been abandoned, but one corner he knew was still dry and completely protected from prying eyes. Lucy's rota at the hospital that night ran from three o'clock till six. Then she was due at six-thirty to join Lady Mainwaring in checking the domestic arrangements. They had less than half an hour.

In the pale damp atmosphere he felt the gloom of the whole Legation and his own spirits were depressed by the relentless courier work. He knew now what it meant to be stomach-sick from seeing war wounds, he knew how nerve-shaking it was to see the man standing beside you talking normally one moment and the next brutally struck and gasping from the blow before he fell to the ground. And the certainty that on a specially selected day your turn would come, that you would be smashed to silence in mid-sentence at ten, twelve, five o'clock — whatever hour laughing destiny fixed without a qualm. And hoping, always hoping, that if it happened it would not mean missing legs or some utterly obscene mutilation which still left you alive to face the consequences. . . .

And then she was there, moving towards him, a ghost figure freshly released from night duty in the improvised hospital and stumbling in her haste before she smothered his words with an embrace and kisses.

"Oh God," she muttered between her kisses. "I can't take much more of this."

"I know," he said. "None of us can."

"I don't mean *this*," she swept one arm towards the Legation buildings. "I mean not seeing you, keeping up this fraudulent front — what does it matter if he knows? We're all liable to die soon, anyway."

"No we're not. We shall come through it."

"Where did you get your optimism?" she asked. "Everyone knows we can't hold out. Kiss me — don't waste time — for God's sake kiss me."

She guided his hands to her breasts. She unbuttoned her semi-uniform dress and as his hands closed over her breasts he shut his eyes and felt the warm glow from her body flowing into him.

They stood there wordless, the roof dripping water into the trench, the acrid odour of expended bullets in their nostrils, unaware of their own smell because to smell was now the natural consequence of being alive or dead. He felt her body moving against his and losing control of his own, responded. He felt her hands moving down his body and boldly finding his central core.

She drew back suddenly. "Let me take these off," she said, and pulling up her skirt was fumbling with her long under-drawers when he stopped her.

"Not here!" he said. "We must wait."

"Wait? You must be mad."

"It wouldn't work," he said.

But she ignored him and was struggling with an impossible undergarment which clung with persistence to her sweating limbs.

"Don't you understand?" he muttered.

"Understand what?" she asked and now she found herself almost helpless with one leg free and threatening to drop in the mud and the other more tightly entangled.

"It's all too clumsy — it will spoil it."

"I know it's sordid — sordid — I know, but if you knew what

frustration is — what dreams I have — " She tugged viciously at the remaining leg and suddenly it split and some malevolent purpose intrinsic to the material twisted it round her leg and now all her attempts merely made it cling more fiercely.

"Damn — damn — damn!" she exploded. "Help me."

He was holding her gently but firmly apart and, as he did so, pulling down her dress and saying, "Don't let's ruin everything — we can't possibly make love standing up. . . . "

"Why not?" she snapped and burst into tears, burying her head in his chest. She lay there sobbing quietly and he stroked her chestnut hair.

"Is that all you want, Lucy?"

"Of course it's not," she answered and suddenly hammered his chest. "You don't understand — you must misinterpret everything — let me go — I want to go — I can't take any more."

With that she pulled back and was about to rush away when she almost stumbled and fell. The loose garment had tangled itself round her ankles and she felt trapped and finally humiliated. A desperate series of manoeuvres at last freed the leg and then she fled — uncaring momentarily where she went, with a desperate need to escape, from Kershaw, the trench, the humiliation.

As she came in sight of Sir Archibald's residence the bullets began flying again and the deeper note of artillery broke the hushed expectancy before the dawn. Instinctively she ducked and moved forward bent double. It seemed absurd. She could not see the enemy — like most in the Legation she had never seen the enemy — the bullets frequently flew high but her humiliation was quickly overwhelmed with fear.

Suddenly she realized she was heading in the wrong direction. Shelham's wound made it necessary for him to sleep alone and he rose late as part of his convalescence. Swerving away she headed off towards the block where the customs officers' wives were accommodated. As she ran the firing suddenly intensified and she flung herself inside the ancient wooden door. Panting, she lay against the door and an arm went round her waist.

"Are you all right, madam?" It was the buxom wife of the

Inspector of Customs, Mrs Nesterose, whose florid countenance and implacable calm had reassured many a woman in the Legation.

Lucy swiftly pulled herself together, thrust the torn garment into her handbag, tried to control her heavy breathing and turning at last to confront Mrs Nesterose said, "Yes, I'm all right — just had to run for it."

As they made their way into the bedroom, with a great effort she gained full control and said, "It's my turn to have a bath today?"

"I'll look at the list," said Mrs Nesterose and ran her big finger down a piece of paper pinned to the wall. "No — your name isn't here. She paused and added with new respect, "Surely, madam, you use Lady Mainwaring's bathroom."

"The waste pipe's jammed."

"In that case," said Mrs Nesterose, "you can have it before the others wake up."

Lucy made her way to the big bathroom with its ancient bath standing upon four lion's paws. Mattresses crowded one half of the enormous floor and in the half light of dawn the sprawled figures, scantily clad, looked like corpses. Not even the exigencies of a siege could modify the Victorian sense of decency, and strung across the room was a sheet reaching above eye level which cut off the bath from the sleeping eyes. Moving swiftly between the mattresses Lucy ducked under the sheet and began undressing rapidly. Three huge laundry bags hung from nails at one end of the bath and she bundled her underclothes into one of them. The coolies had now been organized to collect, wash and deliver laundry every few days, but there was no running water. Old kerosene tins held gallons of water from the well and she struggled in an effort to lift one. Failing, she ducked under the sheet once more and, selecting a woman already stirring in her sleep, she whispered loudly in her ear, "Are you awake?" The woman started up, crying piteously. Like every other woman in the Legation she suffered from the threat of that moment when the Boxers would break in and mutilation and rape begin.

"It's all right," Lucy said. "It's only me." A moment later she recoiled from the stench which came off the woman. It had its own special Chinese quality, particularly evident to European noses, but as Lucy knew, the reverse was equally true.

Lucy went on talking to her for a moment and suddenly realized that the woman spoke no English. She resorted to gesture. At last between them they managed to pour two kerosene tins of water into the iron bath. Lucy stepped into the water and in the coolness of dawn it seemed cold — but refreshingly cold — and after the first shock she sank back in its embrace, wondering suddenly whether any of the Chinese women beyond the sheet had lice in their hair and if so . . .

As usual the mosquitoes began to attack her. There were many reasons why people remained clothed for days on end — modesty, fear of being taken naked and idiotic notions of greater security when clothed — but the lack of mosquito nets added a vital motive. Now the mosquitoes mercilessly enjoyed Lucy's soft white flesh and all her wild flailings did not dismay them. She knew that given time her body would become self-inoculated, but as one huge whirring creature audaciously settled on her left nipple she smacked her hand down so hard she cried out in pain.

And suddenly all the spirit went out of her and she felt miserable. The strains, the anxiety, the dirt, the blood and pain which had so appallingly transformed her life, momentarily overwhelmed her. Above all the impossibility of conducting an affair under siege conditions sent a silent scream of frustration through her head. Affair . . . no, that wasn't what she wanted . . . that underestimated what was happening to her.

Kevin's presence continuously permeated her consciousness. In her dreams, disguised as her brother in far off America, he walked the streets beside her, liberated from the threat of death, laughing happily in the knowledge that soon they would be drifting into a bed of untold luxury where sexual abandon took the place of the horrors of the siege.

Selecting one of the carefully laundered towels from half a dozen hung on pegs beside the bath, she dried herself, and smiled wryly to think how swiftly her sense of personal hygiene had almost disappeared. Before the siege she would never have dreamt of using anyone else's towel.

A new sound came from across the compound: the 91st

Psalm, sung in faltering tones by several nationalities, rising and falling from the direction of the chapel. She knew, too well, how one or other of the endless missionaries conducted early morning prayers in the chapel, inventing unnecessary spiritual duties to keep themselves out of the firing line. She knew that she avoided attending their services because the remnants of her Christian faith made her feel guilty about her desire for Kershaw.

As she dried herself she knew that she must return to her room in Sir Archibald's house because she had no fresh underclothes, and that made her uneasy because she would have to face her husband again. She was pulling her soiled dress over her head when all hell broke loose.

First a rattle of rifle fire began and reached deafening proportions, followed by the high-pitched whine of one shell following another. Then came a new sound which at first worried her because she could not identify it. Slowly she realized that the Chinese were setting off endless fire crackers.

She shuddered as she drew the dress down, and felt very uneasy because she was naked underneath. Before she could relax and snatch a few hours' sleep she had a duty to perform with Lady Mainwaring. Together they carried out a swift survey every morning to see that the domestic arrangements were running reasonably well. Usually they managed to finish the survey before the firing began but this morning they were too late. Common sense dictated that they should wait for a lull, but Lucy knew that the firing might continue for hours.

The strain was beginning to tell on Lucy. She had never seen the attackers, bullets out of nowhere sometimes sang past her head, the temperature as the burning sun came up would mount to a hundred degrees in the shade, flies and mosquitoes would descend on every body in swarms, corpses unburied on the defence perimeters begin to putrefy, and even when the *hideous* cacophony did cease, the silence would become more threatening because her imagination produced far worse horrors under preparation by the Chinese.

Her gloom deepened. She stuffed her fingers into her ears and for a few blissful minutes stood alone in the coolness of the bathroom, trying to isolate herself from the world of the

Legation.

It did not work. The noise penetrated every defence. Noise . . . roaring, hissing, shrieking noise, and always she remembered from the first few days the dreadful chant Kill! Kill! Kill! And then, as Lucy was about to pull the improvised curtain aside and face the world again she stopped dead in her tracks.

Her period. It was late. . . . My God. . . . In all the horror she had completely forgotten, or deliberately pushed out of her mind the monthly anxiety about her period. She sat on the edge of the bath, opened her bag, took out her diary and studied it carefully. Wednesday the 13th the last one finished. The 13th! And now it was Tuesday six weeks later. Six weeks! She felt the colour flooding from her cheeks. What if morning sickness attacked her? He, Shelham, would know at once and he would know it was nothing to do with him because she hadn't slept with him for the last three months. To be pregnant here in the middle of a siege by someone not your husband, with no hope of doing anything about it . . . or was that true. . . ? She came sharply to her feet. She knew Kevin had been struck off as a medical student for performing an abortion — so she did have a means but here, in the close quarters of a siege, with everyone knowing, and Kershaw her lover — no, it could not be.

CHAPTER X

"LUCY WHERE ARE you?"

In an effort to make herself heard above the din Lady Mainwaring's high fluting voice rose to a shout and Lucy pulled aside the sheet to see her standing there, very erect, clad in a remarkable combination of raincoat and pith helmet. At that moment the roar of firing rose to a crescendo and the house shook. The two women hesitated a moment and then embraced wordlessly. It was a remarkable moment. Distinguished for her detachment, Lady Mainwaring had never before conceded more than a kiss on the cheek. Now, as the bathroom shook about them, and the other women cowered in groups trying to comfort one another, Lady Mainwaring's arm remained firmly round Lucy's waist and they looked into each other's eyes with all considerations of rank dissolved.

For a long moment they were silent and then Lady Mainwaring shouted:

"This," touching the pith helmet, "was Sir Archibald's crazy idea. Do you think it suits me?"

"Admirably," Lucy shouted back, dissembling as usual.

"It's an excellent form of protection. We must find one for you."

Slowly Lady Mainwaring became embarrassed by their physical proximity and, making an effort, withdrew from Lucy's arm, saying, "We must really do our rounds."

Lucy looked startled. "You're not suggesting we should go out in all this, are you?"

"Oh come, Lucy — it's all bark and no bite — very few bullets penetrate here."

"I wish I could agree with you," Lucy said. "I suppose our checking does some good."

"Certainly," Lady Mainwaring said. "We need to back up everybody's morale."

At that moment two bullets came hissing through the flimsy wall and buried themselves in the sandbags by the window. Lucy shrank against Lady Mainwaring and again her arm went round Lucy's waist.

Lucy pulled away. "Do you mind if we wait for a lull?" she said.

"If there is one," Lady Mainwaring replied.

The whole conversation had been carried on in half shouts and when suddenly the firing fell away into near silence their voices echoed noisily in the room. They laughed.

"Right," said Lady Mainwaring, cutting her laughter. "Let's try the Chinese millstones."

In the next half an hour they moved around the compound checking and encouraging, Lucy feeling like a ventriloquist's dummy to Lady Mainwaring's performance. There were the Chinese converts busy grinding coarse wheat to make even coarser bread, there was the butcher dividing up carcases of ponies shot dead the night before, the coolies splashing soapsuds in vast tubs which were the laundry, the cobbler reconstructing a pair of someone's shoes. No service seemed neglected in the self-contained community and everything ran smoothly until they came to the damp brick Burmese Hall where scores of schoolgirls were accommodated. They were Chinese, buxom, innocently unaware of being near-women and the two native Christians in charge immediately poured out the same story to Lady Mainwaring.

The V-shaped barricades garrisoned by the Russians faced both ways on Legation Street and their inner lines had reached within a stone's throw of the Burmese Hall and the schoolgirls. The luck of the siege had contrived to leave the Russians more or less idle. They had nothing to do except sleep and mount guard, in boring repetition.

A tall, bent Chinese convert whose face was a mosaic of lines with deeply set eyes tried to convey in broken English his special anxieties. It took some time and Lady Mainwaring grew impatient. "Get it out, man — get it out." At last they pieced together his story. Twice on his nightly rounds he had surprised Russian soldiers trying to break into the Hall and once he had been assaulted. He went to see Baron von Rienstane, the Russian commander, but the Baron refused to believe his story. The honour of Russia was at stake, he claimed, and none of his men would descend to such behaviour. But it was true, the convert said — completely true. He pointed to a big swelling on his left temple — that was where they had hit him. They, the girls, needed some form of protection he said. It was very necessary. Lady Mainwaring said, "We will see the Colonel at once."

She set off immediately, wading through a network of trenches and barricades. "I'm afraid," she said as they strode, "Archie wouldn't approve of this. He would regard this as a man's job."

As they approached, the Russians sent up ironical cheers and whistles and burst into incomprehensible remarks. One quickly converted his cap into the shape of a pith helmet, put it on his head and imitated Lady Mainwaring's stalking walk. As they approached a kind of dugout a fierce rattle of firing sent all the Russians down flat on their faces, but Lady Mainwaring simply strode on clutching Lucy's hand so tightly that her nails dug into its palm. It was beyond her dignity to fall flat on her face before all those men or to admit in public to anything so proletarian as fear. At that moment a bull of a man with enormous shoulders and a heavy sculptured head appeared at the sandbagged door, bellowed something in Russian and a moment later shouted in broken English, "Down — fall — down fall."

Lucy was shivering. Lady Mainwaring said, "I suppose we'd better. . . . " As she spoke she was bending her knees, carefully holding her skirts in position as a preliminary to sinking slowly and with the utmost decency to the ground, but almost as the slow motion accelerated, the firing ceased as abruptly as it had begun.

Baron von Rienstane came striding across with hand outstretched and taking Lady Mainwaring's idle hand raised it to his lips and kissed it, a gesture greeted by a single ironical cheer from an unidentified Russian. Baron von Riestane turned, and glaring in the direction of the cheer, snapped in Russian, "That man will report to me." He escorted Lady Mainwaring into his dugout. There was only one seat — a broken-backed chair — and a single kerosene lamp seemed to create more gloom than it dispelled.

A flow of perfect and peremptory English from Lady Mainwaring was received in aristocratic silence by the Baron. He had not understood a word. "Oh, for Kershaw," Lady Mainwaring said and patiently picked her way through the key sentences in slow motion. When he grasped her meaning he at once became theatrically shocked. It was outrageous: his men were men of honour: they would never behave like that: she could rest assured that . . . Lady Mainwaring cut him short. "All you have to do is put a reliable guard on the place — and especially at night." He immediately replied that he could not spare the men; they were under constant threat of attack.

These exchanges took considerable time as the Baron struggled with his English. At last Lady Mainwaring said, with long pauses between each word, "My husband will post a notice on the bell tower forbidding anyone from approaching the Burmese Hall."

The Baron drew himself up. "If anyone broke the regulation," he said, "I would have him shot at once."

Lady Mainwaring wavered and said, "I don't think you need be quite so drastic as that."

The Baron simply repeated — offenders would be shot.

To Lucy's surprise Lady Mainwaring said, "Well — have it your own way", came to her feet, took Lucy's arm. "We must be getting on." At that moment a swift rattle of rifle fire sent bullets hissing across the barricades. The Baron pulled both ladies back into his dugout and placed himself in front of them, simultaneously snapping out orders. The Russian soldiers leapt into position at the multiple loopholes and an exchange of fire began.

It was very brief and the firing quickly fell into silence. The Baron immediately apologized for such a rude intervention.

At last they managed to leave. Twice in the next ten minutes they were forced to take shelter from bursts of gunfire. After the second attack Lucy said, "I don't think I can go on. . . . I must get some sleep." Her dress was soaked in sweat, her head aching from the growing heat and at the back of her mind the thought kept returning — what if I am pregnant.

"Give me five minutes more," Lady Mainwaring said. "I just want to see how the converts are faring."

In the shelter of a sandbagged wall she paused, took Lucy's arm and said, "You'll be surprised to hear I need the reassurance of your company. I couldn't do this sort of thing alone." Lucy regarded her with astonishment. No one in the Legation had seemed more self-sufficient than Lady Mainwaring.

There were three hundred Chinese refugees and converts scattered in a half ruined house between the chapel and the northern barricades. It was the worst accommodation in the Legation. Large groups were living on the floor without even straw to sleep on. Huddled together, afraid or resigned to their fates, they were dirty, half clothed, surrounded by the few utensils from which they lived and in one corner at this hour in the morning half a dozen kerosene tins were brimming with urine and faeces. The stench as Lady Mainwaring and Lucy entered the door made them pause and draw back. Then they plunged determinedly forward.

Everywhere pallid faces and apathetic eyes regarded them without interest. It was obvious that hope had long ago dwindled and died in the minds of these people without the resignation customary to their race taking its place. In one corner a tiny young mother who seemed little more than a schoolgirl rocked a child at her shrunken breast. There were terrible sores on the baby's shoulders and cheeks and its belly was beginning to swell from malnourishment.

"Boy or girl?" Lady Mainwaring said to Lucy.

"Girl, I think. My God — why aren't we doing something about these people?"

"Yes — why indeed?" Lady Mainwaring said. "But we've got to feed the fighters and ourselves first."

It occurred to Lucy to question the second part of that remark but she was too tired and sickened.

"What is your name?" Lady Mainwaring said, but the girl was lost in hypnotic rocking. Lady Mainwaring touched her gently on the shoulder and repeated her question. She looked up expressionlessly and in a high twanging voice said, "Wang Nai-Nai."

"Good, so you understand English. We must get you some milk if we can. Where did you learn your English?"

"At the mission."

A sudden high whistle and a bullet came zipping through an aperture left in the sandbags to skim over their heads and smack into the opposite wall, scattering brick fragments in all directions. Immediately the girl lay over the child, covering it complete with her body and Lady Mainwaring and Lucy shrank into themselves.

In the next few minutes the occasional stray bullet developed to a throng and the external air was thick with one volley after another. As the din grew, the Chinese converts huddled closer together and some fell into attitudes of prayer. One openly appealed to this new God she had been taught to believe was all-merciful.

"Have mercy! Have mercy! Have mercy!" she repeated endlessly rocking on her heels in time to what became an incantation.

Lady Mainwaring returned to the door but hastily drew back from it as she saw — like rain slanting across the compound — flights of metal flashing in the sun.

"My God!" she exclaimed. "We're stuck — in here of all places." She took the scented scarf from round her long neck and pressed it to her nostrils. A moment later she offered it to Lucy who sniffed and returned it quickly, reflecting uneasily that unless she was mistaken they too were not exactly odourless.

Gradually the noise mounted and became more complex. Flying bricks, broken glass, crashing tiles and volleys of return fire on a higher note echoed and re-echoed round the compound.

But they could see nobody. The compound was empty and the English barricades too far away to reveal any activity. Clearly a very serious attack was meeting very determined resistance — that they could tell — but it was all happening on the French, American and Japanese fronts and here only the swelling crescendo of noise bore witness to the battle. It was uncanny and disturbing. They were in the siege and yet not taking part. They were silent witnesses without the reality of what they witnessed, but the disembodied threat was worse than the actuality.

Wang Nai Nai, still prostrated over her child, was sobbing gently and suddenly Lucy thought she might suffocate the child. She took her shoulder and pulled her gently back but Wang Nai Nai struggled to escape her hand crying "No — No

— " Lucy released her then and slowly Wang Nai Nai recovered some of her composure and sat up holding the child again.

Lady Mainwaring remained standing. They could not face the filthy floor or the threat of lice. A deathly tiredness was beginning to weaken Lucy's legs and there were moments when the room span a little and she had to exercise her will to stop the spinning from gathering speed. Talking was difficult because of the noise, but to concentrate her mind she began talking to Wang Nai Nai, her voice trembling as the crash of falling masonry spoke of a stray shell coming much too close. She tried to discover where Wang came from and what had happened to her. Wang Nai Nai was beginning to tell her of the wholesale slaughter in the Mission House when the child seemed to slump against her breast. She turned in alarm, kissed it many times and when it did not respond shook the small body fiercely. She said something sharply in Chinese but still there was no response.

"Don't do that," Lucy said as she shook the child again, and now a strange low crying sound came from Wang Nai. Lucy said "Let me see. . . . " She lifted the child's eyelids and felt its pulse.

"Don't tell me — " Lady Mainwaring began. "I'm afraid so," Lucy said. "But how — "

Wang Nai's high wailing became loud in the room and Lucy said, "I'm just too tired to cope. I'll send somebody. I'm very sorry, Wang — very sorry — " It seemed hopelessly inadequate.

"I'll arrange it," Lady Mainwaring said. "I'll drop in at the hospital. You get off to bed."

Outside the air was thick and sullen with heat but all seemed quiet again and as they slipped swiftly away Lady Mainwaring said, "Before they became Christians they used to cast dead bodies in the street — think of it. At least it will get a Christian burial now."

"Christian burial — that's a little exaggerated." Lucy paused and added quietly, "Have you seen what happens to the dead here?"

"No," replied Lady Mainwaring sharply. "Tell me."

"Their dead putrefy in the open. Ours — Oh God, I can't talk about it." They embraced and parted.

Lady Mainwaring swiftly made her way towards the British Chancery. Almost immediately she encountered a stretcher party with a man gasping for breath and groaning. He lay on the improvized stretcher with his left thigh smashed and pouring blood but Lady Mainwaring did not see the injury. Her eye first absorbed the stretcher and the two men carrying it and then she saw the blood dripping from underneath the stretcher, leaving a red trail directly in the path she was about to follow. She knew that if she raised her eyes she could see the body and the source of the blood but her eyes remained fixed intently on the dripping blood. She did not want to see its source.

And then wounded people seemed to be coming at her from all directions, one with an arm twisted out of all recognition, one blinded by his own blood from a head wound, another utterly inert, breathing stertorously between two carriers.

She stopped in her tracks as a wave of nausea and dizziness attacked her. She had never seen the hospital or its inmates, and she was suddenly afraid she would not be able to face it. Her hesitating feet seemed to pick up a momentum of their own as they moved forward, while her mind retreated.

Without knowing it she was past the small crowd of wounded at the entrance and still her mind's eye blotted out what her normal eye saw, but she could not exclude the groans or ignore the sudden shrill screaming of a man who writhed so convulsively on an improvised stretcher that he fell to the ground and was suddenly unconscious.

She felt useless, unnecessary, an encumbrance. She knew that the blood had drained from her face and sickness might humiliate her at any moment. And then Doctor Roberts looked up from the man with the shattered thigh and said, "My dear Lady Mainwaring — what on earth are you doing here? This is no place for you."

"No," she said faintly as his image shifted in the shimmering heat. "No." She wanted to tell them something — a message she had to give — about a casualty — a man — a baby that had died — it was all confused in her mind, suppressed into insignificance by the immediate scene.

"I must find a nurse," she began and took a few steps inside.

Doctor Roberts said, "I wouldn't go in there, Lady Mainwaring. We're just dealing with casualties." She hesitated. Yet another part of her mind was driving her to face what lay within but the sickness became more threatening as the thick slurred smell of blood and yet more blood mingled with carbolic and chloroform.

"There's a baby," she said and now she was right amongst it all where men were groaning and bleeding everywhere and the flies, attracted by newly spilt blood, swarmed round open wounds and men were calling in French, German and Russian for help, for water, for release from pain, and one, whose scream was like a scalding jet, regular, stabbing, mutilated the ear.

She caught the arm of a nurse and her lips formed once more the words, "there's a baby", but no sound issued, and as the nurse said, "Sorry, Lady Mainwaring — this is urgent", she knew that her faltering steps were turning away from two long despatch tables. Three weeks before, they used those tables for writing memos to the Foreign Office in London, and crackling parchment documents full of secrets had been solemnly sealed with civil service precision . . . but now a man was struggling on the table with a pad of something pressed to his lips and another man with an ordinary kitchen knife was poised above a leg shattered into a mess of blood and bone.

Everything disappeared from her mind and left a vacuum. She did not faint, she was not sick, but the scene receded, became hazy and vanished into a vacuum. She never remembered how she came to be outside the door again, her faltering steps leading her automatically in the direction of the Residence.

Lucy intended to undress before she fell asleep but she sank down on the mattress fully clothed, utter exhaustion overwhelming her. Her feet twitched momentarily, she turned her nose away from the mustiness of the mattress, she kicked off her shoes and then she lost consciousness as if a black curtain had descended.

She woke at seven o'clock with a furred mouth and a heavy head, glanced at her watch and forced herself to get up. First she must get a clean skirt and shirtwaist. The firing had ceased by the time she made her way swiftly across the compound to Sir Archibald's residence, and there she saw an astonishing sight which stopped her dead in her tracks. One part of the roof had collapsed and the beams were bulging out dangerously. A shell-hit? It must have been. People were hurrying in and out but oddly she passed no one she knew. Not until she was entering the dining-room did she almost collide with Lady Mainwaring.

"My dear!" The embrace was warm and affectionate. "What a morning we had."

A beautifully ironed and embroidered shirtwaist of the purest white silk, a perfectly arranged coiffure and a few artful dabs of papier poudre had completely resurrected the older woman. She was alive and confident, the darker moments of the morning expunged from her mind.

Twenty minutes later Lucy set out to fulfil her rota at the hospital having borrowed a clean skirt and shirtwaist drenched in lavender water. Her limbs were still heavy with tiredness, her mind working slowly, but the feel of clean clothing and underclothing gave her a false sense of freshness.

As she entered the Chancery, a medley of sounds from the wounded greeted her and one man's groaning was so deep her steps faltered. Could she face it all again? Worse still, tonight was burial night and that meant working in that hideous little room like a black cave at the back of the Chancery where the corpses were — so crudely — prepared for what few last rites were possible.

She made her way slowly through the despatch rooms into the back room. John Smithers, a sick berth orderly, was supervising the binding of the corpses. Lucy's hands shivered as she touched the first man. He was a great long fellow with a big head, flopped dramatically to one side — an English sailor called Juniper who had been hit by a shell fragment which blew his chest open. The cold flesh, the fixed eye, the gaping mouth . . . Lucy shut her eyes momentarily. Then she forced herself to reopen them and worked on, under Smithers' direction. There were no coffins. A crude canvas sack had to be drawn over the feet, up to the head and sewn together. It took Lucy twenty minutes to cover the dead man and when it was completed she stared at the coarse sacking. John Smithers' voice broke in on her. "There are two more, madam — if you are up to it."

"Of course I'm up to it," Lucy said fiercely.

When the bearers came they found some difficulty in picking up the dead sailor and as they set out to carry him to the communal trench at the further edge of the compound his booted feet suddenly burst through the sacking as if he were determined to escape the reality of death. Lucy could not stop herself. She gave a short cry and turned away.

For the second corpse they used a plank, strapping the body in place. As they were preparing the third and last, Lucy said, "Surely there should be some sort of service." Smithers looked at her as if nobody but a woman — and a middle-class woman at that — could have thought up anything so sentimental at a time like this. "Too many injured waiting for attention," he said.

"There are scores of useless missionaries lying around — why don't we get one of them to — " she gestured.

"Madam — I think you should ask one of the doctors. I'm just a nobody around here."

Some need to have at least one person pay respect to the dead drove Lucy to accompany the last man to the grave. He was in complete contrast to the Englishmen, a slight elegant Japanese. Below her in the trench she could discern the rough outline of Juniper's body, covered with a thin layer of soil. Now they simply lowered the Japanese on top of Juniper, and as she stood there in the dusk she knew that there were three bodies embracing in a common grave. Three rough crosses had been prepared. The bearer stuck them — cursorily — into the soil. One man stood for a moment with his cap removed, murmuring something. Lucy thought of the words ashes to ashes, dust to dust but they seemed somehow hopelessly inadequate and she could not — to her embarrassment — remember what followed in the burial service. As she turned away a terrible sense of desolation overtook her.

CHAPTER XI

In the dim light of the kerosene lamps Sir Archibald pointed with a ruler to the crude maps spread out on his study desk. "It's a war of attrition," he said to Major Shelham, now on active service again. "They try to shell our barricades to rubble and then push their way forward inch by inch. They have no stomach for fighting in the open. But they don't need to. They are slowly pushing us back into this cramped area." He pointed to a wedge-shaped position on the map.

Major Shelham made non-committal noises. He already knew every detail of the report Sir Archibald was so carefully elaborating. He had not wasted his time while he lay convalescing, dividing the hours between details of strategy and worrying about his wife.

"And another thing," said Sir Archibald. "Kershaw here will tell you we can get no sense out of the French. The French Legation is a heap of rubble. They don't need all those men now. We desperately need some of them here — and here." He pointed to the Russian and American fronts. "But can we get them — no. That's so, isn't it, Kershaw? Tell Shelham what happened."

As he confirmed Sir Archibald's account Kershaw reflected that if he revealed to Major Shelham exactly what had happened on the three occasions when he had managed to carry messages to and from the French lines Shelham would have exploded. After all, Sir Archibald was supposed to be commander-in-chief, but the French commander, Captain d'Arcy, succeeded in accepting orders from High Command with no intention whatever of carrying them out. Preparing his last and third message Sir Archibald had written fiercely on a piece of very official Foreign Office paper: "Must have ten men report to British Legation at once. This is an order." When Kershaw delivered it, Captain d'Arcy had laughed in Kershaw's face. "Order! *C'est impossible.* What's the good of ordering the impossible. We would collapse if ten men left us. *Il est fou, très fou.* But, Monsieur Kershaw, we understand one another. Don't tell him that. Tell him I will send as many as I can spare."

"Meaning none," Kershaw had said.

Captain d'Arcy laughed again. "You understand the French sense of humour. But don't overdo it."

When Sir Archibald finally commanded Captain d'Arcy to report to H.Q. himself in person, the Frenchman smiled again. "H.Q. *Mon Dieu*! Do we have one? But how can I leave my little darlings — they would die without me? Send Sir Archibald — " he blew a kiss " — and tell him I will report as soon as my little war is behaving better."

The stalemate left Sir Archibald inwardly fuming but outwardly calm. What could he do? Short of going himself and levelling his enormous revolver at the Frenchman's head there was only one dignified line of retreat. He must bide his time with the words, "All right, I'll deal with him myself tomorrow. I'll get Monsieur Bleriot to accompany me."

When it came to the point Monsieur Bleriot revealed a remarkable lack of interest in trying to control the recalcitrant Captain d'Arcy. The suggestion that he should accompany Kershaw with the next order and remind the captain that he was liable to be shot for disobeying orders brought a storm of flowery French which evaded the point. This was not really a war: how could there be military discipline? . . . it was a relatively friendly affair: court martials had no place in a siege . . . and shooting! Shooting above all a Frenchman. Did Sir Archibald realize how the French Foreign Office would regard that? It might sour Anglo-French relations throughout the whole of China. The crucial question was lost in the rhetoric. Somehow Monsieur Bleriot never visited the crumbling barricades of the French Legation.

Instead he kept his rifle firmly linked over his shoulder and continued to pace the safe parts of the English Legation with varying catch-phrases according to mood and circumstance. . . . "*Nous sommes perdus*," he would mutter in half soliloquy, followed by a wide-eyed, nose-sniffing, "*Il y a quelque chose qui brûle.*"

Kershaw always remembered Captain d'Arcy's reaction when told that Monsieur Bleriot had decided not to visit the barricades on a certain day. "*Il ne fait que pisser dans ses caleçons.*"

Discreetly censored, some of these events were now retailed to Major Shelham who released a snorting laugh with the single word, "Bounder!" Then he added, "Let me deal with him."

"There's something more important I'd like you to deal with," Sir Archibald said. "I think we have another and much more dangerous spy in the Legation."

"Spy!" Shelham spat out the word. Such an animal was iniquitous beyond conception.

"What makes you think — " he began and left the sentence incomplete.

"They've got a couple of Krupp nine-pounders as you know — couldn't hit anything with them. Now they've positioned them in the burnt-out tower over the Chien Men. But that's not all. Our little Italian one-pounder is the only artillery we've got. It doesn't do much damage — just a morale booster — but we've moved its position four times in three days and each time the Krupps guns have followed it — exactly, practically pin-pointed the damn thing. They want to silence it. Someone is feeding information. Who the hell could that be? You know everybody, Kershaw. Have you any idea?"

Automatically Kershaw shook his head, but in his mind he was wondering — how many of Lu-Ching's agents were reliable, and who amongst them remained long enough in the Legation to check positions.

"The men have nicknamed our gun Daphne," observed Sir Archibald. "But it's not only Daphne. It's the weak spots in the barricades. They seem to know those too. How can that be when they hardly venture into the open — or risk a charge?"

"Why not ask Lu-Ching," Shelham suggested, and at once Kershaw thought the question was ambiguous.

"Good idea," said Sir Archibald. "Can you fetch him, Kershaw?"

As if to prevent any such move, with the abruptness of a thunderclap, the stifling heat and silence of the Peking night was shattered by a reverberating roar of artillery and rifle fire, laced with the now familiar fire crackers.

"You see what I mean," Sir Archibald said raising his voice above the roar. "Either they overheard us — or — better wait, Kershaw."

"I think I know a safe way," said Kershaw.

"They tell me you've gone mad," Sir Archibald replied.

"I don't understand," Kershaw said.

"You no longer understand that bullets tend to kill. We need brave men but not foolhardy."

Foolhardy, Kershaw thought. Is that what this mounting torment amounts to, is that why all this turmoil has boiled up from the past, and what little sleep I get is tortured sleep? Tortured by what — exactly? The evil of the past, the repressed responsibility for suicides and mutilation. . . . That girl had died with her baby — died clumsily. What did it matter with a million such back street abortions faithfully recorded in police reports, a record of illicit love and death familiar to every civilization the world had ever concocted? Concocted — the perfect word — an artificial mixture of—

A crashing roar shook the whole building and Sir Archibald moved swiftly to his study door, saying, "Another direct hit unless I am mistaken."

He had a calm which came easily now. Shelham and Kershaw followed Sir Archibald as he moved swiftly down the corridor to be met by a billow of smoke, the smell of burning and a faint after-roar of crashing bricks and mortar. Doors opened all over the building, voices broke out in alarmed enquiry and one was raised in a burst of hysterical babbling. And then Lady Mainwaring was striding, almost running, down the corridor calling, "They've hit the dining room."

As they met Sir Archibald asked, "Are the children all right?"

"Yes — they're all right — but look at this." She moved back a few paces and flung open the dining room door. The room was full of smoke, dust and floating fragments of plaster and, beside the huge portrait of Queen Victoria, there was a gaping hole in the wall, the edges of which were still crumbling.

Sir Archibald had automatically come to attention and, almost as if he were saluting, said, "Thank God they didn't hit her." He went over and straightened the frame which was awry. The solemn moment passed in a flash, and immediately he added, "Any other damage?"

"Not as far as I know," said Lady Mainwaring.

"Get someone to check, will you, my dear. We must get back to business."

The whole conversation had been carried on in high-pitched voices and once again in mid-sentence the outburst of firing ceased as abruptly as it had begun.

They all paused, listening in the silence, waiting for the uproar to begin again. When it did not Sir Archibald turned away abruptly, saying to his wife, "See you at dinner," and led the way back to his office.

"Perhaps you could get Lu-Ching now," he said to Kershaw as they entered. With his hand on the doorknob he said over his shoulder, "and no mock heroics."

Kershaw looked a question.

"They tell me," said Sir Archibald, "that you take too many risks. We can't afford to lose anyone." He paused with a grim smile and added, "Not even you, Kershaw."

It was for Sir Archibald a subtle remark because the manner of its delivery and the smile convinced Kershaw that it conveyed a meaning the very opposite of the words used.

Heading straight for his own room, Kershaw found it empty. Systematically he searched the Legation buildings and was passing the Chancery when he saw Lu-Ching emerge. Joining him he explained the situation and ended with the question, "Is there anyone you would suspect?"

Lu-Ching said, "It is difficult to tell. There are two who bring me information through the Water Gate — what do I know of what they take away with them?"

"I shouldn't say that to Shelham, I wouldn't put it beyond him to suspect even you."

Lu-Ching padded silently beside him without comment. As they approached the Residence they saw Monsieur Bleriot accompanied by Captain d'Arcy who gave Kershaw a breezy *bonsoir* with a knowing smile. The captain's face was white with exhaustion, his eyes red-rimmed, his face unshaven, his boots covered in black dust. "Monsieur Kershaw," Bleriot said. "I would like you to translate some Chinese for me some time — it is important to my diary."

The diary was the subject of much ribaldry in the Legation. When the firing became particularly hot it was customary now for people to say, "Don't worry, Monsieur Bleriot is keeping his diary."

"Could you come to my room tonight at ten?" Monsieur Bleriot asked.

"I'll try," replied Kershaw. "But we must hurry — Sir Archibald is waiting."

The office was crowded when they entered. The Russian and Austrian Ministers with their respective Commanders were gathered round Sir Archibald and Shelham.

While Sir Archibald talked grand strategy, Major Shelham illustrated each point with a ruler on the map. "We have to defend the northern approaches at any cost. Once they are taken our flanks will be turned and H.Q. a sitting target. Now gentlemen, what I want to know is this — if such an emergency arises will you respond to my call for reinforcements? Twice when I have called on you before you have, to put it bluntly, ignored my request."

The reassurances were immediately forthcoming from the Russian and Austrian Ministers, but Monsieur Bleriot at once began a long and flowing evasion, turning at last to Captain d'Arcy with the question: "I'm sure you will agree, Captain d'Arcy, that we are never — but never — in a position to spare any men."

D'Arcy said acidly, "It is we, sir, who need reinforcements. We shall have to give ground with the next attack unless we get them."

"There will be no giving ground," said Sir Archibald. "There is no more ground to give."

Captain d'Arcy ostentatiously shrugged his shoulders. There was a momentary silence which he broke with, "May I tell you a story?" but Sir Archibald cut him short. "We have no time for stories."

"A report then."

"All right."

Kershaw translated. "When the Chinese captured the

eastern half of the French Legation they pushed their barricades to within a hundred yards of ours. They brought up heavy guns, firing segment and shrapnel. They blasted away at us with devastating effect. The main blockhouse and the last line of trenches should have been abandoned — but we received orders from you, Sir Archibald, to hold the line at any cost. For once we did. As a result scores of men were wounded and a French volunteer had his entire face blown off, dying a horrible death. I then ordered my bugler to sound the retreat. We dragged our wounded and dead back to the fortified line of the Peking Hotel. If we had retreated earlier none of this would have happened."

Sir Archibald could not allow his distress to show on his face. He simply said, "I am sorry — but very sorry, Captain d'Arcy. I appreciate your dilemma and your valour. Especially your valour. But there is something you must understand. Here we see the overall picture. There you see only one fragment. It was vital to fight that battle to save the whole of the northern sector from collapsing."

Was the word muttered by Captain d'Arcy "*merde*" — nobody clearly knew, but Sir Archibald finished his lesson in strategy with "Am I understanding you aright, Captain d'Arcy? Are you saying that because of this episode you will disobey my orders in future?"

Captain d'Arcy took out a cigarette and lit it without answering. "You sir," Sir Archibald continued, addressing Monsieur Bleriot. "It is up to you to tell the Captain that I am in command here."

Bleriot spoke to Captain d'Arcy in such rapid French that only Kershaw understood. Captain d'Arcy replied in equally fluent French, spiked with racy colloquialisms. "He says," Monsieur Bleriot addressed Sir Archibald, "that he will obey in future."

Kershaw intervened.

"Excuse me, sir, but what he in fact said was he would *do his best* to obey."

Sir Archibald slammed his fist on the desk and exploded. "You go too far, Bleriot. You sit around here in my Legation all day, you have to be forced to visit your troops and now you are deliberately mis-reporting what this man has to say." He leaned forward over his desk, his bony face set. "I warn both of you. I keep daily reports. Everything will go down in writing. Unless you conform to my orders there will be serious trouble when all this is over."

"If we are still alive," put in Captain d'Arcy. There was a long uneasy silence.

At last Sir Archibald asked, "Do I have your assurance, Captain d'Arcy, that you will obey my orders." D'Arcy shrugged his shoulders. "*Mais oui,*" he said and exchanged a venomous glance with Kershaw. Half an hour later the remaining Ministers and their commanders gave Sir Archibald fresh reassurances and one by one left the room. When they had gone Sir Archibald turned to Shelham and said, "One more evasion by Captain d'Arcy and I'll have him arrested. As for Bleriot —" he made an explosive noise of total disgust.

By now the firing was a continuous barrage but they managed to keep talking without difficulty. The question of a possible spy in the Legation surfaced again. Sir Archibald approached it with what seemed to Kershaw surprising tact. Shelham had no such scruples. Within fifteen minutes his suspicion came through clearly.

Lu-Ching answered his persistent questions with unfailing composure until Shelham repeated all over again one key question.

"Do not understand why you remain in Legation. Plenty lulls."

Kershaw felt it necessary to interpret Shelham's cabalese and Lu-Ching received the question in silence for some moments. Then he began a statement which Kershaw found difficulty in memorizing.

"I repeat that my fundamental loyalties are to my ancestors but there is a division within the Chinese people — a temporary division — between those whose desire it is to — " Kershaw searched for the word and chose "obliterate — the foreigners in our midst and those who want to compromise. From many moons' experience it has seemed to me there are situations where compromise is a better solution."

"Then you're not on one side or the other," Shelham

interpolated sharply.

"That is the unfortunate position into which I am forced since I cannot abandon my country, but I disagree with what they are doing now. I disagree very strongly."

"Tell him, " Sir Archibald said to Kershaw, "why we know someone is passing information."

Kershaw said, "I think that is unnecessary, Sir Archibald. He understands perfectly."

"Well, tell him," Sir Archibald persisted. "We must find out who it is — and quickly. Look what happened just now — a direct hit on my house. I'm just waiting for the next one."

It occurred to Kershaw that Sir Archibald's logic had gone awry. Whereas the field gun could be moved and followed by enemy fire, the house remained an immobile sitting target.

A sudden cresendo of firing which set the house trembling momentarily silenced everybody and out of the din came a long high-pitched whine which held them on the taut edge of another direct hit, but the crash and roar of subsiding masonry came from the direction of the Russian lines.

Sir Archibald drew a deep breath. "Just before we break up — Kershaw — I would like you to know that I appreciate your work on behalf of the Legation." Kershaw found himself falling back on a cliché in his embarrassment: "It's nothing."

"You seem to have mastered English modesty too," Sir Archibald said, unaware of the implication that the British had a monopoly of bravery as well.

"Just minute," said Shelham. "Puzzle me, Kershaw. Often talk oddly. You think Chinese have a case."

Kershaw considered the question. He wanted to say "Yes — I think the Chinese have a case". But it was easier to lie — once Shelham got his talons into him he would suspect everything. "No — no-one could have a case for what they are doing now." Shelham looked at him searchingly. "Half Chinese? Yes?"

"Yes, I am half Chinese but if you think . . . " Sir Archibald interrupted. "I don't think we should go around suspecting everybody, Shelham, if that's what you're getting at."

"Not getting at. Has expressed sympathies."

"Yes," said Sir Archibald. "Quite openly expressed them I think. He'd hardly do that if he were a spy. I think we should concentrate on Lu-Ching's agents. That's where the leak lies. Don't you agree, Lu-Ching?"

Once again Lu Ching considered very carefully what had been said and replied. "I think, Sir Archibald, that it would be better if I ceased communicating with the Chinese and took no further part in this unfortunate incident."

"Now we've offended you," Sir Archibald said. "'Unfortunate incident.' Is that what you call it?"

A half smile was suppressed on Lu-Ching's face. "Tell them," he spoke to Kershaw, "that we are not unaccustomed to offence."

Kershaw repeated his words and before either Sir Archibald or Shelham could answer Lu-Ching spoke again.

"This *is* an incident. It will pass."

"We with it," Shelham muttered, "if the Chinks have their way."

The word 'Chinks' hung on the air with embarrassing persistence until Sir Archibald said very firmly, "If you are going to remain in the Legation, Lu-Ching, you must find out whether your agents are reliable or not. They are converts, aren't they?"

Lu-Ching nodded.

"Then the missionaries could tell you."

"I would rather question them myself," Lu-Ching replied.

Shelham shifted uneasily. "How would we know — " he said and left the sentence unfinished, but everyone in the room knew how it ended . . . that you weren't double-crossing us.

"Perhaps I had better leave the Legation," Lu-Ching observed.

"Which means," said Kershaw, "that he would either be shot or decapitated."

Sir Archibald rolled up the map on his desk, saying, "Yes — I suppose he would — but those are my terms. If you stay I want you to check on your agents." He gestured. "And now I have much to do . . . gentlemen. Shelham, could you tell my wife I would like to see her. And Kershaw — can you deliver this order to the Americans? God knows what they are up to on the Wall. Goodnight, gentlemen."

Shelham and Kershaw left the house together. Moving

across the compound the bullets were sizzling overhead but Shelham made no concession whatever, walking bolt upright. Crouching at first, Kershaw slowly straightened up. Self-preservation did little good inside the compound. It was pure chance whether an unlucky bullet picked you out or ricochetted from a wall. In the open air the noise redoubled and Shelham raised his voice, "Noticed something, Kershaw."

Kershaw said nothing.

"Fond of my wife."

Kershaw concentrated on reaching the protection of the Chancery wall. As they paused under the shelter of the upswung eaves Shelham asked, "What's it mean?"

The need to raise his voice destroyed the inflections and a question which could have been menacing became a straight question.

"I don't know what you mean," said Kershaw.

Shelham gave his chortling laugh. "Think you do."

"I must get up to the Americans."

"Warn you," Shelham said. "She eats men like you alive."

"I'm dead already." Kershaw strode away into the darkness. Shelham hesitated in the doorway of the Chancery. The muffled groans, the smell of carbolic and the blackness with the intense white light of the operating table picked out in the centre, were repellent to him. Steadying his nerves he strode on amongst it all, looking for his wife.

He found her trying to comfort a Japanese captain who was lying on a mattress with a coat thrown over him. His side had been torn open by a bullet. He could not have been more than five feet high and his sword which was a tiny blade not more than thirty inches long was still strapped to his wrist by a cord which he refused to release. Beating his arms up and down, the tiny sword bobbed with them as he struggled to master the pain, but he could not stop his groans. Shelham waited patiently while Doctor Roberts gave the man an injection.

He caught his wife on the wing as she broke away in search of absorbent dressings. He was dismayed to see her hands covered in blood.

"You shouldn't be doing this," he said.

She ignored him and hurried to the far end of the room. He

followed her and while she washed her hands, persisted, "Must see you — "

"Can't you see this is an emergency?" Drying her hands she grabbed up two absorbent dressings.

"When off duty — tomorrow."

"You want me to come and wake you up in the dawn?"

"Yes."

"All right — you won't like it."

"Awake anyway — no one sleeps."

With that he left, abruptly, but it was a long time before the smell of blood and antiseptics diminished. It seemed to have permeated his clothing. It carried for him a foreboding of what was to come.

The quarrel which followed in the dawn was bizarre. The background of bullets and shellbursts continued to roar in the half light, and as Lucy entered the room her husband reared up out of uneasy sleep to confront what momentarily seemed to him like a ghost. This was not his wife but some disembodied figure back from the makeshift graves to warn him how close he lived to that gaping communal ditch.

"I'll sleep here today," she was saying as she struggled to remove her shirtwaist. Her fingers were stiff with unaccustomed bandaging, her legs weak, her whole body ready to collapse into instant sleep.

"Breakfast?" he asked shrugging off sleep as swiftly as a skin.

"Had some," she replied.

Frequently his cabalese drove her to answer in kind. Now, it seemed appropriate to the situation and her mood.

"Must talk," he said.

"Not now."

"Yes — now."

She was struggling with the fastenings at the back of her skirt. Moving swiftly round her he did what he had always done over the years: tried to take over the unfastening. It had been a welcome attention in the past but now she brushed him aside: "I can do it."

"Listen," he said. "Kershaw".

She shrank into herself at the sound of the name.

"Look," she said. "I'm liable to collapse any minute. I don't know why you want to talk about Kershaw but for God's sake choose some other time."

"No. Now."

"Not if I can help it."

"Listen — love this man?"

Naked to the waist she turned slowly and confronted him for a long moment. As she very deliberately slipped out of her skirt she was silently repeating the words — yes, desperately — yes, desperately — but aloud she asked, "What on earth are you talking about?"

"Dawn assignations," he said.

Her mind jumped. How could he know about that. No one saw them — or did they? The Legation compound in the dawn was a rabbit warren of hiding places where unidentified shadows flitted from one duty to the next, and who knew what private behaviour might suddenly become public.

"I don't know what you are talking about. Have you finished with the bed?"

"You do know," he said.

She slumped down on the bed in her long underdrawers, pulled the sheet over herself and turned away from him. He grabbed her arm and turned her back.

In the half light she had the illusion that his eyes were blazing in a grey mask of a face. He took her shoulders, drew her up towards him and staring straight into her eyes, asked, "Slept with him?"

She struggled then. "Damn you — can't you see I'm dead — leave me alone — I must sleep. For God's sake let me sleep."

He did not relax his grip.

"Slept with him?" he repeated.

"Of course I haven't slept with him." She tried to pull away.

"Tell truth!"

"I am telling truth."

"Not."

"Sometimes you sound like a robot," she exclaimed, "and you've got just about as much feeling. Do you know what I went through last night? Do you know what happened to that Japanese? Died in my arms — all blood and horror! Let me go

— let me sleep."

She was beating on his chest but he did not relax his grip.

"Must know," he persisted.

"There's nothing to know. Kershaw is a friend."

"Lying!" And now he shook her and repeated, "Must have truth."

She blazed at him then — "You've got the truth." And as she said it she was thinking — my period, what has happened to my period . . . that will tell him the truth one day . . . but what does it matter . . . I want him to know — I must tell him . . . tell him now.

As he threw her roughly back on the bed the resolve to tell him — arrogantly, with pride — welled up in her and she turned and began.

"All right — I will tell you — "

But he had gone out into the morning.

CHAPTER XII

THE RAINS NEVER came and the heat beat up at noon to 110 degrees in the shade until sweat accompanied every movement. People went mechanically through rota duties — four hours on and four off — and as mechanically fell asleep, sometimes fully clothed.

Everybody smoked heavily to smother the smell of accumulated dirt, sweat and putrefaction. Rationing had intensified. White rice, butter, milk and flour were minimal, and four cubes of sugar a day a luxury for those who could get them. Coarse Chinese bread made from brown flour stuck in European throats and horse meat became a delicacy replaced by the tough hides of mules. The hard bread needed intensive chewing: swallowing enough to satisfy hunger was difficult. There was still water, wine and foods looted by the Legation defenders from sorties into abandoned shops. But people were tired . . . tired . . . and visibly drooping, and women pinned deeper pleats each week in their skirts and shirtwaists. Two hours' continuous sleep was a luxury. If the sheer suffocation of heat did not bring people awake, the sound of blaring Chinese trumpets broke open the night when they heralded yet another attack.

At four o'clock in the morning the alarm from the Bell Tower sounded the emergency note. Reserves poured out, half dressed, some grasping improvised weapons, all stupefied with sleep and the inferno of noise began again from thousands of Chinese rifles.

Kershaw arrived late, fully clothed and weaponless. He had abandoned the big Colt, symbol of his new aggression, which he had grown so accustomed to carrying in the day. Night attacks and alarms of this kind were now too familiar. Thousands of rifles he knew would crash away at distant barricades, swarms of bullets pass overhead and occasionally find a human target, but here, in the Legation compound it was — fantastically — as safe as Piccadilly Circus in peacetime London. As if to confirm the unnatural security Sir Archibald sauntered out from his house wearing nothing but pyjamas.

Monsieur Bleriot emerged with his rifle still over his shoulder and paced on the fringes of the gathered group. Two more plenipotentiaries joined him and strolled at the correct distance, carefully preserving rank. Very few women troubled to join them. They had become familiar with the routine emergencies, and the demands of decency made a sudden rush into the open difficult.

It was a curious scene. The still safe centre of the British Legation concentrating many of the able-bodied reserves with Sir Archibald dominating the group: all hell let loose a few score yards away: the women mostly safe in their beds, whether indifferent or in fear: the plenipotentiaries preserving protocol and a holocaust of bullets passing harmlessly — for the most part — overhead.

As Kershaw waited patiently for the crescendo of firing to falter he thought of the Chinese finding the barrels of their rifles becoming hotter until they pulled them out of loopholes and stood them against the barricades. Or would this be the occasion they all feared when, instead of faltering, the firing came nearer and nearer and at last an ugly rush of Chinese with screams of "Kill! Kill!" would burst through the flimsy barricades? It was a common nightmare now. Women started up out of sleep on the note of a Chinese trumpet as if the Chinese had already burst into the room.

As the firing continued anxieties multiplied. It was unusually prolonged. Could that possibly mean that tonight the routine would in fact be broken, that the guns were creeping closer until they could blow holes in the barricades at point blank range? The background talk dwindled away, the group fell into uneasy silence and on the fringe Monsieur Bleriot and his colleagues stopped pacing and stood still, listening. There was a long moment when the scene froze into a tableau.

And then the crescendo slowly fell away, the heavier note of the artillery diminished and the bullets overhead became sporadic.

As Kershaw turned away Monsieur Bleriot caught him by the arm. "Do you sleep well?" he said in French. Kershaw smiled grimly and asked, "Who does?" Coming from Monsieur Bleriot the question had a special poignancy. "Good, — good," said Bleriot. "Perhaps you would not be averse to a little brandy?"

Kershaw hesitated. What could these sudden overtures mean? Obviously Bleriot needed something, but the last thing he desired was Bleriot's company, though he knew he would not sleep, and brandy was a luxury that perhaps would kill the painful emptiness which always followed a major attack, when he lay fully awake, alive in every strained fibre.

"All right," he agreed.

"I need to have a quick word with Sir Archibald," Monsieur Bleriot said. "You know where my room is." Kershaw shook his head.

"Down the main corridor of Sir Archibald's residence, take the first on the right and the second on the left — you will see my name on the door."

"But Madame Bleriot — " Kershaw said.

"She is staying with Lady Mainwaring. I won't be a few minutes."

With that he moved away and walked with Sir Archibald towards the Residence. For a moment Kershaw wondered whether this move was some madly subtle interpretation of protocol whereby Monsieur Bleriot could not be seen walking away with Kershaw in public on such an occasion.

The room when he reached it was in total darkness. He struck a match, peered round and found a big kerosene lamp with an ornate brass stem and a great swelling globe. It was an object of considerable beauty. In the dim light he saw that the room was furnished with yellow brocaded chairs — clearly imported, a leather-topped desk, and a number of small Chinese lacquer tables.

Papers were scattered over the leather desk and at one side lay two big, black volumes, one with the pages open. Moving over to the desk, Kershaw peered at the volumes. One was hand-written . . . could it be . . . a journal, a diary . . . a diplomatic notebook? He went to the door, looked down the corridor, shut the door firmly and returned to the desk. Pulling the lamp closer he peered at the written page and drew breath sharply. The words were in French, sprawling, as though produced under stress.

"Leaving compound to visit front line — narrowly missed by shell. It lodged in the Residence. Later found it had passed through dining room narrowly missing Queen Victoria. What a blow to British morale if she had been — shattered — British damned patronizing. Anyone would think they were winning siege. They simply sit in Legation safe and sound."

Something had been struck through in the next paragraph. Picking up the diary and holding it to the light Kershaw was able to decipher the first words: "I don't know what Sir Archibald" and then thick black ink blotted out the rest.

He turned back to another page.

"Had to reassure my wife Christine. She cannot settle to anything. Better if she had a job and did something. Busy myself all day. Countermanded Sir A's instructions to Captain d'Arcy — madness for him to spare a single man."

"Helped a wounded Frenchman to the hospital. Had him picked up on a plank at barricade. Our positions hard pressed. Don't like being under heavy fire."

There were footsteps coming along the corridor. When Bleriot entered Kershaw was sitting in one of the brocaded chairs, well away from the desk, and immediately came to his feet as a mark of respect.

"*Pardon! Pardon!*" Bleriot said effusively. His eye immediately fixed on the diaries and he strode over to close the open page, pushing both into a drawer.

"*Asseyez-vous — asseyez-vous!*" He moved swiftly to an ornate Chinese cupboard and took out a bottle of brandy and two glasses.

"Better to drink than lie awake," he commented.

Kershaw nodded agreement. He noticed that one of Bleriot's fat white hands was still shaking as he poured the drinks.

"There was a small favour — a very small favour — I wanted to ask you."

The brandies were large and Kershaw was tempted to drink his down in one gulp. Instead he sipped it discreetly and tried desperately to stop himself yawning. Always it was like that. Immediately after an attack he felt geared up, strung taut, wishing for some form of action to release the coiled springs and then within a few minutes the tensions relaxed, but he could not sleep. He drew deeply at the brandy and dimly heard Bleriot saying,

"I stumbled on some Chinese documents but I cannot read them. I should be eternally grateful, Monsieur, if you would give me the advantage of your skills. Am I asking too much?"

He leaned forward and proffered two Chinese parchments. Kershaw took them and began to read in a monotone. He did not register the meaning of what he read because he was too tired to care.

"The great city of Peking which surrounds the Legation defences will never march away. They are trapped in one large windowless cell because, on all sides, treetops and roofs restrict their vision to that of ten lengths of silk or less, and where this is not so, to the north and south, a wall of more than forty feet so dominates and encloses their life as to render it one of blind imprisonment. It is a situation which offers little sustenance to the human spirit and thus I feel their morale must fail before long."

As he finished reading Bleriot said, "Most interesting. Most interesting. Tell me, Monsieur Kershaw — would you know what rank of person had written this document from the handwriting — I understand it is easily possible to distinguish one rank from another?"

"Sometimes," Kershaw began and stopped. The handwriting was familiar. Where had he seen such writing before? There flashed before his mind's eye a letter Lu-Ching had shown him, which he had himself written to the Empress. It remained undelivered because the chain of communication from one so humble to one so high had broken down. Could it be? Was it possible that Lu-Ching had written this document?

"Do I see recognition?" Monsieur Bleriot asked.

Hesitating a long moment Kershaw said, "Can I ask, Monsieur Bleriot, where you got this?"

"I found it."

"Where did you find it?"

"I cannot tell you that."

"Then it is difficult for me to tell you who I think wrote it."

Monsieur Bleriot bridled. "Difficult? Why should it be difficult."

"Because it seems a compromising document."

"Why compromising?"

"It's not exactly calculated to boost our morale, is it?"

Monsieur Bleriot noticed Kershaw's empty glass. "Let me re-fill you," he offered. His hand still shook and he over-filled the glass. "I'm sorry," he said, and a moment later: "All right, I will tell you where I found it. Outside the door of Lu-Ching's room."

"Outside?"

"On the floor. I think he must have dropped it."

"That is also my room."

"*Mon Dieu*, is it? But you surprise me." It was some time before Bleriot broke the silence. "I have some cigars. Would you like one?"

"No thanks."

"You don't mind if I smoke?" Kershaw shook his head.

"Tell me," said Bleriot. "That is Lu-Ching's handwriting, isn't it?"

What was there to lose, Kershaw thought. They could so easily check and Lu-Ching would have a perfectly innocent explanation. Kershaw knew that he had long been in the habit of keeping a journal about events in the Legation. Several people did.

"Yes," he replied. "It is Lu-Ching's."

"Most interesting," said Bleriot. "Most interesting. You see, Sir Archibald asked me to keep an eye on him. I don't know why. I think he suspects something."

"What exactly?"

"I don't know."

"Come now, Monsieur Bleriot. You know why."

"Maybe I do."

"Lu-Ching," Kershaw said, "is a man of integrity — unlike a number of people in this Legation."

Bleriot bridled again. "Really Monsieur Kershaw — there is no need to — " he stopped abruptly as the sound of rifle fire began again. The firing increased and within a few minutes echoed round the Legation. "*Mon Dieu*! Will it never end? *Nous allons tous mourir ce soir*."

A moment later he came to his feet, automatically picked up his rifle, slung it over his shoulder and began pacing round the room. All thought of Lu-Ching seemed to have vanished from his mind. Kershaw swallowed his brandy and stood up. At once Bleriot was all smiling charm. "But no — Monsieur — there is no need to go so early — there's much brandy left. Look." He held the bottle up to the light. It occurred to Kershaw that Bleriot was afraid to be left alone, and he weighed the knowledge against his sudden desire to go on drinking the brandy. Sleep he felt would not come easily. He had long ago learnt that when physical exhaustion was prolonged it became a form of nervous excitement which defied the body's powers of relaxation. He was to meet Lucy again in the dawn, down by the abandoned trench. Afterwards it was his turn to be on duty with Sir Archibald.

People were stirring in the Residence once more. Suddenly he saw Bleriot stop walking and stiffen. "Listen," he said. "Those bullets. *Mon Dieu*! They are. . . . " He stopped and listened again. "Yes, yes! They are hitting the walls — the outside walls — of this house. What does it mean Kershaw — what do you think it means?"

"I will have another brandy," Kershaw said. "Don't worry. A few stray shots."

But the bullets were thudding thickly against the wall of the house and suddenly he thought of Sir Archibald's suspicions that someone from inside the Legation was directing the fire.

"I nearly got hit by a shell fragment yesterday," said Kershaw. "It crashed down from a shell-burst. It doesn't mean a thing."

"Doesn't mean a thing!" Bleriot was indignant. "Of course it means a thing — everything. They have found the range and are hitting the target. Who gave them the range? Who — who?"

Kershaw thought — I suppose that damned alarm will go off at any moment and we will all troop out again . . . but no — leaving the house would be too dangerous under such close fire.

Bleriot's hand was shaking again as he poured more brandy.

"How is it going to end, Kershaw? How is it going to end? We can't go on like this, can we? Can we?"

He thrust the glass back at Kershaw with the force of a punch and half the contents spilt again. "*Pardon! Pardon!*" he said and taking his silk handkerchief from an inner pocket mopped the brandy from Kershaw's trousers. The question of rank had undergone a curious inversion. Monsieur Bleriot was appealing for reassurance from Kershaw.

Slowly the note and sound of the bullets changed again. They ceased to slap into the walls of the Residence and once more whistled overhead. Bleriot brightened visibly.

"You know the Chinese," Bleriot said. "What do you think they will do next?"

"Everything depends on Seymour's lot," said Kershaw. "Once he approaches Peking they will beat it."

"You are the only optimist left in the Legation." As Bleriot spoke a howl began in the compound which mounted to such a maniacal pitch it left him fumbling with his cravat as if he were about to be decapitated.

Kershaw strode over to the sandbagged window. Between the interstices he saw a thin scarecrow of a man in a loose Chinese tunic, with his hands raised to heaven, apostrophizing what was evidently his god in a high-pitched wailing which broke off abruptly to be followed by a stream of language.

"Be thou forgotten of the Lord if thou confess not they sins. . . . Take a flaming sword and forge a weapon for the greater glory of God, but woe be unto you who kill for the sake of killing. . . . " His voice fell away in a kind of chorus:

"Woe be unto you
Woe be unto
Woe be
Woe! Woe!"

A moment later the voice rose again: "Then shall the heavens split in anger and the Lord shall appear in all his might and strike your enemies down. . . .

"Strike your enemies down
Strike your enemies
Strike your
Strike! Strike!"

Now he had picked up a staff with a carved head and was hitting the ground in time with the words Strike! Strike!

Bleriot, sitting in the corner of the room furthest from the window, kept repeating, "What is it? What is it?"

At last Kershaw turned and said, "It's the American missionary. His name's James something or other. It's all got too much for him. He seems to have gone crazy."

There was a moon breaking through the clouds, converting the Yankee's tunic into opalescent white and his figure into sharp silhouette. The scene took on the artificiality of a stage set with an actor declaiming his lines but the gaunt face and beard had a reality which only madness could achieve. . . .

"Save us Lord ere we come to the brink. . . . Save us and the living shall praise you beyond the reach of the dead."

There was a pause when the gaunt figure prostrated itself and as it unbent, and once more flung its hands and almost its whole body towards the heavens, it declaimed again, "Look down we do beseech thee oh Lord on the depth of our misery and snatch us we beseech you oh Lord out of the jaws of death before we are swallowed up by eternal night. But if we are to die — if we are to die, let it be thy benediction that we die without pain.

"Without pain
Without pain. . . ."

Again he repeated the last words like an echo.

The sound and direction of the bullets now changed once more. Some continued to whistle overhead but others thudded into buildings around the compound, almost as if they were changing their direction in an effort to destroy the mad figure in the moonlight.

Bleriot moved over to the window and peered through the sandbags.

"You see," he said. "Someone's directing them. They must be. They want to get him."

"We must get him out of that," Kershaw muttered and turned towards the door.

"You're not going out!" exclaimed Bleriot.

Ignoring him, Kershaw hurried down the corridor and paused in the protection of the portico.

"Hi, you!" he shouted but the scarecrow figure ignored him.

Kershaw picked up a stone and threw it with some accuracy. The stone struck the missionary on the left shoulder, and he staggered slightly in bewilderment. "Ah God — My Lord God Almighty — Is it thy hand, oh Lord, on my shoulder?"

"This is the voice of the Lord," Kershaw bellowed, "telling you to return to the Residence. At once." The missionary half turned in amazement, took a few steps, hesitated and stared up at the sky.

"Not there," Kershaw bellowed. "Here!" As he spoke a spattering of bullets dug a diagonal across the compound and the missionary fell on his knees. "I beseech thee, oh Lord — let me be the voice of thy message . . . what is thy message. . . . "

Kershaw suddenly dashed across the compound, grabbed the missionary by the hand and dragged him back to the safety of the portico.

Once inside the hall a terrible smell hit Kershaw's nostrils. Then he was aware of two burning eyes staring straight into his and a quavering voice trying to say something.

"Where do you sleep?" Kershaw said. "Are you in the Fu?"

But the face had hardened and the eyes intensified and now suddenly the voice said, "I smell an unbeliever. I smell an unbeliever."

Kershaw had the impulse to slap the man's face to bring him to his senses but whatever madness gripped the missionary it was probably capable of violent retaliation.

"We'll wait till the firing stops," he said. "Then I'll take you to the Fu."

"Do you believe, or don't you?" the missionary demanded, drawing his gaunt frame up to its full five feet two. Kershaw ignored the question the first time but when it was repeated with greater vehemence, on the impulse he replied, "Of course I don't."

Some strange power seemed to blow up the missionary's small frame and shake it as he roared with a voice out of all proportion to his size, "So you are the unbeliever we must root out — you are the evil one prolonging our fate."

His voice and words began to mount again and presently sonorous periods apostrophizing God were once more ringing on the air, and in between the rolling sentences Kershaw became aware that the firing had ceased. Suddenly seizing the missionary by his two arms he twisted them behind his back and frog-marched him across the compound towards the Fu.

Fifteen minutes later, back in the compound, he stood for a moment staring at the moon, hesitating. Should he go back to Bleriot and the brandy — no. Not even the brandy redeemed Bleriot. Instead he made his way to his small room in the west corner of the Residence, expecting to find Lu-Ching asleep. The room was empty.

Slumping down, he was too tired to remove anything except his shoes. The air was heavy and foetid and smelt of kerosene. He staggered up again, went to the window, removed the sandbags and opened it. He stood there a moment breathing the cooler air and the words, "So you are the unbeliever we must root out", came back to him and he smiled grimly. Unbeliever or not, how much longer could they go on like this?

Discipline was breaking down with increasing frequency; sailors off duty and some volunteers looted the foreign stores enclosed in their lines; Chinese converts were beginning to forget their Christian codes: dealing with the culprits became more and more difficult. Short of shooting one or two nothing seemed to deter them, and shooting such a precious commodity as manpower was madness.

Kershaw turned back towards his bed, lay down and tossed restlessly. Fifteen minutes later the calm outside drove him to rise again and make his way swiftly down the corridor once more. Out in the open the silence was deep enough to seem uncanny. He walked — almost sauntered — to the Bell Tower and peered at the many notices pinned to its walls. The sentry at the Tower seemed half asleep. A clerk from the Customs Office, he looked absurdly theatrical, standing there with his rifle askew and a pith helmet which was too large for him crushed down on his head. He seemed disinclined to talk. The notices on the Tower were just visible in the moonlight and domestic in a madly normal way: a pair of shoes missing, an iron for hire, the cobbler ready once again to repair shoes and a wonderfully simplistic notice from Sir Archibald Mainwaring in his own handwriting:

"Loopholes should never be left open except when being used for looking through or firing through. A brick placed at the narrowest part is quite sufficient to prevent the enemy firing through and hitting people passing."

It was beautifully matter of fact and touched with naivety.

Kershaw climbed to the small verandah and stood looking out over the Legation. It seemed unbelievably calm, with just the light from the hospital. The air was soft and balmy, the moon perfect in a cloudless sky, the exotic architecture of Peking rising in ghostly symmetry in the background with the black might of the Tartar wall rearing up and over the huddle of buildings and the great pink walls of the Imperial Palace — grey in the moonlight — still dominating the city. It was a drearily familiar background to Kershaw, but tonight compounded of mysterious elements which could stir his blood as if with some ethnic quality.

The unbeliever we must root out. If, by that, allegiance to God was meant, yes, but if loyalty to the Legations, nothing was more confused. What did this handful of predatory Europeans matter beside the surging millions of Chinese whose culture for centuries had subsumed half the earth? What did men like Sir Archibald and Shelham weigh in the balance beside the stirring of a sleeping giant stung into action by the foreign interloper: and what clash of codes could resolve the claims of superiority; one based on dynamic laws reaching back into a mystical past, the other on commercialized Christianity and primitive democracy? The unbeliever we must root out. Had God devised this pretty little battle between his minions in order to watch the spectacle of decapitation, mutilation, courage and cowardice? What sense could there be in furthering the Grand Design with a siege in which the meek had certainly failed to inherit the earth? The Chinese converts were the easily expendable pawns in this particular episode of God's game. They were approaching starvation, they were herded like cattle, and two of them he had now marked out to see the effects of that most splendidly ingenious master bacillus — cholera. And the missionary's madness was the final tribute to the divine torturer who committed himself to an all-embracing love and drove his faithful to insanity when that love gave no protection. The missionary could not face the truth. His God had abandoned him. Oh Lord, oh Lord, why hast thou forsaken me. Save my mind from snapping that I may die in dignity and not become a howling dervish desiring only to escape the death you have so fiendishly devised for me. . . . And why should I deserve such a death?

"Can't sleep — can you?"

If the voice startled Kershaw its owner was much more disturbing.

"Funny place," Major Shelham said. "Why here?"

"Cooler," replied Kershaw, once more imitating Shelham's staccato speech.

"Quiet worse than noise," said Shelham. "Never know what buggers brewing."

"I like the quiet," Kershaw said.

"Also like Chinese — yes?" Shelham gave his neighing laugh. Kershaw said nothing.

"You move around. Know everything."

"Not exactly," said Kershaw.

"Discuss things with Lu-Ching."

"If you mean do I discuss our defences with Lu-Ching, the answer is yes. Why shouldn't I?"

"Must tell you. Don't trust him. Simple as that."

"I have no reason not to trust Lu-Ching. As I've said before — " he paused and then decided to risk it — "Lu-Ching has a damned sight more integrity than some of the people in the Legation."

"Integrity, yes. Not our kind. Chinese integrity for Chinese."

"Lu-Ching has been very useful. His sources are better than ours."

"Sir Archibald says — don't tell him anything. That's an order."

"An order?"

"Yes — an order."

Kershaw drew a deep breath and was about to challenge the words when it suddenly seemed unwise. He shrugged his shoulders and reflected that he would go on talking to Lu-Ching in confidence.

"Seen anything Lucy?"

Shelham turned towards Kershaw as he said it, and his cold eyes stared at his face in the moonlight.

"No," Kershaw lied. "Nothing."

"Better that way," said Shelham.

Kershaw wanted to ask why it was better, what the hell it had to do with Shelham, why couldn't he take his stuffed shirt military presence back to the Residence and leave him alone out here in the moonlight whose soothing beauty he was disrupting. But he said nothing.

"Try sleep. Goodnight." With that Shelham strode down the steps and off across the compound. Kershaw remained staring out over the upswung eaves and dragons to the ghostly pink walls of the Palace. A scheming old lady whose finger nails were six inches long slept soundly out there in a most luxurious bed, surrounded by innumerable eunuchs. What incredible quirk of the Divine Intelligence had given this old lady powers equivalent to God's when clearly it was her own fate, not that of the Chinese people, which concerned her? Equally, what debased imagination had conceived a race of people called Boxers who destroyed the civilized ideals of ancient China and made the foreigners the occasion for indulging their own blood lust? It was too simple of course. Foreign merchants had their blood lusts too: Lord Elgin had bitterly complained of that.

And suddenly there came up at the back of Kershaw's mind the day he went to witness the ritual of the *lien chu-üan*, or boxing, from which the Boxers took their name. The recitation of the cabbalistic message, the slow change of breathing of the speaker, the mounting intensity, the frothing at the mouth and the crowd of red-sashed Boxers shouting at the climax — God descends! God descends! Possessed by the spirit of *lien chu-üan* the man was said to be invulnerable but all the sword thrusts went deliberately wide and no one dared to fire directly into his body.

What crazily confused divinity had proliferated so many twisted minds to act out such third-rate purposes in a universe which tonight slept momentarily under the great arc of the sky and the mystery of the moon with all the sublimity of a noble conception? Noble conception! Yes, but cold, uninterested, driven by forces which did not share the elevated emotions which it inspired.

Somewhere up on the Tartar wall a trumpet blare echoed round the compound and died away. It was all about to begin again . . . or, was it . . . Kershaw waited for the first fusillade but as the minutes ticked away nothing happened. His eyes closed and an immense burden of weariness overwhelmed him as he moved down from the verandah and walked back to the Residence. The room was still empty. He slumped down on the bed and was instantly asleep.

The background firing woke him before the dawn and he lay there wondering what had happened to Lu-Ching. As the first morning light seeped through the cracks in the sandbags he forced himself to get up. His mouth was dry, his body dirty, his clothes rumpled but he had a rendezvous with Lucy at six o'clock and it was already five-thirty. He poured some water from the big Chinese jug into a bowl, stripped off his shirt and washed his torso. With a big open razor he hacked unsatisfactorily at his beard. His toothbrush was showing signs of wear and there was no tooth powder. Ten minutes later he set out towards the abandoned trench. Once more the bullets were whistling overhead with an occasional stray one penetrating the compound. As yet the shelling had not begun. Moving along every convenient wall, he quickly reached the northern perimeter. The trench was heavily carpeted with thick black Peking dust and so dry it stirred in clouds round his shoes. This time as he approached the meeting place his heart beat fast, and that marked a change he did not overlook. He knew now that his expectations were high. The mere sight of Lucy was sufficient to stir his blood. But she was not there. He waited ten minutes and she did not appear. And then he noticed, stuck between the wooden beams, the tip of something resembling an envelope. He snatched it up and read, "Meet burial ground." It was printed in almost undecipherable block letters obviously intended to preserve anonymity.

The quickest way to the burial ground lay through the hospital. From a back room he peered through a small slit in the wall. The scene was empty, desolate. Waiting a long moment he slipped quickly away down towards the canal. Part of a burnt-out house was still standing and as he picked his way through the ruins her voice came softly — "Kevin — I'm here."

She had secreted herself in the remains of a room with three whole walls offering some privacy. She fell into his arms and was kissing him so passionately he staggered back a pace. Then she dragged him into a corner and as he tried to speak said, "Don't say anything — just kiss me."

Sexual arousal came slowly with him but now months of deprivation and Lucy's urgent body brought him instant passion. Then he was kissing her as she wanted to be kissed, his hands embracing her breasts, his core hard against her deeply thrusting body. For five minutes they said nothing but embraced until she was shaking in his arms, and at that moment came a sudden crumbling of brickwork in the next ruin and he pushed away from her, covering her mouth with his hand. It was nothing more than a stray bullet; and then she said urgently,

"Kevin, he knows."

"Knows what?"

"He knows what's going on between us."

"How can he know that?"

"I think someone saw us last time in the trench. That's why I changed the place. No one's ever here except in the evenings."

"It had to happen, I suppose," he said.

"There's something else," she said.

"Tell me."

"My period — it's overdue."

"How much?"

"Two weeks now."

He made a swift calculation. "You think it's me," he said.

"I know it's you," she said. "But there's more. I don't know how to tell you."

He kissed her again but she held him back and looked deeply into his eyes.

"You *do* believe I love you, don't you," she said.

"Yes," he said.

"I was so scared I had to do something terrible."

"Tell me."

She buried her face on his chest and burst into tears. "Now I feel ashamed — now I hate myself — now I don't know how to tell you."

He held her gently back and said, "You've slept with him."

"Yes — yes — yes." She punched his chest as she spoke as if to make sure he clearly understood the depth of her iniquity. Then the words poured away from her. "I had to have a safeguard — it's only for the time being — while we are locked up in here. I can't escape him . . . if I'd started being sick in the mornings and I hadn't slept with him — he would — oh, I know it sounds ridiculous — I don't know what he'd do. He's so ruthless when he's roused. The horrible thing is he still loves me. He's capable of anything — you don't know. Oh, my God, when will this awful siege be over — we can escape then, can't we? We can go off together . . . we can . . . we can. . . ?" Her words tumbled into silence and she stared at him through her tears. "Can you forgive me?" she asked.

He said nothing but embraced and kissed her gently. Suddenly she pulled away, glanced at her watch and said, "I must go — I'm staying with him again. I didn't want it. He insisted!" She buried her head in his chest once more and her muffled voice said, "What are we going to do, Kevin?"

He held her close. "There's nothing we can do now. We must wait until the siege is over."

"Do you think we will survive?"

"I don't know. But we must stop meeting like this. It doesn't do us any good. If he finds out and tells Sir Archibald it will ruin everything."

She pulled away from him, her face hardening.

"Kevin — how can you be so brave about all the bullets and so afraid of stuffed dummies like Sir Archibald? How *can* you?"

"I'm not afraid," he began but she cut across him — "Oh yes you are."

"Listen to me," he said. "It's bad enough that he suspects already. If he finds out the truth he'll go straight to Sir Archibald and that will be the end of us."

"Why?" she said. "Why?"

"I wouldn't put it past Sir Archibald to have me arrested."

"Arrested? You must be mad."

"You don't seem to realize we're in a war. We must be more

discreet."

"Discreet! In the middle of death and disaster you talk about discretion! What does it matter what they think — we're liable to die any minute, anyway."

"Your argument's getting very mixed up, Lucy. A moment ago you told me you slept with your husband to protect yourself. You're afraid of him and I am afraid if they find out about these meetings."

"It's all such a mess. When will this awful siege be over — when will we be free?"

She embraced him again then, and began kissing him so passionately she forced him to take two paces backward. He stumbled over a piece of charred wood which snapped with a sound so loud in the silence of the dawn they both froze in alarm, but there was no one to hear. The smell of carbolic came drifting on the air from the hospital and seemed to alert her to passing time. "I must go," she said. "He'll be waiting. I wouldn't put it past him to come to the hospital to collect me. We'll meet again tomorrow — here."

"Not tomorrow. I'm with the Americans — the day after."

"All right — but there's another thing, Kevin. For God's sake give up this stupid bravery of yours. They told me you rescued the missionary the other night. They tell me you rush around ignoring the bullets. For my sake — just for my sake —" she laughed as the phrase occurred to her — "show a little cowardice."

He laughed too then and for the first time they were momentarily relaxed. "After all," she said, "we know it isn't genuine bravery, don't we. We know it is just your damned guilt driving you to search out punishment. Well, you've had enough punishment — you've paid — now think of me. Think how I would feel if anything happened to you. I must go. . . . "

She pulled away. "You go first," he said. "I'll follow later." She gave him one last fleeting kiss on the cheek and said "Wednesday. You promise?"

"I promise."

She fled then and as he stood there, against the charred wall feeling the sun already hot on his face, he tried to suppress all thought of Lucy and her period. As part of his escape he tried to analyze the many faces of bravery. . . . Sir Archibald, who was brave because he could not let the old country down, because fear of what they would think of him in the Foreign Office drove him on, or was that true? Partly, yes, but at a deeper level something bred in his blood from generations of expectations, something known as an old-fashioned sense of honour, held him together with greater certainty than fear of Foreign Office opinion. But what confusion would overtake him if someone asked him what he meant by honour. "Honour? Everyone knows what I mean by honour." He would recoil from the disturbing implications of anything so obvious. And Shelham. Precise, military Shelham whose ordered reactions had been programmed by Sandhurst and were inescapable? What awful fears sometimes shook that façade and left him struggling with the same feelings which gripped the viscera of everybody under fire? Or did his lack of imagination fail to communicate the true nature of pain, and leave him living in a bland desert? And Lucy, who had so swiftly adapted to the horrors of the hospital. Lucy, brave in a different way — Lucy — whose battle with her husband — whose . . . period . . . what if she were pregnant . . . a child . . . he, Kevin Kershaw, the father of a child. It would change — revolutionize — his life. Did he want that? Did he want to settle to the bourgeois life, the respectable father of a family, doomed to earning a living in a secure job instead of disappearing in the vast embrace of China and finding an utterly different — he hesitated on the word — destiny. Destiny . . . the air in this siege seemed heavy with destiny and at the still centre was his personal *Chinese* destiny.

A sharp crackle of fire followed by blaring trumpets brought him back to his senses. Avoiding the hospital he made his way through the ruins into the main compound towards the Residence, and there he joined the morning conference in Sir Archibald's office.

CHAPTER XIII

"It's almost impossible now," Sir Archibald was saying pompously, "to keep a check on what is happening. The ebb and flow of reinforcements is confused and not by any means always in my control."

There were six people gathered round his desk including Sir Robert Hart, Major Shelham, Captain d'Arcy and a huge, fat American sergeant, Chuck Winterburn, who sat with his hands balanced on his wide-apart knees, eagerly scanning every point on the map.

"Roughly it amounts to this," Sir Archibald continued. "We have a defensive square. Eastern and northern sections are manned by the Germans, French, Japanese and Italians. In the face of a mass attack, post commanders supply each other with reinforcements without consulting me, and that won't do. It's a flagrant violation of regulations. I am trying to work out a new liaison. The other fronts and the Americans on the Tartar wall work with me. But we've had trouble with the Americans too. I am sending Mr Kershaw with you this morning, Sergeant Winterburn, to find out exactly what is happening. But first I want you to go to the south-west corner of the British Legation. The Chinese have pushed up a gun which is annoying everyone. It hit my Residence yesterday. Captain Halliday is awaiting my instructions. Tell him to attack and disable the gun at once."

"And me?" Winterburn said.

"After that, Winterburn — I want your detachment to tackle the guns firing from the Ha-ta Gate."

"Sure thing. When do we go?"

"At once."

"Okay."

"Captain Halliday tells me the British have developed a new technique. Go and watch it Winterburn. You may learn a trick or two." Winterburn grinned. "Sure thing," he said. "We're babes in arms." As he rose to leave with Kershaw he dropped his voice and whispered, "Six campaign medals and I haven't learnt a goddam thing."

Hurrying across the compound, his big fat body seemed to progress by rolling, not walking, and he talked as fast as he moved. He told Kershaw of his feud with Captain Meyerstein, ostensibly in command of the Americans. They hated each other for the simplest of reasons. Meyerstein was in command and frequently frightened: Winterburn second in command and seldom frightened. It was Winterburn who had rallied the Americans to return to the wall, not Meyerstein. It was Winterburn the men identified with, not Meyerstein whose outward show of forceful authority always wavered at the crucial moment.

But there were deeper troubles. "Look at this sonofabitch Meyerstein—he's a goddam cavalry officer, we're Marines. We don't want the army telling the marines."

"Anything goes in a siege," Kershaw said.

"Goes too far," replied Winterburn. "Sonofabitch." He broke off with a broad grin. "Say, Kershaw — you're a great guy. Didn't know Limeys came in such different sizes."

Somehow Kershaw couldn't bring himself to say that he was American too.

Immediately night fell reinforcements began to make their way in pairs up the wall. It was then that the wild dervish figure came waddling along, threatening to wreck the whole undertaking. Wearing a long black cassock and a top hat, the mad missionary sang:

> "In death's dark vale I fear no ill
> With thee, dear Lord, beside me,
> Thy rod and staff my comfort still,
> Thy cross before to guide me."

Stumbling blindly along in the darkness, his eyes fixed on some divine host in the heavens, his voice rose to a howl:

> "Look down in mercy, oh Lord,

We ask but for your justice.
None shall gainsay our darkest day — "

Winterburn was furious. "He'll screw everything. Shut that bastard up." He set off down the ramp at a run. Confronting the missionary, he grabbed him and said, "Stow it you stupid bastard."

The missionary's voice rose to a scream. "King Oscar, hear me — Your Royal Majesty, listen to my plea — I plight my troth to you and God — can a man do more. There is an evil man among us — there is an unbeliever. He must be exorcised — *exorcised*!"

Winterburn tore the scarf from round his neck, grabbed the man's wrists in one giant hand, whipped the scarf round the missionary's face, tried to tie it and failed. The scarf dropped, the missionary rushed on up the ramp and Winterburn, calling softly for help, pursued him. Two English sailors joined the chase and grappled with the missionary. Now they pulled a shirt clean over his head and Winterburn made a gag which left him gasping. "Lock him up — he's nuts," Winterburn said and the two sailors frog-marched him back down the ramp.

Towards ten o'clock in the evening Kershaw looked out over the Chinese city and saw its lantern-lit beauty full of civilian activity. There was a distant sound of music, voices called across the plain, somewhere a far rumble spoke of the movement of traffic and only once a blare of trumpets sent the Americans grabbing up their weapons, but no attack followed. Slowly the sounds subsided, the lights went out and by eleven everything was quiet with that kind of dead quietness which heat, lethargy and the Chinese landscape so easily induced.

There was no moon. Kershaw lay on his back staring up at the stars. How many times had these scenes repeated themselves in Chinese history with a different cast of characters playing out similar rôles. Once the self-contained culture with its so different roots had successfully resisted attempts by Westerners to break into its porcelain structures, its beautiful rituals, poverty, scholarship, misery and shameless display of wealth and privilege. Now the hairy ones had penetrated these defences. Age old battles were repeating themselves but differently. Hence this small excrescence on the smooth Chinese skin that had to be excised ruthlessly. Ruthlessly . . . Kershaw thought of the battle about to begin. It was a mistake to be taken prisoner. Mutilation so often preceded death. He could accommodate sudden obliteration from a stray bullet. Indeed he now knew the nature of the mad song which beat up at the back of his head under fire as if he desired to be the exact target of any bullet, because a kind of redemptive ecstasy held him in thrall. But mutilation — torture — decapitation . . .

The night was beautiful. Nature had reasserted its grace over everything. The lines of the Imperial Palace far to the north grew out of the landscape with a new symmetry. Everywhere awkward shapes were softened by the darkness, and there, stretching into eternity was the Chinese plain, an endless glimmering presence which spoke of changelessness. This small blemish would be removed when nature found it convenient and leave no trace. . . .

At midnight Captain Meyerstein gave everyone a whispered briefing. Then, at 1.45 a.m., someone interrupted Kershaw's musings. "You playing Socrates, buddy?" It was Winterburn whispering in his ear. "We're ready to go. Remember. Not a sound — one peep out of you and you're stone cold dead."

In the event it was all too simple. Sixty men with fixed bayonets suddenly charged the Chinese barricades and the sight of those blades glittering and thrashing in the semi-darkness was more effective than hails of bullets. The Chinese had no stomach for close-quarter fighting. They retreated in disorder. Captain Meyerstein became a tower of strength, urging everyone on, shooting with great accuracy and deliberation. Suddenly he shouted in the darkness, exultantly, "A horse! A horse! Where is my horse?" His old cavalry days were too much for him.

Following close on the heels of the Chinese, Kershaw saw Winterburn transformed into a monster who dug and twisted with a devilish delight. Some savage side of his nature was free at last to indulge its intentions. Brutality, blood lust, savagery — all were let loose in his so comfortable, so soft, round person.

And then Winterburn seemed to stop abruptly with his bayonet uplifted for another disembowelment and for a moment he was fixed there, rigid, like a cut-out figure against the night sky and Kershaw was aware of a mess of blood and something blowing past him so close that it stained his ragged tunic. The cut-out figure crumpled at his feet with its head oozing blood and Kershaw thought with a shock that it must be Winterburn's brains which had blown past him on the night air, and he fell on one knee, lifted Winterburn by the shoulders and spoke to him but the head fell back and the mouth gaped and blood began to spill from the lips. Kershaw lowered him gently down and stood looking at him. His reactions were frozen and he felt nothing.

Half an hour later, making his way down the wall to report the success of the action to Sir Archibald, the cut-out picture of Winterburn came back to him, his head began to spin and he nearly fell. Somehow Winterburn was so much more a full-blooded human being than most people that when he died, death was a starker reality.

Recovered again, Kershaw decided to return through the Russian lines. The luck of the Russians still held. Protected on one side by the American Legation and on the other by the English, they continued to escape the full brunt of any attack. In all the storm and stress around them they mounted guard, turn and turn about, looted the vacant houses nearby and drank anything which came to hand. Now as Kershaw approached their lines he became aware of a remarkable phenomenon.

There was no sign of an attack. The Chinese were quiet and no trumpet blared. Yet shots were coming from within the Russian lines, and not merely shots. The occasional burst of rifle fire slowly mounted until a howling fusillade whipped high over Kershaw's head and he dived into the narrow lanes of burnt-out houses, heading fast for the Russian barricades. As he approached them he saw an even more remarkable sight. The Russian sailors were laughing and jeering at each other as they moved steadily backwards into the narrow lanes firing their rifles in the air with blood-curdling yells.

Suddenly Kershaw remembered the occasion when the Russians were accused of trying to seduce the Chinese schoolgirls housed behind their lines. Now — *force majeure* — a "major attack" was driving them back to safety in the self-same dormitories. He found himself laughing at first to think how convincing it all sounded, and he simply stood there wondering whether it was any part of his rôle to intervene.

In that interval two elderly Chinese converts in charge of the schoolgirls fled through the passageways cut into the British Legation and disappeared, chased by a big Russian corporal. Then began a series of screams. Kershaw hurried into the main passageway only to be met by a barrier of rifle butts turned horizontally to hold him back. Russian was the language he found most difficult, and now his available expletives had no effect and an attempt to issue orders met with drunken ribaldry. Clearly the sailors had been drinking steadily for hours and now they guyed his accent and one kept saying, "Speaka no Engleesa."

Demands to be taken to an officer were met with winks and smirks and it was quickly apparent to Kershaw that they were not going to let him pass. As he continued to push against the rifle butts the men grew angry.

"Keep out!" they shouted in Russian. "This is our affair."

Should he head direct to the British Legation and call out the British guard, or would that cause an international incident? Should he follow the lanes round to the back of the dormitories and see for himself what was happening? Turning swiftly he moved through a burnt-out house-shell, climbed a wall and circled back towards the dormitories. The rear door was open and a hubbub of voices grew to a roar as he ran into the passage and burst into the main dormitory. The scene was Hogarthian. Soldiers and sailors dancing, stamping their feet in time to a lewd song as they circled around two girls whose nightdresses had been pulled up round their waists. One sailor had penetrated his victim while another man drunkenly tried to achieve the same end with the second. Other girls cowered on their mattresses, some hidden under sheets, some weeping in that curiously soundless Chinese manner.

Kershaw hesitated. The sailors were still armed with pistols, most were hopelessly drunk and the mood was one of such total abandon that anything could happen. He decided to avoid a frontal assault and ran down the corridor to the back door.

Grabbing up a dropped sword he hammered on the door and then rushed down the passage roaring at the top of his stentorian voice, in Russian, "The guards! The guards! For Chrissake break it up — the guards!"

Pandemonium ensued. The man who had brutalized one girl desperately tried to withdraw, found it impossible and dragged her with him as he fought to escape. The second sailor dropped his would-be victim, turned and running blindly crashed into the wall and collapsed. Everyone else broke and ran, choking the corridors, fighting one another to escape. Kershaw stood by the back door, pressed flat against the wall. Furniture was smashed, mattresses were flung aside, one man threatened another with his gun.

As the noise and confusion at last subsided, another sound rose — the soft rhythmic moaning of the children, somehow achieving a unison in their terror which failed to find any expression whatever on their round, doll-like, watchful faces.

Three days later Baron von Rienstane court-martialled the two rapists. One was shot and the other — for lack of anything resembling a cell — was locked in the laundry cupboard until an alternative prison could be found. Sir Archibald ordered two British civilians to mount armed guard henceforward over the dormitory every night and Kershaw wondered at the twisted morality which shot men driven to rape by sexual starvation, but allowed poltroons to go scot-free.

CHAPTER XIV

THE DROUGHT BROKE early in July. Torrential rain flooded the trenches and shelters, burst the fabric of flimsy sandbags, cascaded through bullet-riddled tiles. The children danced half naked in the pitiless downpour, the mad missionary stood face upwards embracing the torrent. Everyone relaxed in the sparkling coolness, listening to the splashing water as to music, but the mood did not last. The rain ceased as suddenly as it began, the sun distilled a haze from the flooding waters and the foetid heat slowly returned.

Forty people now ate scrambled meals twice a day in Lady Mainwaring's elegant dining room. Missionaries, Royal Marines, Customs officials, railway engineers, Sir Robert Hart, Major and Mrs Shelham, Lu-Ching and Kershaw, rubbed shoulders in changing groups as coolies and maids fought to cope with their demands.

Sir Archibald sat at the head of the main table, with Sir Robert Hart on his left and Monsieur Bleriot on his right. From his vantage point at the opposite end of the table, on the twentieth day of the siege, Kershaw observed the grey faces, red eyes and shabby clothing, and especially he was aware of the droop in Sir Archibald's usually very square shoulders. Everybody showed signs of strain. Curious bursts of hysterical laughter about nothing at all released pent up nerves in sometimes embarrassing moments.

Normally Peking was a malodorous city, especially in the summer. And now many factors combined to produce stenches of such intensity that they penetrated closed windows, barricades, clothing — everything. The big tin cans set in wooden thrones which constituted the sanitation of the Residence were emptied into the latrine trenches, newly dug to run into the canal, but the canal was stagnant and did not carry it away. Common latrines consisted of smaller trenches, connected with the main trench which sometimes failed to flow in the right direction and overflowed. In the burnt-out Chinese houses adjoining the Legation, putrefying corpses were alive with maggots; new corpses were torn at by dogs and pigs, and within forty-eight hours began to exude overpowering gases.

Every few days more Chinese refugees down at the Water Gate died of starvation. Diarrhoea attacked every other person. Above all the lack of any consistent sleep produced a grey lethargy which spread its depression like a living presence.

The happiest man was the Dutch Minister who slept in a cupboard in the small house allotted to the Russian Minister and the fifty-one members of his family and staff. The cupboard turned out to be soundproof and the round jovial Dutchman kept his glowing cheeks and clear eyes because he slept well. He moved energetically round the Legation in the day, busy about a dozen undefined tasks and no one ever managed to pin down precisely what it was he did. Kershaw suspected he did nothing and made a splendid show of it. Monsieur Bleriot continued to fuss, fret and pretend. Monsieur Pokotilov, once head of the Russo-Chinese Bank and a manipulator of millions, now cut a sad figure as he chose to tend the solitary remaining cow which gave hardly any milk from lack of grazing. A forlorn air surrounded a squadron of perambulators in which ten babies were thought to be safe from bullets. One had already died and another, born in the middle of a heavy bombardment, was immediately named Siege.

One evening while the regulation bullets were flying in all directions Lucy Shelham hurried into the Residence, sought out Lady Mainwaring in her still immaculate bedroom and collapsed on the bed crying hysterically, "I can't go back, I can't go back." She was punching the pillow as she spoke.

"Go back where?" Lady Mainwaring said, sitting down beside her and stroking her chestnut hair, now hanging limp and greasy to her waist.

"Back to the hospital," she said. "I cannot bear it any more."

Lady Mainwaring put her arm round the girl and drew her upright. "There . . . there . . . Lucy," she said. "Of course you won't go back. You've done your share. We'll find someone to take your place."

She brushed Lucy's hair out of her eyes, took a tiny scrap of cambric and began drying her tears.

Lucy pushed her hand away. "Don't do that!" she said. "You make me feel like a spoiled child."

She opened her handbag, took out a bigger handkerchief, blew her nose and said, "I must pull myself together."

"Don't try too hard," retorted Lady Mainwaring. "Everybody's in the same state. Why don't you take over the rationing for a bit?"

"And who'll take my place?"

"We'll find someone, don't worry."

"How do you manage to remain so calm?" Lucy asked. "I've never seen you even flustered."

"Calm!" Lady Mainwaring exclaimed. "It's all a fake. I'm seething inside — like you, I can't stand much more of this. I wonder what in heaven's name has happened to that relieving force? Archie tells me privately even he has lost faith in its arriving until it's too late — but please don't repeat that to anyone."

Lucy took out the packet of papier poudre she carried in her bag and began dabbing her nose, but as fast as she applied the powder the sweat overwhelmed it. Simultaneously the tears began to flow again and she found herself powerless to stop them. She snapped the small hand-mirror into its case and lay back on the bed.

"I'm such a weakling," she said.

"Nonsense!" Lady Mainwaring snapped. "You've faced things in that awful hospital I couldn't face. You're a braver woman than I am — but you need a rest and change. Just get out of your clothes and climb into bed and sleep."

It was at that moment that a series of stomach cramps seized Lucy and she doubled up on the bed.

"Are you all right?" Lady Mainwaring asked, once more putting her arm round her.

"I hope — " Lucy began and a moment later changed the words. "I think it's my period. I must go to the lavatory to see."

The tears were still running down Lucy's cheeks into her blouse but she seemed unaware. She dragged herself from the bed.

"I'm so tired," she said.

"I'll give you a piece of towelling. You must get into bed," said Lady Mainwaring, rolling back the beautiful satin counterpane and removing the ornate bolster which did service as an ornamental pillow.

In the small dark lavatory with its window sandbagged Lucy sat on the wooden throne, and as her eyes closed she leaned against the wall and was at once asleep. Five minutes later Lady Mainwaring hammered on the door and escorted her to bed. As she lay back on the soft whiteness two thoughts dominated everything else: there was still no sign of her period, and if she gave up the hospital she would be unable to see Kevin during the day. She fell asleep, then, and despite two artillery bombardments slept for twelve hours.

They met by accident. He was leaving Sir Archibald's study as she came to report her resignation from the hospital. For a brief moment they hesitated and she whispered, "Visit you tonight." He whispered back, "Don't be a fool," and they passed on.

At nine o'clock he returned to his room to find an envelope containing a note. "Burial ground nine o'clock."

He sat for a moment staring at the note. Here was a chance to break off this ever deepening and now dangerous relationship. The siege had tested so many aspects of character and personality. For him, all the suppressed conflicts of twenty years had welled up to shape his attitude to events. So far he had survived a hundred moments of redemption. But fate, luck or destiny must run out soon. Flouting danger was an elemental process but simplified to the point of meaninglessness when every hour offered a new chance of death. As yet he had survived every test — yes — but a new plan to shape his ends was forming in his mind and it was a plan which did not include Lucy.

Almost unaware he found himself walking through the starlit compound towards the burial ground. Often, now, some deep impulse took charge of his thoughts and movements, at a level beyond the rational, and worked out a pattern whose true nature he only discovered afterwards. Momentarily he came to a halt as his rational self asserted the folly of keeping this assignation.

Then he surrendered again, moved forward and five minutes later with a leap of his pulse, saw the wraith of her white dress in the corner of the ruined pavilion. They embraced silently. When he tried to speak she kissed him to silence. At last she spoke herself.

"I had to see you," she said. "He's cooking up a conspiracy against you. He's arranging to have you shadowed."

"I don't understand."

"He's trying to convince Archie that you're giving information to the Chinese."

"Why would he do that?"

"Because if you're watched he will know your movements. Know whether we meet."

"You must be joking."

She shook her head. "He's already convinced Archie that all those direct hits — on the Residence, the water tanks, the guns — are something to do with you. The only other possibility is Lu-Ching. Colin defends him. Says he's a Chinese aristocrat. His Confucian principles would never stoop to spying."

"But this is crazy — I don't — "

"Listen to me!" she interrupted. "A couple of coolies swear you've been out of the Water Gate twice."

"Lies. Absolute lies."

"You'll have trouble convincing Archie, I had to warn you. Colin is mad — mad with jealousy. You wouldn't believe — with all that stiff upper lip — how jealous he could be. He's also ruthless when roused. I can't stay. Lady Mainwaring's expecting me. I must get back. Oh, my God — when will this awful siege be over?"

He kissed her gently. The moon fell across her hair and face and both seemed to him beautiful. He knew it was a trick of light and shade, a biological deception because love meant reproduction and reproduction was the imperious command of the evolutionary process. But now, in all the stink of decaying bodies, the sweat of passion and the hunger which always grew as evening wore on, it was beautiful to hold her, to feel the warmth of her quickened blood, to know that somewhere within the horror of the siege this island held its own — the word magic seemed absurdly romantic — a schoolgirl's word.

She had been speaking without his hearing and she thumped his chest saying, "You're not listening."

"I am now."

"Remember," she said. "When this is over I'm leaving him."

He began to protest but she overwhelmed him.

"Whether you will have me or not — I'm leaving him. I must fly — I'm late."

She kissed him and slipped away back towards the Residence.

As Kershaw made his way across the compound towards the barricades, the maniacal howls of the mad missionary began again. Then came the words picked out with clarity in the silence: "Let not Thy demons loose amongst us again, oh Lord, that we may be consumed. . . .

"Look down in mercy, oh Lord, that out of the night may come a flaming angel —

"Look down, oh Lord

"Look down

"As we look up

"And may your awful gaze not blind you to our need. For we are but the broken playthings of destiny. . . . Look down in mercy, oh Lord!"

As he reached the barricade Kershaw saw the white figure moving across no-man's-land towards the Chinese lines. For a whole week this man Nostegarde had remained, hysterical and starving, locked up in the stables. Now, driven by the demons which possessed him, he had broken out and as Kershaw watched he suddenly began to run. Dressed in a white smock, picked out in silhouette by the moon, his figure seemed to skim the ground, impelled by unnatural powers, and his voice rose in such maniacal howls as only direct contact with the devil could inspire.

But not a shot was fired.

That was the odd thing.

The Chinese let him run until he vanished safely in their lines. The howls died away and the night was quiet.

CHAPTER XV

THERE WAS A lull lasting the whole of the following day. That evening four people met after dinner in Sir Archibald's dining room at his express invitation — Sir Archibald, Major Shelham, Lu-Ching and Kershaw. Drinking ersatz coffee, almost at once Sir Archibald said to Lu-Ching:

"I understand they are putting a price on our heads."

"Yes," Lu-Ching replied. "History is repeating itself. In 1860 an edict inspired by the concubine who now rules the Imperial Palace offered fifty taels for the head of a black barbarian. Now they are offering fifty for a male foreigner, forty for a female and thirty for a child. I have a cutting from a newspaper — perhaps you would like Mr Kershaw to translate it."

Kershaw took the tattered cutting and read aloud: "As foreigners are not easy to obtain all Chinese having high noses and deep eyes have been beheaded by the Boxers. But so many heads have been brought in that the offer of blood money has been withdrawn."

Sir Archibald did not react but Major Shelham smiled grimly.

"Where get newspaper cutting?" he asked, and Kershaw rapidly translated the conversation which followed.

"From one of my spies."

"A reliable one?"

"Not very."

"How know when telling truth?"

"I can tell from questioning them. If they are lying they break down on detail. If not . . ."

Sir Archibald said, "We too have spies — one says that the Boxers and Chinese are quarrelling after all this time without success."

"Can I ask the names of those who said this?"

Major Shelham looked at Sir Archibald, who nodded. "His name is Fi-Chu," Shelham said.

"Yes — " said Lu-Ching. "I know him, but I must warn you. He is one of those Chinese shopkeepers who work on the principle that the customer is always right. If you want the relieving forces to advance rapidly he will produce evidence to show it is happening. If you want disaffection in the Chinese army he can arrange that too. I observe that there are two notices on the Bell Tower announcing gratifying victories of Allied troops approaching Peking. There are neither victories nor are they approaching Peking. . . . Surely you have discovered his unreliability by now."

Sir Archibald showed no surprise. "Yes," he said. "We have come to suspect him — but he insists on one thing which we believe."

Lu-Ching waited for Sir Archibald to continue. "He says that there is not one spy in the Legation but several."

Lu-Ching said nothing, and when Sir Archibald pressed him for an answer, said, "There are always spies."

"And would you know who they might be?"

"It could be anybody," Lu-Ching replied, and after a long pause: "I have known Customs clerks who accepted bribes."

"European Customs clerks?"

"Yes."

"Why are you so certain the relieving force is not approaching Tientsin?"

"My most reliable man, Choo-Li, says that no foreign troops have even reached Tientsin."

"And are you sure Choo-Li is not passing information to the enemy — is not in fact a double agent?" Sir Archibald asked.

"What is a double agent?"

Kershaw explained and Lu-Ching shook his head.

"I really don't see," Sir Archibald continued, "how anyone can be quite sure about the behaviour of a Chinese coolie."

Lu-Ching's hands sank even more deeply into his ornate sleeves and he said nothing.

Major Shelham broke the silence. "Other facts indicate knowledge beyond British Legation."

Everyone was puzzled by this piece of cabalese and Sir

Archibald spelt it out. "Yes — our Post Commanders tell us enemy fire has become even more accurate. They continue to find our bits of artillery whenever we re-position them."

"But Sir Archibald," asked Kershaw, "wouldn't the simple firing of the guns reveal their new positions?"

"In a limited way — yes — but not with the pin-point accuracy shown by enemy fire."

"Someone," Major Shelham said, "knows positions — passing information."

Kershaw shifted uneasily in his chair. There was a long pause and at last Sir Archibald broke it.

"Kershaw, is there anyone you have reason to suspect?"

Kershaw shook his head.

"There are, I believe," Sir Archibald persisted, "certain views of the Chinese which you have come to share."

"I don't understand?"

"Several reports your sympathy Chinese cause," Shelham put in.

"Which reports?" asked Kershaw.

"My wife for one."

Kershaw drew breath sharply. "Has she told you I'm sympathetic to what the Chinese are doing?"

"In a way — yes."

"Which way?"

"You accuse us of abusing Chinese in past."

Lu-Ching said, "Would you not say, Major, that there might be some truth in that?"

"Enlightening, not abusing."

Sir Archibald smiled. "Both sometimes, I think. . . . But other reports have reached us, Kershaw."

"Which reports?"

"Monsieur Bleriot and Colonel Rienstane. Both think you speak too much in favour of the Chinese."

Kershaw sat up. "Sir Archibald," he said, "if you suspect me of being the spy I shall be happy to be arrested."

"Why happy be arrested?" Shelham asked suspiciously.

"I find my job too goddam dangerous," Kershaw replied. It was the first time he had ever shown anger in front of Sir Archibald.

"You do see," said Sir Archibald, "that your job makes you one of the few people fully familiar with all our dispositions."

Kershaw nodded. "Why not take me off the job and see whether the shooting remains accurate?"

"We have in fact other evidence," Sir Archibald went on. "One of your coolie spies, Lu-Ching, says he's got information from Kershaw who agreed that he could pass it on to the Chinese."

"Which coolie?" Lu-Ching said.

"A man called Fung-Ling."

"I know him," Lu-Ching said. "He is not one of my spies. Did you pay him?"

Sir Archibald looked uncomfortable.

"Lives are at stake," he said. "He has already given us valuable information about the positions of the Chinese artillery which turned out to be accurate."

Lu-Ching shrugged his shoulders. "I repeat what I said before. Certain spies work on the principle that the customer is always right. May I ask one question?"

"Certainly."

"Did he know that you suspect Mr Kershaw?"

"I'm not sure — he may have known."

Lu-Ching's hands came out of his sleeves and made a wide gracious gesture. "Then he would have invented evidence to confirm it — provided you paid him."

Kershaw found himself in this prolonged exchange in the embarrassing position of being both suspect and interpreter, and it was difficult to exclude from his renderings his own implicit comment simply by the tone of voice in which he delivered the words.

There was a long uneasy pause. To everyone's surprise Sir Archibald deliberately turned the conversation into an entirely different field.

"I have always wanted to ask you, Lu-Ching. Am I right in thinking that the old teachings of Confucius are undergoing serious changes today?"

Lu-Ching sat very still, reflecting on the question for some minutes and the silence became so prolonged that Shelham fidgeted uneasily and Sir Archibald was on the point of speaking again when Lu-Ching said:

"The answer is long and difficult. It would need much time."

Sir Archibald glanced at his watch. "It's ten o'clock. Unless the attacks begin again we have plenty of time."

It seemed to Kershaw that Sir Archibald desired above everything to stop the conversation returning to spies. As Lu-Ching spoke again Kershaw continued translating, but now in a monotone.

"Considerable patience as well as time," Lu-Ching began, "is required to enquire into the changes which have overtaken Confucianism." He paused again and stared at the assembled company. Sir Archibald smiled. "I think the siege has taught us all to be patient and not to — " Kershaw rendered the next phrase as "jump to conclusions" but in the Chinese it was much more subtle. No one missed the double meaning.

"Let us look at the past," Lu-Ching continued. "For two thousand years Confucianism kept its hold on Chinese thought and culture, but as it became more and more conservative it lost its vitality. However it never lost its spirit of rationalism, humanism and moralism. The biggest changes began to become apparent when a kind of empiricism led to a revolt against the excessive use of textual criticisms and flowery compositions. A new emphasis appeared which stressed the reforming aspects of Confucianism. China's defeat in wars and the introduction of certain aspects of Western technology meant that China had to change. A famous saying was now embodied in our teachings — a saying which, because of its subtle texture, is difficult to translate. But my friend Kershaw is a very good translator and I am sure he will approach the reality of the words I use."

Here he delivered the quotation very deliberately and made a special pause for Kershaw to consider it. Without hesitation Kershaw gave a rendering. "Chinese studies are for the fundamentals of life and Western studies for the practical purposes of life."

"Nineteenth-century Confucianists agreed," Lu-Ching continued, "that Western knowledge should be used for building houses, roads and railroads, but that Confucian teaching was far superior for moral and spiritual values. The two conflicting currents met in the supreme person of K'ang Yu-Wei who led the new approach in radical reform only two years ago. Confucius, he argued, was a great reformer who conceived the history of mankind to be proceeding in three stages towards the Epoch of Great Harmony. But there was a flaw in this belief when applied to our present condition. We were ready only for an Epoch of Small Peace, not Great Harmony. He therefore suggested reforms in the civil service of China, in the schools, the building of railroads and open mines. He also believed in the translation and publication of Western works, a revolutionary departure from the past. In some ways it encouraged the invasion of Western peoples with the result that you — and I — now sit in this Legation, you as representatives of the new ways of commercialism and I as a relic of the old China. We are pathetically trapped between two cultures."

Lu-Ching paused and drank the remainder of his coffee. "I think perhaps," he added, "I have said enough to tire your ears with this present subject and we should perhaps find a new one."

"Where," Shelham asked, "Empress Dowager stand in all this?"

"She is trying to save a crumbling Manchu empire. She wishes to raise the traditional sacrifice of Middle Order for Confucius to the sacrifice of the First Order which has been reserved for Heaven. Thus this will make Confucius the Counterpart of Heaven. If we — "

"Rubbish!" Shelham interrupted. "No such thing. She's simply trying to murder us."

Sir Archibald smiled. "It would seem as if Major Shelham might be right."

Lu-Ching said nothing.

"Have things changed very much concerning filial piety?" asked Sir Archibald.

As usual Lu-Ching considered the question for a long minute and then he began:

"It is difficult to answer your question without returning to the past again. The root of all moral life used to centre around filial piety, because it was a central belief that no person would become a good person unless he was good to his parents.

Parents gave children their lives, care and upbringing. A natural bond and obligation arose which must be fulfilled. But the moral obligation was mutual. Parents were expected to choose wives for their children, to take all family decisions, to hold property in the name of the father. A kind of equality was part of the fabric of this way of life. But as silk and cotton are different, men and women remained different. A Confucian saying states, 'To be a ch'i—or wife—is to be Chi's equal.' It is of course a pious hope. But ancestor worship remained . . . until now. . . .

"I regret that now a long process of erosion has begun. Arranged marriages are beginning to be questioned by intellectuals and scholars. The authority of the father is under new scrutiny. Ancestral rites are losing their grip. I foresee a time when few temples — if any — will be built for Confucius or the great men of history. It is a watershed for the Chinese culture and way of life. Our attempts to divide off the practical from the spiritual are proving steadily more difficult. Western values are beginning to press against the age-old pillars of Chinese thinking."

Lu-Ching paused. "I deeply regret this."

"Balderdash!" exclaimed Shelham. "Chinese way of life beheads and murders. We the victims."

Sir Archibald addressed Lu-Ching, "You talk as if you had moral superiority. This siege is the living contradiction."

"We do not lay claim to superiority," Lu-Ching explained. "There are bad sides to both our cultures. The Boxers are not part of our culture. They are the living presence of evil in mankind from which we all suffer."

"Nonsense!" Before he could stop himself, Kershaw had spoken.

Everyone looked surprised. Until then he had remained a ventriloquist figure in the background, never asserting his own views; but slowly moral indignation had built up.

"The Boxers are symbolic of the exploited poor of China," he said. "They are driven to violence by poverty. It's not only the Chinese culture which exploits the poor — it is — "

He cut off abruptly, but everyone knew the end of his sentence. . . . "The English, the French, the Germans. . . . "

Shelham gave his snorting laugh and looked sharply at Sir

Archibald. "See what I mean?" he said.

Carried on the wave of indignation, Kershaw found himself talking fast, and later he could not recall the words he used but now Sir Archibald received them with growing astonishment.

"Do you realise what is going on in this Legation. . . . Do you know some Chinese are starving to death. They strip the leaves off the trees and eat them. Drink gallons of water to stop hunger pains — have swollen stomachs — stick-like legs. . . . "

"Rice has to go to worker coolies," Shelham interrupted.

"The Europeans have enough food — the Chinese are half starved," Kershaw continued. He wanted to add, "That's what our culture produces", but his courage failed him.

"Do you really mean to say Chinese are starving?" Sir Archibald said. "I knew nothing about this. Is it true, Shelham?"

"Has to be true."

"Why?"

"Not enough food. Only defenders and workers. Otherwise all die."

"I suppose," observed Sir Archibald, "it could be said that some Europeans in the Legation are neither workers nor defenders, but they eat."

"Injustice unavoidable," snapped Shelham.

"Where *are* these Chinese?" Sir Archibald asked.

"In Prince Su's Palace," replied Kershaw.

"I will see them tomorrow," Sir Archibald said. "But I must ask you something, Kershaw. Do you approve of what the Boxers are doing?"

Emboldened by the mood of the moment Kershaw replied, "We all believe in violence when it suits our purposes."

"That's a cynical remark," said Sir Archibald. "Beheading and mutilating people is different from fighting a war. You would agree with that."

"Yes — certainly, but. . . . "

Once again Kershaw stopped. The die was cast. He knew he had confirmed Shelham's suspicions, but there was a limit to the provocation he was prepared to risk.

"What were you going to say?" asked Sir Archibald.

"Nothing," Kershaw said, "except that I regard the Boxers as murderers."

"I'm sure all glad to hear that," Shelham said.

"I think," remarked Lu-Ching, "if you will excuse me — I am tired."

"Yes, it's time to drop all this philosophizing." Sir Archibald came to his feet. "Well, gentlemen, we'll meet again tomorrow — " he laughed. "There's no escape from one another."

As Kershaw rose to follow Major Shelham and Lu-Ching, Sir Archibald said, "I'd like a word with you before you go, Kershaw."

Immediately they were alone Sir Archibald began pacing round the room with his long loping stride. "You know, Kershaw, I respect you. I don't share your views — in fact I think you are very wrong-headed. But tell me honestly — do you really believe what you were saying just now, or were you carried away by anger?"

Kershaw sat down again and stared moodily at the mahogany dining table. At last he replied.

"I don't want to believe it. It may have been exaggerated — but we all know the Chinese have been exploited."

Sir Archibald sighed. "Yes, I suppose they have — but isn't that in the nature of things. . . . "

"Nature of things?" Kershaw repeated and immediately regretted the challenge in his voice.

"You don't believe in God or destiny, do you?" Sir Archibald asked. Kershaw did not answer.

"If you did," he continued, "you would see that there is a natural law at work in these things — a law which finds its compensations — not necessarily on earth. It is not up to us to try to interfere with that law."

Inwardly Kershaw was laughing, but the laughter, as Sir Archibald talked on, became qualified once more by anger, and the anger again reached a pitch where only iron control prevented its vehement expression.

"You say nothing?" Sir Archibald finished at last.

"I have nothing to say."

Suddenly it was as if weeks of exhaustion had contrived to crumble away the striding authority of Sir Archibald's figure. His shoulders drooped, and he slumped down in his chair. His voice became hoarse.

"I didn't ask you to stay behind to lecture you," he said. "The truth is, Kershaw, Major Shelham seems to hate you — why is that?"

Kershaw shook his head.

"Someone said it was to do with his wife Lucy."

Kershaw said nothing.

"Can you assure me that nothing is going on between you and his wife?" Sir Archibald said.

Kershaw replied immediately with great firmness: "Absolutely." Lying, to be convincing, had to be rapid and cogent.

There was a pause and then Sir Archibald threw what was obviously a prepared question at Kershaw.

"If you had to choose between saving the life of an American or a Chinaman — which would you choose?"

"What a question!" Kershaw said. "The American."

"And you still swear that you do not pass information to the Chinese?"

"Yes."

Sir Archibald came wearily to his feet, walked round the table and shook Kershaw firmly by the hand.

"Good fellow," he said. "I knew I could trust you."

As he walked out into the cool starlit and for once silent night vivid images jostled in Kershaw's mind, one replacing the other with the rapidity of a kaleidoscope: the shot and shell crashing round the Legation; the starving Chinese; the rotting carcases festering in the sun; the broken bodies in the hospital; the face of the Commander-in-Chief whose lieutenants continued to ignore his orders. The glory of the siege had long since departed. There was nothing now but the brutal realities. One image persisted above all others. It was of an old rag-picker stumbling along outside the Tartar wall towards the Water Gate which ran under the Great Wall into the dry canal. Chinese sharpshooters had seen him and mistaken him for a spy. As their rifles crashed out, he had fallen to his hands and knees, wounded, and begun crawling towards his countrymen like a stricken dog. Pitilessly the bullets hissed round him until they found their mark again. He rolled over and was motionless. His white beard seemed to raise an eloquent protest to heaven.

CHAPTER XVI

Everything happened on Friday July 13th. Heavy firing continued ceaselessly throughout the day: the Japanese were dislodged from the seventh of their nine defence lines: the Germans risked a bayonet charge to avoid being over-run: the Americans gave ground under continuous pressure on the Wall: the British barricades were heavily attacked, and at four o'clock in the heat of a tropical afternoon an emergency sounded from the Bell Tower.

As dusk came the roar of rifles and artillery was overwhelmed by a new and long-drawn-out explosion which shook the earth of the inner compounds as if they were about to erupt. The Chinese had tunnelled under the French Legation and detonated two land-mines. Three French sailors were buried in the debris, others blown to bits, and the Austrian Chargé d'Affaires wounded. Into the smoking ruins hundreds of howling Chinese poured, firing at random and throwing incendiary torches. The French and Germans fought back, but it quickly became a matter of holding bridgeheads. As the roar of earth and masonry subsided, a sinister tapping noise was detected under an advanced British position. Another tunnel, to carry another mine, was obviously in progress.

A young Harrovian, on leave from the barricades, suddenly remembered that Friday the thirteenth was the day of the Eton and Harrow Match. He wrote in the diary which he kept for his parents, "Am wondering if you will go to Lords today. We are gradually being closed in upon and unless relief comes soon we shall be in an awful fix."

A member of the Chinese Customs Service broke open the central horror in his diary:

"In the no-man's-land beyond the barricades droves of ravening dogs tear up the buried bodies of the Chinese dead and eat them. They fight furiously over the slightest scrap of a man's arm or thigh. Nothing will drive them away. They rush down on the outposts in maniacal bands with such wild cries the defenders open heavy fire. No matter how many are shot, others push forward, frantic with hunger and tear even the English dead to pieces in front of the garrison's eyes. Toughened campaigners turn away from the sickening sight."

Monsieur Bleriot wrote: "*C'est le massacre final qui se prépare.*" He had successfully avoided the defences of the French Legation, but continued to keep a tally of the number of shells — "*Quatre cents cinquante coups de canon.*" Chain smoking, he stalked round the British compound only to break off suddenly, hurry into the Residence and bring out his secret archives. Setting fire to the papers, some promptly blew away with Madame Bleriot in full chase. As she recovered half-burned fragments he zealously re-burnt them. Returning to his room in the Residence he was astonished to see his diary lying open on the bureau. On the point of shutting it, he suddenly noticed some alien writing on the open page. Underneath his latest entry a sprawling hand had written in green ink, "*Il ne fait que pisser dans ses caleçons.*" "*Merde! Merde*!" he roared at his wife who covered her ears. Snatching up his pen he viciously scored through the offending words.

As darkness fell that day Sir Archie sat in his study gloomily examining battle notes. It had been a bad day. Seven men killed, twenty wounded and new mines being laid under the British Legation. *The British Legation*! It was insufferable. Sir Archibald sat up, squared his shoulders and rang his bell. An orderly arrived. "Find Mr Kershaw for me — at once," he said and began scribbling an order which read, "Begin a counter mine at 11 p.m. at the precise spot where tapping heard."

Lady Mainwaring in her bedroom was trying to quieten the two children, awakened by the blast and now for the first time on the edge of hysteria from constant confinement. No amount of rifle and shell fire had disturbed them. They had continued to play battle games in the drawing room and, when Lady Mainwaring was absent, beheaded captives wholesale: but confinement in the house was proving too much for them. When Andrew continued to weep hysterically she slapped his face and he was so astonished he attacked her like a bull with his head down. Simultaneously Vanessa began screaming. Momentarily winded, Lady Mainwaring's dignity collapsed and she sank down on the bed, weeping herself. "I did not mean it Andrew," she said, "I did not mean it. Oh! this terrible, terrible, war — will it never be over!" Within seconds she had pulled herself together, gathered Vanessa in her arms and was comforting her. As the children at last dozed off she moved over to her dressing table and turned away from the haggard image she saw reflected in the mirror. A knock came at the door.

"Who is it?" Her voice was hoarse with weariness.

"It's Lucy."

"Come in," she said and, as Lucy entered, "Sssh! Speak softly — the children."

"I'm sorry," Lucy whispered. "I can't sleep. Do you have any laudanum?"

"Yes — but we mustn't use it. It's reserved for the wounded now."

"I see," said Lucy. "Well, I won't disturb you any longer."

"Stay a minute, but keep your voice down."

Lady Mainwaring turned and braced herself to face her image in the mirror again.

"Do you need any more Jourdain?" she asked as she took up her scent spray. She sprayed it lavishly over her shoulders and arms, and said, "There's only one thing worse than death — that's smelling."

"I *would* like some but — " Lucy began and Lady Mainwaring turned with a half smile. "Let me spray you. . . . "

"Perhaps I'd better take my frock off."

"Don't bother. Why should you? Here — it's so refreshing." She sprayed her, laughing as she did so.

Lucy said, "I can't take much more of this, can you?"

Lady Mainwaring stopped spraying. "I sometimes think it would be better if they broke through and got it over with. We could shoot ourselves then."

Lucy was astounded. "To hear *you* talk like that," she said.

Suddenly, to Lucy's astonishment, Lady Mainwaring took her arm. "I didn't mean it, dear," she said. They stood there then, the warmth of their bodies intermingling with the scent and the sweat. "Your eyes are a wonderful green," said Lady

Mainwaring. "I prefer them grey," Lucy said. Lady Mainwaring leant forward and kissed her on the cheek.

"I didn't like you very much before this siege began," she remarked. "Now I see what a different person you can be."

"You won't mind — if I say the same about you?"

"Of course not. Listen — what's that?" Lady Mainwaring drew back from Lucy as she spoke and moved over to the sandbagged window.

It was the sound of a phonograph grinding out a Dixie melody accompanied by American voices.

"It's the American missionaries," said Lucy. "Eighty of them are crammed into the chapel. Do you know that tune?"

"No. What is it?"

"It's famous in America — *De Ringtailed Coon.*"

"Where did they get the gramophone?"

"They looted Kieralff's store — with his permission."

As if to rival the first phonograph, a second — more distantly — began playing *Marching Through Georgia*, and within minutes a third broke in with *Nearer My God to Thee.*

"Good heavens," cried Lady Mainwaring. "How many of them are there?"

"I don't know. They're new toys. Everybody's trying them out."

"All looted."

"With permission."

"This siege is revising our morality." She paused for a long moment and then said, "By the way, I don't want to probe but Archie tells me you're having some difficulty with your husband."

"Oh, just a routine tiff." Lucy shrugged, and thought — of course you want to probe.

"I'm glad it's nothing more than that," said Lady Mainwaring, clearly disbelieving her.

She waited for some further comment and when nothing came, her whole mood changed. "Something's got to be done about the hospital. It's horrifying the way the flies settle on the wounded men."

There flashed through Lucy's mind a scene she had witnessed two days before, when swarms of flies settled on an open wound, tormenting the man to madness and defying all efforts to disperse them.

"We must make or find some mosquito nets. And if we can't . . . " Lady Mainwaring stopped and added, "Somebody will have to surrender their nets."

Lucy looked carefully at the nets protecting the windows. "I think Monsieur Bleriot has some."

Lady Mainwaring smiled. "Or were you thinking of mine?" she asked.

Lucy shook her head and lied.

"Oh, no!"

"You're very sweet, my dear, and I think you *were* thinking of mine — but I must confess I'm going to try to find them elsewhere first. Or will you take on the job?"

"Certainly," Lucy said, "and if you've no objections I'll begin with Bleriot."

"You'll need Sir Archibald's authority to do that. Monsieur Bleriot can fully justify every small luxury he possesses — " she dropped her voice. "Like, I suppose," she added, "all the rest of us."

"I must be going," said Lucy. "Do you have anything I could read? I haven't read a book since it all began."

Lady Mainwaring went over to her bedside table. "I've just finished this," she said and handed Lucy a copy of *The Relief of Lucknow*. "We're circulating two copies of it as fast as possible — Archie says they're morale boosters."

"How did you manage to get them?" Lucy turned the pages.

"Mr Cockburn preserved his library. We've asked him not to circulate *The India Mutiny* — or *The Fate of Cawnpore*."

Lucy stood hesitating in the doorway and Lady Mainwaring went over to kiss her on the cheek. "You don't look well," she said. "You must get some sleep tonight. Here — wait a minute."

She went back to her dressing table and measured out a thimbleful of laudanum.

"Take that at a gulp — it tastes nasty."

Lucy swallowed the laudanum, felt momentarily sick, said "Goodnight — thank you" and moved reluctantly down the corridor. She hesitated outside the door of her bedroom, praying that Shelham was not inside. She opened the door. The room was in darkness but by instinct she felt that someone lay on the bed. He spoke almost at once.

"Where you been."

"Talking to Lady Mainwaring."

"Have you seen him?"

"Seen who?"

"Kershaw."

"Of course I haven't seen him."

"You're such an accomplished liar."

"If you think that, why ask me?"

"Come to bed."

"I want to sleep."

"And I don't."

"I've just taken some laudanum."

"Who the hell gave you that?"

"Lady Mainwaring."

"She had no right to."

Slipping off her dress Lucy slumped down on the far side of the double bed.

He reached out a hand and pulled her towards him. She resisted his embrace and he said, "Get your clothes off."

"I don't want to take them off — the alarm is certain to go again."

"What does that matter? Get them off."

"Look, I'm finished — dead tired. Let me sleep."

He sat up without answering, turned on his knees, reached down and began pulling off her drawers. At first she struggled but sheer weariness made her abandon resistance. If he wanted to — rape? — her there was little she could do about it. She was tired with a deathly tiredness, her limbs were heavy to the point of numbness and nothing could inspire passion in her — not even Kevin. As the thought occurred she knew that she was lying again. If the man now tearing at her underclothing had been Kevin. . . . But it wasn't Kevin and she felt so detached that the whole scene might have been happening to someone other than herself.

And when she was naked from the waist down and he tried to enter her she lay like a log. It seemed a matter of mere curiosity whether he succeeded or not. Pain stabbed through her vagina but it was muted pain because the tiredness was anaesthetic. Suddenly he stopped and turned away from her. His voice was choked with emotion when he spoke. "What's gone wrong, old girl. Why are you doing this to me?"

She didn't answer because the laudanum was beginning to take effect and the image in her mind was Kevin's image.

"It's Kershaw, isn't it," he said but the furious anger she expected was not in his voice, and his distress seemed so genuine she said, "I'm drugged — I must sleep — I'm too tired for anything. I could scream with tiredness."

He turned round again then and took her in his arms almost tenderly. "All right," he said. "Tomorrow, maybe."

As she lay there she felt her skin prickling with revulsion, but she did not move, and just before the clouds began to settle over her mind she remembered him saying what seemed to her an extraordinary thing. "I need you old girl. I need you."

Then she was asleep.

CHAPTER XVII

Sir Archibald made several attempts to smuggle couriers through to Tientsin but none survived — until July 14. News came from the outposts that a frail old Roman Catholic had safely returned to the Legation lines. As he at last entered Sir Archibald's study he collapsed, and had to be revived with brandy. He had been captured, and his letter to the English commanders confiscated. Hurried to the H.Q. of the Chinese commander, Jung Lu, he had been treated kindly and given a letter to Sir Archibald with the express instruction that he must bring a reply within twenty-four hours.

Kershaw translated the letter. Couched in far less lapidary style than that used for even the most disobliging pronouncements, it was signed by Prince Ch'ing and Colleagues: "For the last ten days the soldiers and militia have been fighting and there has been no communication between us to our great anxiety. The yamen has just learnt from a captured convert that the Ministers are in good health which causes us very great satisfaction. The yamen's original idea of escorting the diplomats to Tientsin is no longer possible because we should be very apprehensive of misadventure.

"Under these circumstances the Ministers are requested to proceed in detachments to the Tsungli yamen, but at the time of leaving the Legations there must, on no account whatever, be taken any single armed foreign soldier, in order to prevent doubt and fear on the part of the troops and people, leading to untoward incidents. This is the only way of preserving relations that we have been able to devise in face of innumerable difficulties and if no reply is received by noon the day following this letter even our affection will not enable us to help you. Compliments."

Sir Archibald at once summoned a meeting of Ministers. They were relieved and delighted to be dealing once again in the true currency of diplomacy — deception and power struggles on paper. For once they were unanimous that a negative reply be sent immediately in unequivocal terms: "It is customary in dealings with civilized states for foreign envoys to be regarded as sacrosanct even under the stresses of war. This canon has been grossly disregarded by the Chinese troops who have fired on the Legations with rifles and artillery since June 20th. Should any harm come to the property or person of diplomats there is every possibility that personal reprisals against all officials in the city would in due course be taken. Meanwhile the Ministers see no merit in the proposal that they should proceed to the yamen and will continue to defend themselves and their Legations."

This message was placed in the hands of the frail old convert but at first nothing would move him to risk once more entering the enemy's lines. Given a white flag and every encouragement he twice set out, only to return again. On the third occasion he at last disappeared from sight heading approximately in the right direction.

On the following day a marine reported to Sir Archibald that the frail old convert was again approaching the main gate of the Legation. Sir Archibald and Shelham, Kershaw and Sir Robert Hart hurried down to watch him staggering uncertainly through a diminished field of fire, carrying but not waving a white flag. With his arms wrapped round him and his head down the old man looked as though he must crumple and fall at any moment. The group gathered outside the main gate, waved white handkerchiefs to encourage him, and at length he tottered over the barricades into the Legation.

He carried two messages. One was written on a telegraph form in an American State Department cypher and read "Communicate tidings to bearer."

It was of little significance, but the actual physical reality of such a message brought its own encouragement. This was the first communication to reach the besieged from a non-Chinese source in the outside world since the siege began.

The second missive was far more interesting. Kershaw translated rapidly. Apologizing for the misplaced suggestion that the Ministers should move to the yamen, it reaffirmed, in stylish Chinese, that Prince Ch'ing was continuing to exert all his efforts to give protection and keep order. Even as Kershaw was reading the message a shell from a Krupp's gun exploded over the compound and they all ducked as fragments scattered widely.

"God preserve us against protection," Sir Archibald said. "What do you make of it, Sir Robert?"

"Worthless," he replied. "Not worth the paper it is written on."

As with so many of his more recent statements this one turned out to be false. First the guns fell silent, then the rifles slowly died away and the following morning a most remarkable phenomenon became evident. Cautiously the Chinese soldiers were beginning to expose themselves, waving white flags and grinning with horrible affability. A first few stray shots at such sitting targets were summarily stopped by Sir Archibald, and then one — two — no less than three Chinese messengers carrying white flags were seen coming towards the barricades. Handing in their messages they crouched down and waited to be given safe conduct back to their own lines.

Men were now exposing themselves to enemy fire recklessly, on both sides, with every shred of white cloth brought into play. When the snipers failed to pick off obvious victims, and the total absence of gunfire continued, men became bolder. Both sides climbed over their barricades and stood there in the open, unprotected, waiting for the next move. One thing emerged as certain. Unaccountably a truce had come into force.

By mid-day confidence had reached such a pitch that half the Allied garrisons were climbing over the barricades and advancing — with huge smiles and placating gestures — to meet the Chinese soldiers in the neutral zone of intervening rubbish and ruins.

Since the Chinese advanced unarmed it was agreed by the British and Americans that they should leave their rifles behind, but Shelham and Kershaw who marched out together both carried revolvers in their trousers pockets. "You can fire through the trousers," Kershaw said, "like the Americans in Western saloons."

Wandering in no-man's-land a Chinese captain with violet

embroidered coat and blue trousers beckoned Kershaw and Shelham towards his own barricades. When Kershaw broke into fluent Chinese the Captain smiled and said there was no danger if they followed him. Shelham looked at Kershaw who shook his head. "Not me," he said.

"Come on Kershaw — think what we can pick up."

"Information?" Kershaw asked.

"Yes."

"And bullets?"

"That doesn't worry you."

Kershaw shrugged. "Not really." He wondered for a moment whether Shelham was deliberately trying to get him shot.

Ten minutes later the Chinese were openly walking around the British barricades and Kershaw and Shelham were in the midst of a military position whose intricacy surprised them. Not only did they contain the British Legation with frontal trenches and barricades but flanking these were large numbers of parallel defences so placed that any sortie from the Legation would be met with withering cross fire.

The mid-day sun was scorching down and Kershaw pulled out his Chinese cap and put it on to the delight of the Captain.

"Very much me," the captain said in Chinese, and when Kershaw translated, Shelham suggested, "Why not offer your services."

The Captain insisted on introducing the two men to a cavalry officer dressed in a red and black tunic and "tiger skirt" with a huge, blank face and gleaming bald pate. A moment later the two Chinese took Shelham and Kershaw by the hand and performed a quick circular dance. Hundreds of deeply bronzed men, wearing black fighting caps, applauded smiling, and pressing forward round Shelham and Kershaw.

"Better move on," Shelham said to Kershaw. Smiling and bowing they managed to extricate themselves. But there was no escaping the swirling mass of brightly coloured tunics. Standing atop their fortifications, the Chinese soldiers were a brilliant fresco against an appalling setting. Whole streets of houses lay in ruins with broken rifles and empty brass cartridge cases everywhere and human skulls picked clean by the pariah dogs and a whole litter of bones polished by the sun.

"Hope you're noting everything," Shelham said. "Look there — "

He pointed to a semi-circle of wooden forks with rifles resting on them, all trained on one spot. Kershaw's eye travelled back to the English barricades. On the north western perimeter there was a notorious weak spot.

"Who told them that?" asked Shelham, and Kershaw was on the point of challenging him but thought better of it.

"Let's talk to the Shansi," suggested Kershaw. "They are more talkative than Fu Hsiang's lot."

The Shansi levies were very happy to enlarge on why they were trying to kill as many foreigners as possible. They came from the provinces and they had been sent to prevent the Hairy Ones from breaking into the Imperial Palace and killing their Empress. They did not want to fight or be killed. The foreigners invited death because they had brought so many of their own soldiers into Peking. When Kershaw mentioned the Boxers the levies said the Boxers were finished, driven away, discredited. They could no longer be a reason for fighting, and since there was no other reason why did the foreign troops remain in the capital killing people indiscriminately? The logic was unanswerable.

A sudden commotion in the middle distance drew Kershaw's attention to three carts laden with melons, vegetables, ice and flour, heavily protected by guards, heading towards the Legation Main Gate. Overtaking them Kershaw asked, "What are these?"

"Gifts by command of the Empress Dowager," the captain of the guard replied. "We are to deliver to your commander-in-chief."

"My God!" Shelham said. "Mean business!"

Kershaw found his mouth watering. It was weeks since they had tasted fresh vegetables or fruit.

Soon many contradictions arose. An illicit trade in eggs sprang up, and a Japanese captain haggled for half an hour before buying the very rifles some levies were using. A young Frenchman disappeared behind the Chinese lines saying he was going on a long journey and returned having been fed sumptuously at Jung Lu's headquarters. His pockets bulged with fine peaches.

But at twelve noon on the following day came a secretary from the Tsungli yamen, dressed in full official uniform accompanied by a trembling t'ingoh'ai (card-bearer) frantically waving a huge flag of truce which threatened to throw him to the ground. Gripping the free arm of his card-bearer the secretary walked with spasmodic steps urging his card-bearer to wave — wave — wave until his fear became farcical.

Arriving at the main gate blockhouse he was curtly stopped by a heavily armed marine, given a chair and told to await the arrival of the Ministers. It was great loss of face for a yamen secretary to be sat outside an evil-smelling dungeon surrounded by the garbage of war and stenches from every form of detritus.

As Kershaw approached the blockhouse with Sir Archibald he smiled to see the elegant secretary holding his nostrils. Sir Archibald took a second sedan chair, beside the secretary, and a whole retinue of minor officials gathered in the middle distance as befitted ministers without portfolio.

Kershaw found translation unusually difficult: the secretary spoke in dialect. Regrets were expressed on both sides, mutual reassurances exchanged together with the crocodile tears of diplomacy. Vague threats delivered first by the secretary were forcibly capped by Sir Archibald. It was like a Gilbert and Sullivan opera with the stenches increasing as the sun intensified. Sir Archibald's attitude stiffened as he failed to find a satisfactory explanation for the truce and Kershaw was driven to re-formulate his demands in polite Chinese. Continuously, refinements of translation maintained negotiations otherwise doomed to abrupt failure. Sir Archibald, his face pink under his pith helmet, was mopping the sweat with a useless silk handkerchief and demanding of Kershaw in English, "Do you think we shall get anywhere?"

Kershaw shook his head but recommended patience. He was interested in the reversal of roles. This was the first time Sir Archibald had openly sought his advice in official negotiation. The Ministers in the middle ground seemed reassured that the world of diplomacy had suddenly been resurrected. They fidgeted and shifted, edging slowly nearer, trying to pick up scraps of the exchanges.

It all led nowhere, but one hour later, back in his study, Sir Archibald found yet another missive from "Prince Ch'ing and Others".

"What do you think 'others' means?" he asked Kershaw.

"I doubt they exist, Sir Archibald. It's a bluff."

"I couldn't agree with you more. It's pretty obvious, isn't it, why we've got this truce."

"Yes, I suppose it is."

Sir Archibald smiled. "You know, sometimes, Kershaw I think you would have made a splendid diplomat — you play every card close to your chest. Why do you think we've got the truce?"

"They think the relieving force has taken Tientsin."

"Is that an inspired guess?"

Kershaw shook his head. "It comes from Lu-Ching."

"That man is omniscient," Sir Archibald said. "I came to that conclusion reading between the lines of this sort of thing." He flung down Prince Ch'ing's missive with distaste. "How did he arrive at it?"

"He's constantly in touch."

"And you still deny he's a double agent?"

"Certainly."

Later, in his report to the Foreign Office, Sir Archibald wrote: "Some of these letters take the usual Tsungli yamen form and are accompanied by the cards of all the yamen Ministers but these are the more formal communications. The important part of the correspondence purports to come from Prince Ch'ing and Others, or Prince Ch'ing and Colleagues and to Prince Ch'ing accordingly I addressed my reply, but there is no ground for supposing that all the letters came from him.

"On the whole we assume that we really are in direct correspondence with the Heads of Chinese Government, the changes in tone being due to the effect produced by events at Tientsin and possibly to fluctuations in the influence of different advisers of that Government."

As he finished writing he sat back with a sigh. Why, of all Her Majesty's Plenipotentiary Ministers sent to lie abroad on behalf of the Imperial Crown, had he been chosen for this godforsaken destiny. And why did he continue every evening to join his wife in futile prayers to the Almighty who must by now be deafened by the din of appeals from every member of every Legation? Religious fervour flourished readily when attacks were fierce.

As the truce ran into its second day another cart laden with ice, melons and vegetables entered the perimeter by command of the Empress Dowager. On the third day the restless marines began to play cricket, explaining the mysteries of the game to the Chinese levies.

By then the cessation of gunfire and the continuous silence pressed on Kershaw's nerves. It was madness, of course, but the total absence of action disturbed him more than its opposite. Ignored in the heat of battle, the mosquitoes created a new and ceaseless irritation, descending in such masses that the drone of their wings became a roar; no one noticed the roar in rifle fire. With the threat of death a daily presence, Kershaw was driven out of introspection; but now, in near idleness, his thoughts turned inward again.

Looking into his mirror one morning he saw an unfamiliar face. It was haggard, bearded, with dark blotches under the eyes and — yes — he peered more closely — a small almost undetectable twitch at the right side of the mouth. He fingered the twitch and it stopped. When he lifted his finger it began again. Geared up by nervous energy, driven by bursts of overworked adrenalin, he had lived on his nerves for weeks, and now, when peace and almost complacency had descended, his system could not take the sudden change. He did not want to get out of bed in the mornings. He had an overwhelming impulse to slip down again and lie there, inert, all day.

The past came crowding in. The smell of his mother's restaurant and the stink of formaldehyde from his medical days. Stinks — the living background of the Legation linked him with their counterpart in the past. And then as he struggled with a blunt open razor to tidy his beard he saw the peeled body of the young girl student with her swollen belly and shaved pubes waiting for the dilator of steadily increasing size as his inexperienced hand fumbled with her vagina and her scream made the razor jerk in his hand and the blood began to run down his chin. He knew then that he should get out of the bedroom, do something active, lose himself again in the whirl of siege life . . . but there was no whirl.

A knock on the door. "Come in." It was Lu-Ching, but a different Lu-Ching. His hair was tonsured, his clothing a dirty tunic, his paper shoes in tatters and his face pouring rivulets of sweat between a mask of dirt.

"What in God's name — " Kershaw began.

"I have been through the Water Gate," Lu-Ching said, his voice a hoarse whisper. "Someone recognized me. I had to go into hiding. Fortunately the truce came and I was able to get back in again." He saw the blood on Kershaw's face. "Has anything happened?"

"Just a razor cut," Kershaw said.

Lu-Ching staggered towards his bed and collapsed on it.

"Do you need a doctor?" asked Kershaw.

"No."

"Some brandy?"

"Just sleep — let me sleep." As if a lever had been pulled he immediately fell asleep.

Reporting to Sir Archibald's study Kershaw found it empty and his secretary said, "He's at a melon-tasting party."

"Melon tasting?"

"They've divided up the melons and organized a tasting party. It's in the theatre," she said.

As he walked towards the theatre Kershaw thought that normality could get no further — a melon-tasting party. Amateur dramatics must begin again soon, a village fête would offer coconut shies and of course the horses would be racing past a re-built stand.

The theatre was full of people all wearing fresh clothes, some women in Ascot hats, one man with a monocle, and they surrounded a table with six half melons placed in ice buckets. Two melons — purple with claret — were being ceremoniously tasted and a mock discussion of their merits followed. A series of melons underwent similar philosophic exposition at the end of which Sir Archibald finally announced that one huge fat yellow half globe dripping with pips, juice and claret was the appointed Dowager Empress of the melon empire. He sank his teeth so deeply and viciously into it he received a roar of applause. Immediately afterwards he said:

"We have work to do. Every able-bodied man must strengthen the barricades and trenches. We must not waste time. I regret to say this truce may not last."

There was a groan of disappointment. The truce had given rise to the wildest expectations. To hope till hope creates from its own wreck the thing it contemplates! Someone had quoted that one day, and the quotation appeared in elaborate script on the Bell Tower. Sir Archibald's words fell like lead.

The gloom was temporary. As the day wore on, spirits revived and by noon scores of people were lying in the shade drinking and gossiping, talking about England and what they would do when they got home. Elaborate fantasies of gorgeous meals predominated and when someone mentioned an overwhelming desire to see a Gilbert and Sullivan opera he was accused of philistinism. The palate had been elevated above music, its refined satisfaction developed into an art.

One other luxury they indulged orgiastically — sleep. People were found sprawled in public places, dangerously exposed to the sun, so sound asleep that nothing short of wild shakings brought them awake again. The shade of the theatre became a living mortuary with apparent corpses collapsed in fantastic attitudes, snoring indiscriminately.

Sir Archibald sent minions scurrying to every Legation insisting that this was no time for relaxation. Kershaw found himself part of the galvanizing machinery. Men and women had to be roused from exhausted torpor to patch, repair and rebuild. Somehow, half the coolie population filtered away as the day wore on, and abandoned handcarts were everywhere.

At three o'clock in the afternoon, returning to his room, Kershaw found it empty, but a false pigtail lay beside the bed, the greasy tunic had been folded away and the rich official jacket no longer hung on the back of the lacquered chair. On the table was a small white familiar envelope. Tearing it open

Kershaw read, "Tonight as before. 10.0 p.m."

He sank down on the bed. For the tenth time the resolve formulated in his mind — he must make an end of this — but the outlines of the room became a haze and within minutes he was deeply asleep, his mouth open, his face twitching.

When he woke it was dark. His mouth was dry and sour, his limbs heavy with unaccustomed relaxation, and he stumbled round the room feeling for the kerosene lamp. In its dim light he peered into the mirror and smiled grimly. The exaggerated shadows from the limited light gave his face a ghoulish air. Suddenly he remembered Lucy's note. He snatched up his watch — five minutes past ten. Damnation and hell. He moved swiftly out into the night.

Whether his mood or the thought of seeing Lucy transformed the reality of the Legation he could not be sure, but the air seemed like a soft caress on his bearded cheek. The stars were so insistent they seemed to spell out a brilliant message and the moon made opalescent even the rotting heaps of rubbish.

It was a night of illusion. Nothing seemed — true. Slops pouring out from under the laundry door were molten silver, the blur of a tree elaborate filigree, the Residence, rising safe and secure, a silver palace.

But he was late. Lucy would be waiting. She had no time. . . . He stumbled over the handles of an abandoned cart left beside the cemetery and the noise seemed alarmingly loud. Then he was there in the sheltered remnant of the ruined pavilion and she was cursing him — You're late! You're late! — but kissing him relentlessly and with a purpose which brooked no interference.

"Not here!" he exclaimed and she put her hand over his mouth. "Ssh!" she whispered. "Follow me." She led him between the ruins to an inner part of the pavilion with four walls intact and, lying sprawled diagonally across the floor, a modern European mattress.

She was dragging him down ignoring every protest. This time there was no mistake. Under her long skirt there was nothing and when she deliberately pulled up her skirt he was amazed by her audacity and astonished at the beauty of her slender limbs.

They made love instantly, savagely as if life was about to leave them. She could not stop the cry, and it went out echoing across the Legation. He put his hand across her mouth to stop the repetition as one wave mounted to the next, but his own body sucked him down to its ferocious centre and his own cry came, tearing his throat.

Afterwards they lay listening, their ears tuned to every sound, starting up when a distant door shut and a night voice called something unintelligibly, but no one came, and slowly their tense bodies relaxed and they lay in each other's arms tenderly.

It was some time before they spoke. His first inquiry seemed so ordinary she could not bear it. "Where does he think you are?"

"Helping out in the hospital again — but don't let's talk about him — or anything."

He tried to speak and she put her hand across his mouth.

"Ssh," she said. "You'll break the spell."

She had soaked herself in Lady Mainwaring's scent, because its expensive subtlety would have been overwhelmed in smaller quantities, and now some chemical alchemy blended the real and artificial to produce an aura which fitted the romantic unreality of the night.

They lay in silence aware of nothing but the sensuality of their bodies and the perfection of the night. The moon moved round and found a shell hole to flood their refuge with light. It crept slowly across their faces and still they said nothing. And then at last she said very quietly:

"There's something I've been wanting to tell you."

He waited, his hand settled over her breast, his body renewing now its sexual tensions.

"We never really consummated that marriage."

"I don't understand," he said.

"Colin was desperate to show himself a man — I pretended."

"Pretended?"

"I never had a genuine climax. I became very skilled at pretending — he really believed it."

There was a long pause and in the pause her hand slipped down to caress him and he drew away shuddering with delight.

"Why do you do that?" she said.

"There's no time," he said.

"You're afraid, aren't you."

"Yes. I'm afraid."

"You face all those bullets — you behave like a hero — but you're afraid of being found like this, here, with me."

"Yes," he said quietly. "I am."

"I'll never understand you," she said.

"I'll never understand myself."

She turned over on her side then and tried to guide him into her. He stopped her. "Just once more," she pleaded. "Just once."

"We must go," he said. "It's dangerous."

"Oh, my God — what a damned coward you really are."

She turned away and there were tears in her eyes, when he said, "We can't go on like this."

She turned round furiously. "Why should we worry — he knows all about it, he's accepted it — but I'll tell you something."

He remained silent.

"The awful thing is I think he still genuinely loves me."

He pulled away from her then and sat up. "You must go," he said and then he bent again and very tenderly kissed her breasts, tasting the sweat-soaked skin with deepest pleasure.

"We must go separately," she suggested. "You first."

As she readjusted her dress and came to her feet she added, "One more thing. Be careful. He may shoot you."

He started. "Shoot me? — that's crazy."

"Think," she said. "With all these stray bullets and stray deaths — what would be easier than to shoot you and fake it all?"

She waited for him to answer but he did not reply. "Tomorrow," she said. "Here?"

He shook his head. She grew angry and her voice rose. "Quietly," he said. "For God's sake keep quiet." They wrangled on for several minutes and at last he agreed. "All right, the day after tomorrow."

She took two steps away and came back again.

"There's something you haven't asked me."

He was puzzled.

"My period."

"Oh — yes."

"No sign." With that she went.

CHAPTER XVIII

THE LAST OF the kerosene had given out and at midnight in his study Sir Archibald wrote a memorandum to the Foreign Office by the light of three ornate Christmas candles:

"A certain reserve and reluctance to give free expression to one's feelings cannot be described as an unusual feature of diplomatic correspondence but such reserve can rarely have been so irksome and at the same time imposed by such cogent motives as in our case.

"We need to prolong the Alice in Wonderland negotiations as far as possible, because reliable news has reached us on this day, July 18th, that Tientsin has been captured by the relieving force. We get this news from the remarkable stranger in our midst upon whose presence I have remarked before — the Chinese magistrate Lu-Ching who sought sanctuary in our Legation, six weeks ago and has been unable to leave for fear of death at the hands of the Boxers. I have at last come to the conviction that he is neither an agent nor a double agent, but a man with genuine convictions of his own which are consonant with the old Chinese philosophy of Confucius and far removed from the expediencies of the Dowager Empress.

"The truce we are experiencing at the moment can only be explained by the taking of Tientsin and the threat that poses to Peking. Clearly the Empress does not want to be discovered in the process of destroying the Legations if the relieving forces are about to enter the city. However I am advised by Lu-Ching that any show of impatience at Prince Ch'ing's plain prevarications might bring the truce to an end and the truce is such a God-send to us that we continue with this long-drawn-out charade of hypocritical communications. . . ."

"Why are you working at this time of night?" Lady Mainwaring had entered the study, come up behind him and kissed the beginnings of a bald patch.

"I must keep the record straight my dear."

"Damn the record," she said. "It's sleep we all need — and here we have this wonderful truce and you don't take advantage of it. Come back to bed."

"I won't be long. I must write this out while it's on my mind — you know how easily I forget."

She put her arm round his shoulders and he felt her breasts pressed against him. Turning to kiss her he was surprised to see that she was naked. Even in the heat of Peking no one wandered the corridors of the Residence after dark without even a nightdress.

"My dear," he said, slightly shocked. "Suppose you had met someone."

Her breasts he thought were surprisingly well preserved and but for the middle-age spread of her stomach she could pass for a much younger woman. Only her face showed the ravages of the siege. Ignoring his remark she continued, "You looked so tired at dinner. Worse than tired — ill."

"You don't exactly look yourself, either," he commented.

She plumped down in the gold-brocaded armchair. "I'm not going back to bed until you come too," she said. "It's such a marvellous night outside. Does it remind you of something?"

The pen was drooping in his tired fingers, his eyes closing, and all he could find to reply was, "No m'dear. Let me finish this."

His pen began scratching its way across the page again.

"But there is a serious qualification of the whole truce brought to my attention by another valuable member of my staff whose importance has grown beyond that of an interpreter for which he was originally employed. Mr C. K. Kershaw reports to me that the Chinese Imperial Troops are busy deepening and strengthening their fortifications around us. He, along with other observers such as Major Shelham, have come to believe that the lull is really a temporary device to put us off our guard. It would be appropriate at this moment to . . . "

The pen simply slipped from his hand as his eyes closed and at once Lady Mainwaring came to her feet, took him by the arm saying, "That's enough. We're going to bed."

Slowly they made their way along the corridor towards the

big bedroom, still preserved intact for their use. As Lady Mainwaring sank down on the satin stool before her dressing table to apply her face cream he came up behind her and stared at the two images in the mirror.

"This way of life does not suit either of us, does it?" she said. "I look like an old witch."

"I was just reflecting, my dear, how little changed you were."

She took his hand and looked up at him.

"Flatterer," she said and, turning back to the mirror, "My skin is ruined — dry, wrinkled, great pits under the eyes — we must take advantage of this lull to get some sleep. Otherwise I'll end up prematurely old. Thank goodness it's a bit cooler this evening. I'm permanently drenched in perspiration."

They climbed into bed and as he reached out a hand to draw her to him she protested.

"It's too hot, Archie."

He lay there silent for a long moment and then he said, "Do you think we will ever make love again?"

"Of course we will," she said, lying with as much conviction as she could summon.

"I don't," he said. "I think our sex life has — " he hesitated for the word " — run dry."

There was a long silence and then she reached out a hand to him and said, "Even if that were true, and it isn't, it wouldn't be the end of everything, would it?" She paused and added, "You know my views. I think sex is for the young."

As they lay at opposite sides of the bed Lady Mainwaring fell suddenly asleep but Sir Archibald's restless twisting woke her five minutes later.

"Can't you sleep?" she asked.

"No," he said. "I've reached a stage beyond sleep."

She turned to him then and put her arms round him. "Don't be absurd, Archie — just relax and forget all this and put the whole thing out of your mind. Did you know what I meant when I asked you whether the beautiful night reminded you of anything just now?"

"I'm sorry — no."

"The first weekend we spent in this house. The weather was perfect — it was all so romantically new — the Chinese seemed so splendidly friendly — and the moon went on shining night after night . . . "

"And night after night we made love."

She turned away abruptly; "I wish you wouldn't keep talking like that. You're as bad as Lucy Shelham."

"How do you mean, Lucy Shelham?"

"She's having an affair with Kershaw, isn't she."

"Why do you say that. And how can anyone have an affair under these conditions?"

"Come on Archie — you know her reputation as well as I do. . . . And you also know she's having an affair. Wasn't there some scandal in Singapore? Didn't they get posted here because of that?"

"I don't think we should talk about that."

"I like her — but her behaviour is becoming outrageous."

"She's been working in the hospital for weeks — a very brave thing to do."

"Yes — I must say I couldn't face it — but that doesn't alter the fact that. . . "

As she talked she became aware that Sir Archie was snoring beside her. If there was anything which seemed to her to degrade human beings it was their ability to produce these stertorous animal noises and she turned over on her side and pulled the sheet over her head. A moment later the heat was too much for her and she pulled the sheet back again. It was now her turn to twist restlessly, unable to sleep, mopping the sweat from her face. At last she rose, took the sheet and rolled it back to the foot of the bed. As she did so — incongruously — she resolved that she really must speak to Lucy Shelham about Kevin Kershaw.

Diplomatic exchanges by letter continued between Prince Ch'ing and the Legation Ministers. They seemed hopelessly repetitive to Sir Archibald. The Prince wrote: "It is possible that the Foreign Envoys do not fully realize the keen desire of our Court to protect the Legations and we feel bound to give a detailed explanation. . . . There is existing a general ferment absolutely beyond our control which nothing but the destruction of the Legations can satisfy and the diplomats are requested that a day of departure be fixed in order that we may make ready boats and provisions."

Sir Archie returned a circumspect reply which explained the dangers of leaving the Legations, without actually refusing to do so.

Three days later a scattering of fire from the Chinese lines momentarily rose to a fusillade which caught people unprepared, killing an English marine and wounding three coolies. It subsided almost at once, but Sir Archibald wrote to Prince Ch'ing to complain. The reply annoyed him. "The firing was due to a misunderstanding and it was more or less on the same footing as the sounding of the evening drum and the morning bell, an everyday matter, hardly worth a smile."

As the days of the truce multiplied food shortages became more acute and the last ponies were killed one by one. Many were personally owned by members of the Legation staff. One, a young Customs officer, wrote in his diary: "Went to say goodbye to poor old Memory. He was wretchedly thin. Very sad — sad."

It amused Kershaw that the Ministers automatically granted Europeans first claim on any available food even though some Chinese converts were doing work no less important.

Checks on the Legation defences were made continuously. One day Kershaw accompanied Major Shelham on his rounds. It was a long, tedious day's work and Shelham's unconcealed hostility reduced the two men to rarely broken silences. Some of the enemy's barricades seemed abandoned but others were being extended and a secret traffic of eggs and ammunition continued with the renegade soldiery from Fung Fu-hsiang's camp.

The scene changed dramatically in the Fu Palace. There, the converts pleaded for any scraps of food, and some aggressively drew attention to their skeletal ribs. One man was bent low, weeping silently over a boy with a huge pot belly who had died of starvation that morning. There were six others he said, and more would die soon. One woman lay quite still in the burning sun with a dead child clasped to her withered breast. Converts clung to Shelham dragging at his sleeve as he moved away. He shook them off.

Worse scenes followed at the Water Gate. Hardened as he was, Kershaw found difficulty in confronting the herd of ordinary native Chinese, trapped by the siege inside the Water Gate. Their eyes stood out from sunken flesh and their bones seemed to be pushing through their skins. Sharpshooters regarded them as traitors and even during the truce simply picked off every man who tried to escape. Scores of them staggered up pointing to swollen bellies and pleading for rice. Kershaw tried to tell them that he would insist on some rice being sent but they clearly did not believe him. And then two marines came down the slope dragging a dead dog and crow which they had just deliberately shot for one purpose only. They threw the bodies towards the starving Chinese. With maniacal cries the stronger Chinese set on the still warm bodies, tore them apart and began gnawing at the bleeding flesh. Kershaw turned away.

Shelham said, "Disgusting. Must get something done."

To Kershaw's astonishment, when they reported back to the Residence, the first thing Shelham did was to bring up the plight of the native Chinese. Kershaw found himself supporting Shelham with an emotion which surprised Sir Archibald. "They've obviously got under your skin, Kershaw," he said. Kershaw thought how accurate a description that was. "But what can we do? Our own people are malnourished. Others are sick and dying — we must keep the fighters fit."

"Just one sack of rice," Kershaw pleaded.

"What's the use of that — they'd fight over it and it wouldn't provide one decent meal. Believe me, I sympathize with them. I was near starving once in the Cairo campaign."

"If you can spare the time," said Kershaw, "take a look at them yourself, Sir Archibald. You may change your mind."

"I will," Sir Archibald assured him. "I will. But tell our sharpshooters not to waste ammunition shooting stray dogs. If we run out of ammunition — everybody knows what that means — and we are running out."

There was a knock at the door and Elizabeth Smythe, Sir Archibald's secretary, entered. She had changed dramatically. The plump, well nourished young woman had visibly diminished until her shirt hung loosely on her body and her cheeks had lost their innocent symmetry. She held herself rigidly as if expecting a blow and her voice no longer carried its rich throaty quality. "There's a messenger," she said with apprehension as if any messenger meant bad news. Continuous strain and fear had drained away the resources of her body as much as rationing. "He's just a boy."

"A boy — I know who that may be. Show him in at once."

"He's very dirty sir."

"That doesn't matter."

The boy who walked with a limp into the room was barely fifteen years old and his tattered clothing stank, but Sir Archibald came to his feet, walked round his desk and shook him warmly by the hand. This was a vital moment. Lu-Ching had selected this boy to carry a letter concealed in a beggar's rice bowl to Mr Carles, the British Consul at Tientsin.

"Congratulations! Congratulations!" Sir Archibald kept repeating, his nostrils quivering with a stink even stronger than that familiar to the garrison. The boy did not understand a word and Kershaw began to translate. His thick dialect made it almost impossible, but the boy kept fingering the collar of his tattered coat, and at last Kershaw understood that a message had been sewn into it.

They tried with a pair of scissors to free the message, but inexpert hands threatened to reduce it to shreds and Sir Archibald showed signs of anger. He rang his silver bell. Pretty Poo appeared and with a pair of nail scissors expertly extracted a closely folded sheet of European paper.

Sir Archibald read aloud:

"Your letter of July 4. There are now 24,000 troops landed and 19,000 troops here (Tientsin). General Gaselee is expected at Taku. When he comes I hope to see more activity. The Russians are at Peitsang. Tientsin is under foreign government and the Boxers' power here is exploded. Do try to keep me informed of yourselves. There are plenty of troops on the way; if you can keep yourselves in food for a time, all ought yet to come out well. The Consulate is mended to be ready for you when you come. Almost all the ladies have left Tientsin. Kindest remembrances to all in the Legation. W. R. Carles."

"What do you think of that?" Sir Archibald said to Shelham.

"Stupendous stuff," he replied ironically.

Sir Archibald repeated a phrase: "*When he comes I hope to see more activity*. My God, — they were supposed to be on their way here. *More activity*! What does that mean?"

He sat back in his chair. Clearly he was stunned by the message. The high hopes of relief which had spread through the Legation were completely dashed. No relief was in sight.

"The question is, should we post it on the Bell Tower?"

"Must tell truth," Shelham said.

"You don't say anything, Kershaw — what do you think?"

"I think Major Shelham is right," replied Kershaw.

"If a relief column was setting out from Tientsin he would have said so, wouldn't he?"

Sir Archibald seemed to search for reassurance.

"Certainly," Major Shelham said. "No relief force."

"Everyone must have seen this boy arrive. We must say something. Perhaps we'd better censor it."

Sir Archibald took up his pen. "Come," he gestured to Shelham and Kershaw, "tell me which you think are the most damaging phrases."

There was no doubt. Four phrases were removed from the text. "*When he comes I hope to see more activity.*" "*Do try and keep me informed of yourselves.*" "*All ought to come out well.*" "*Kindest remembrances to all in the Legation.*"

The last phrase was the most insensitive of all. It might have been a funeral phrase in expectation of death.

No one in the study noticed that the boy messenger had collapsed on the floor. Five minutes later they carried him out and revived him. When at last Lu-Ching managed to extract his story, it was humbling to all would-be heroes, and when the revised message was pinned on the Bell Tower it sent a wave of gloom through the Legation. As Monsieur Bleriot recorded in his diary, "Men moved away from the ladies to express their feelings. Mr Carles, the British Consul, is an idiot."

As if to underline the emptiness of hope, rifle fire began again as dusk fell and everyone drank champagne, wrangled, argued and tried to adjust once more to the threat of starvation waiting at the end of a not very long line.

CHAPTER XIX

Somewhere high above the orchestra of shell and rifle fire the shrill rising and falling of maniacal cries out of all proportion to any human sound made a fearful counterpoint to the pandemonium which a full scale attack produced one week later.

Lu-Ching and Kershaw were standing sheltered behind the advance barricade of the British Legation and there, once more, a familiar figure like a whirling dervish dressed in brilliant white was picked out by the all-persistent moon. It did not run straight across the bullet scarred no man's land. It performed a mad ballet, one moment running forward, the next backward, and then whirling on its heels as if trying to spin like a professional dancer only to fall, pick itself up again and advance once more. But whether it dipped, turned or pirouetted, miraculously the bullets cleared a space for it and if the phrase 'a charmed life' had any meaning then this was its living incarnation.

As the figure approached Lu-Ching and Kershaw, they began to pick out the words hurled with demonic howls at the unheeding bowl of the night sky:

"Thou hast saved me oh Lord
And I am sanctified —
Be Thou thrice blessed Oh most high of all divinites that none can say me nay —
In death's dark vale I fear no ill
With Thee dear Lord beside me
Thy rod and staff my comfort still
Thy cross before to guide me."

As he approached the barricades it seemed impossible that the fusillades could miss him, but it was as if he twirled a mad challenge between the bullets until he reached the last ten yards. And then suddenly he straightened up and, goose-stepping his way forward with military precision, he roared at the barricades:

"Onward Christian soldiers
Marching as to war — "

Dumbfounded marines stared at the apparition fully vulnerable in the sights of their guns.

As Kershaw helped the man over the barricade, they knew they were dealing with the mad missionary, Nostegarde.

A whole hour elapsed before they succeeded in piecing together his incoherent story. At the most illogical moments of that story he would suddenly cluck triumphantly like a hen laying an egg and flap his arms. Another time his burning eyes threatened to release fire and brimstone on his Satanic questioners clearly intent on claiming his soul for the devil. Towards the end he became physically violent and the energy of the possessed gave him such strength that it took four coolies to hold him down. There was nothing for it but to bind his hands and feet and lock him up but — where? They discovered that the cupboard under the stairs had been vacated by the Dutch Minister, and Nostegarde was strapped into the cupboard with the door open, hysterically invoking "Our Father that art in Heaven — why hast Thou forsaken me". But the roar of his voice was too disturbing, and finally they carried him away to the stables and tethered him like a pony. There he spreadeagled himself against the wall and appeared a self-immolated Christ demanding,

"Did I not do your bidding, Lord?
Why do you not do mine? Damn you, Lord you
do not listen. Damn you and your son Christ — I am
your living son. For I have been thrice crucified. . . . "

Late that afternoon as Kershaw and Lu-Ching entered Sir Archibald's study he snapped, "Five minutes, no more — what is it?" He was enmeshed in telegrams, interviews, committees, spies, the whole network which circled round his alleged command, a command which issued orders with less and less effect.

The story they unfolded astonished Sir Archibald. Nostegarde had been accepted unharmed into the Chinese lines and taken to Jung Lu's headquarters where he was treated with great respect, fed well, and searched. He carried personal papers which identified him, and among them was one apologizing for indecently exposing himself to Madame Bleriot, the wife of the French Minister.

"But why didn't they shoot him out of hand?" Sir Archibald remarked, to cover his embarrassment.

"Because," Lu-Ching explained, "the Chinese stand in awe of madness. A person who behaves in that manner is living in another world and may be speaking with the inspired voice of many ancestors. Mad people are respected and receive special consideration."

"Well, what happened next?" Sir Archibald asked impatiently. Kershaw took up the story and revealed that Nostegarde had answered every question put to him about the strength of the garrisons, the position of guns, and morale.

Ecstatically happy that these people took his outpourings seriously he had given away depositions and strategies with the joy of someone dispensing largesse to the poor. Subject, like many madmen, to periods of sanity, the Chinese patiently waited for one of these, treated him with opium to prolong it and released him back to the Legation lines, suitably converted into a Chinese peasant. Three times he was treated and returned with more information, but on the fourth occasion, threw off his peasant disguise, put on his white robes and howled his way once more to a dubious freedom.

"But if he's mad, how could his information be of any use?"

"The Chinese are adept at detecting periods of sanity," Lu-Ching said, "because their treatment establishes understanding of the madman's logic. The opium also helps."

Sir Archibald had been following his usual habit of stalking round the room as he listened to their story and now he slumped down in his chair and said: "Well, that at least clears up one source of spying. I think, Kershaw, Major Shelham may have to apologize to you."

Kershaw said nothing.

Sir Archibald glanced at his diary.

"See me again after dinner this evening," he said, dismissing them.

It was nine o'clock before Kershaw returned to Sir Archibald's study to find it in darkness. Outside — monotonously — the bullets were hissing through the darkness. As he moved towards the dining room Kershaw suddenly wondered what was stopping the Chinese from bringing up enough artillery to blow their barricades to pieces and bring this farcical siege to an end.

The servants were clearing the debris of a meal for forty people, by the dim light of a few candles. Lady Mainwaring and her husband were sitting at their own side table. She wore a chiffon evening dress, and Sir Archibald was in full dress uniform with his decorations all perfectly in place. Both were poised, correct, talking flawless social clichés from years of diplomatic dinner parties. The fact that they were forced to raise their voices to be heard above the gunfire did not seem to discourage them. Why protocol had flowered once more Kershaw could not fathom but the scene preserved the correct dispensation of class and creed expected of God's Englishmen by Her Imperial Majesty Queen Victoria when defending the humblest outpost of Empire.

Seeing Kershaw enter, Sir Archibald waved. "I'll be with you in my study in ten minutes," he said, puffing at a cigar.

As Kershaw turned away he added, "Oh just a minute, Kershaw. Join us for coffee."

Kershaw looked down at his crumpled shirt and dirty trousers, and gestured.

"Don't worry," Sir Archibald said. "We'll all be back in the firing line in ten minutes. Here — " he drew up a lacquered chair. "Make yourself comfortable."

From a slender silver coffee pot Sir Archibald poured a liquid, which smelled like real coffee, into a fragile cup and Sir Archibald picked up a cut glass decanter. "Some brandy."

"Thank you — " Kershaw was on the point of saying "sir" and stopped.

The napery was spotless; the silver, real silver; the discarded dishes on the table, of fine porcelain. Beads of sweat gathered and ran down the face of Sir Archibald and his wife, soaking into her bodice and his collar.

It was at that moment that Major Shelham marched over from another table wearing his regulation uniform, bowed to Sir Archibald and said, "If you will excuse me." He turned then to Kershaw, almost clicked his heels, thrust out his hand and said, "I was wrong. I am sorry. I apologize." Kershaw came to his feet, hesitated for a fraction of a second while Shelham's hand seemed to quiver on the air, the marriage ring on his third finger glittering dully in the candlelight. Then Kershaw took and shook the hand and again with a half bow Shelham retired to his table.

Lucy sat waiting for him, her braided hair piled high on her head, reflecting a yellow glow from the light of a big candle and Kershaw felt her eyes fixed on him. Their expression was lost in the shadows.

Presently Lady Mainwaring rose, excused herself and left the room followed by Major Shelham and Lucy. Then Sir Archibald said, "Let's go to my office."

When they were settled opposite each other Sir Archibald offered Kershaw a cigar which he politely refused. Sir Archibald unbuttoned his tunic, stripping it off with relief. He turned over some papers on his desk, picked up a ruler and began measuring distances on the map pinned to a board.

"They're closing in on us," he observed. "We've lost more than half the ground we used to occupy." He pushed the board aside. . . . "But that's not what I wanted to talk about. . . . " He sat back and paused again. Clearly he was delaying the awkward moment when he had to come to the point. It came out suddenly with greater force than he intended.

"You must know Kershaw that the whole Legation is talking about you."

Kershaw was genuinely surprised.

"Talking about me," he said. "Why?"

"We must be frank with one another. As you know I've come to like and respect you — but this simply cannot go on."

"You mean — " Kershaw began and stopped.

"Yes, I mean whatever it is that exists between you and Lucy Shelham."

Kershaw was silent.

"What *is* there between you?"

Kershaw thought a moment and then said quietly, "She loves me and I love her."

"My God!" Sir Archibald said. "Who would believe such an experience could overtake people in a situation like this!"

Kershaw was silent.

"I wondered why Shelham seemed to — well — have it in for you. Now I know. But there's something I don't know. How far has this gone?"

Kershaw's mind said what in hell has it got to do with you whether your petty bourgeois morals are upheld or not, especially in a life and death situation like this.

"Have you spoken to Mrs Shelham?" Kershaw asked.

"I haven't, but my wife has. I can't tell you what she said until I've heard your version."

What would Lucy say to a woman like Lady Mainwaring? Clearly she would never acknowledge those sadly inhibited, clumsy moments of love-making in the ruins of the Fu, and to betray her now would bring all hell down on her head.

"We simply love one another, that is all."

Sir Archibald leant forward across his desk and stared straight into Kershaw's eyes. "You know Kershaw, in your own curious way I think you are a man of integrity. Now, as a man of integrity, have you made love to her?" Again Kershaw's impulse was to say what the hell has it got to do with you? Instead he said "No — certainly not" and at that moment his mind resolved the conflict between his own integrity and loyalty to Lucy.

Sir Archibald released a sigh of relief. "Good — but this has got to stop."

"What — exactly — has got to stop?" asked Kershaw, and Sir Archibald seemed surprised at the challenge.

"You know very well what I mean."

"If you mean we have to stop loving one another that is going to be difficult."

"I don't mean that. I mean you've got to stop seeing one

another. It's disturbing the whole Legation and above all it's humiliating to Major Shelham — an officer and a gentleman."

"Can I ask what Mrs Shelham said about this?"

"She refuses to give the required undertaking. It's up to you."

Brave, brave Lucy, Kershaw thought, but oh, how foolish. Why not give the undertaking and still follow their clandestine habits?

When Kershaw did not answer, Sir Archibald said, "I'm asking you now, Kershaw, to give an undertaking that you will not see her again."

"But we are bound to meet under present conditions."

"That is different from making assignations."

Kershaw decided to risk expressing his thoughts.

"Doesn't it strike you, Sir Archibald, as being — odd — that we should be worrying about niceties of morality in a life and death situation?"

"They are not niceties," Sir Archibald said curtly. "They are fundamentals. And we shall all survive to face the consequences of our actions here."

"You are so sure?"

"Yes — certain. But there's something else I have to tell you which may help you." Sir Archibald picked up his ebony ruler and tapped for nearly a minute. Then he began. "What I have to say must be treated in the highest confidence. You agree to that?"

Kershaw was thinking — how much longer is this farce going on? "Of course," he said.

"You see — you are not the first man to become entangled with Lucy Shelham." He paused to let the words sink in. "Major Shelham was Second Secretary to the Embassy in Singapore four years ago. His prospects were very good. But his wife became involved in a scandalous affair — there was a threat of divorce — and as a result they posted him here — the whole thing was hushed up."

His voice dropped to a sad note. "You see, the odd thing about Major Shelham is that despite that unfortunate clipped manner of his, he is a very clever man. He also happens to be devoted to his wife."

His cigar had gone out and he paused to re-light it. Puffing thickly on it he continued, "Nor is that the whole story. There was yet another — er — lover — earlier . . . in Cairo. Mrs Shelham is a very strange woman. She is undoubtedly a very brave woman but she is totally unsuited to the marriage state, and in my view disgustingly immoral."

He sucked on his cigar until the end was glowing. "To put it bluntly, Kershaw, you are the third man she has been — " he paused to search for the right words, and chose " — mixed up with. That may make you feel differently about the whole affair."

The shock was considerable. A love relationship of such power and reciprocity that it could only happen once in a lifetime had been reduced to a commonplace affair with many predecessors.

"Perhaps you will see it in a new perspective, now," Sir Archibald said, coming to his feet. "I take it I have your word that you will — er — discontinue this relationship."

Kershaw also rose but without answering. He was thinking, suppose she is pregnant — what will they say about that? Sir Archibald waited for him to speak and, when he did not, said, "You force me to tell you — I will not tolerate it continuing."

At last Kershaw replied, "I must talk to Lucy first."

"I see no need for that." As Sir Archibald spoke, a huge rumble passed through the Legation, the floor of the study shook, books fell from their shelves and the ebony ruler went crashing to the floor. Cries and screams echoed through the Residence and then came an after-roar as if a massive wave of destruction was withdrawing from a desolated beach.

"A land mine," Sir Archibald said, looking no more than startled. He picked up his jacket, swung it round his shoulders, strode out of the room, out of the Residence, into the night.

It left a crater twenty feet wide. Standing on the rim Kershaw saw the strange amalgam of earth beneath Peking. Thick layers of black Peking dust, followed by stones, soil and detritus and then tightly packed clay. Thrown up by the explosion were two solid iron canon balls, from battles fought centuries before, and a single skull withered away as if the bone itself had shrunk.

Out of the smoke emerged a missionary with his arm blown off and, half buried in the debris, lay a marine, screaming, with blood pouring from his head.

People were appearing in doorways and Sir Archibald coughed his way through the smoke calling for volunteers.

"Get some coolies," he said to Kershaw, "and find Major Shelham."

Kershaw strode off in the direction of the Fu and within moments he was aware of someone walking beside him. It was Lucy.

"You must keep away," he said fiercely. "They're watching us."

She had some difficulty in matching his pace but she continued to walk beside him and said, "I must talk to you."

"Do you know what's happened?" he asked.

"Yes," she said. "I suppose you've had a dressing down too."

"You don't seem very worried."

"Why should I be? Everyone seems to know — what have we to lose?"

He stopped suddenly, grasped her shoulders and shook her. "Look Lucy, you really must stop behaving like a free woman — you are not a free woman. You belong to Queen Victoria. You can't get away from it."

He strode on and she half stumbled, half ran after him. "Meet me later," she begged breathlessly. "The same place?"

"It's impossible," he replied.

"I'll be there waiting."

"I'm sorry — it won't work."

She stopped and as he walked on she repeated softly, "I'll be there."

When the coolies had done their work they took a count of the casualties — three dead and twenty injured. "We simply cannot go on losing men at that rate," Sir Archibald said. "Where's Kershaw?"

"Not here," replied Major Shelham.

"Find him, will you?"

As Sir Archibald spoke Kershaw arrived at the ruined room in the Fu palace and Lucy flung herself into his arms. Gently disengaging himself Kershaw held her at arm's length. "Is it all true?"

Lucy struggled to kiss him, but as he held her back she asked, "Is what all true?"

"The other lovers — the scandal."

Lucy stopped struggling. "I see. Who's been talking?"

"Does it matter who?"

"Was it Colin?"

"No."

"My God! Not that monstrous old puritan Archie?"

"Well — is it true?"

"What did he tell you?"

"Look, we must hurry. I'll be missed."

"There are times when I despise you. What does it matter if you're missed?"

Kershaw began, "It matters because — " and stopped dead in his tracks. Christ — yes — here he was, a full blown man with no official allegiance to Sir Archibald, trapped in his way of thinking, his values, and responding to events with his ventriloquist voice. It was humiliating. "Yes," he agreed at last. "You're right — what does it matter."

He told her the story Sir Archibald had unfolded to him. She tried to embrace him again and as he finished she lay against him.

"There's only one flaw in it all," she said. "None of them mattered as you matter."

"Which is what you told the others I suppose."

"Do you really believe that?"

"How will I ever know?" As he said it he detected undertones of another set of values in which he did not believe. Romantic values, the ideal woman, the one and only relationship which transcended all others and meant commitment for life. Dear God! Life — was she aware that he would in all probability remain in Peking if they survived, and not as a European?

"Do you realize" she was saying "that if you said to me let's take a risk — break out of here and go off together — I'd go?"

"Since we're not that mad it's no test, is it?" he said.

"But there's something else." Her voice hardened as she drew back from him. "Did Archie tell you about Colin's behaviour. Did he tell you about *his* women. About two, three, four women, one of them a kept mistress in London. Did he tell you that? — No, of course he didn't. It's all right for a man to behave like that, but a woman — oh, no. We've got to sit sewing while they get away with it all."

Her voice was rising as she spoke and he tried to put his hand across her mouth but she brushed it aside.

"I decided I wouldn't let him get away with it and deliberately took a lover — and what explosions that caused. It wasn't worth it in the end. But I did it on principle. The double standard. It's built into our society, but one of these days women are going to revolt . . . and I'll be in the vanguard."

The pressure of her body against his had become irresistible and he took her in his arms and kissed her and she looked into his eyes and said, "I do — love you — differently. I mean it. You must understand — you *must* — I am hopelessly in love."

"Listen," he said. "If we survive this I don't know what will happen, but here and now we've got to play along with them. We must stop seeing each other, for the time being."

"I'm going to leave him anyway."

"We've just about enough iron rations for two weeks, excluding the Chinese. They will starve to death. Let's play it quietly for two weeks — and then, if we're still alive — "

"I don't want to play it quietly — " she began but he cut her short.

"Sir Archibald more or less ordered me to stop seeing you. He seems to think in this siege he's military master. It's nonsense of course and I don't take orders of that kind — but your husband's a different matter."

"You mean he might shoot you?"

"That's what you told me."

"Don't be absurd."

"I must go — they'll be looking for me."

"There's something not even Archie can control," Lucy said. "You so easily forget."

For a moment he was at a loss and then he said, "Your period?"

"No sign. And I'll tell you something Kevin. I'm glad." She swung away from him, performed a pirouette and came back in his arms again. "Glad! Glad!" she frowned. "Oh God, I wish I didn't love you."

"I must go. . . ."

"When do we meet again?"

"We don't."

She laughed. "In this confined space we're bound to meet again, anyway."

"We can meet when all this is over — if we survive. All this is too clumsy."

"Just tell me that somewhere behind that tired hard face of yours there lies just a hint of love for me."

"All right."

"All right! Don't just say — all right. Say — Yes, I *love* you."

"Yes I love you."

"And I mean it."

"And I mean it."

"And I hate leaving you."

"Loathe . . ."

"Kiss me."

"Kiss me."

Five minutes later he tore himself away.

Lu-Ching was sound asleep when he entered their room at midnight. Another deceptive lull outside was distantly broken by baying dogs tearing at decaying corpses and a medley of sounds from the hospital. Suddenly, out of the background murmurs, came a scream of such pibroch shrillness it rose and exploded in the silence, sending continuous echoes round the compound. Kershaw shuddered to think what hideous brutality of amateur surgery had removed what piece of shrapnel from a man's groin in the hospital, because the marine buried in the pit had been hit in the groin.

He wanted above all to read — quietly — Confucius, but to light the candle would probably awaken Lu-Ching. Awaken Lu-Ching! Nobody slept for more than two hours at a stretch. What did one more interruption matter in a much better cause?

There were very few matches left, and the candles were running low. He lit one, felt wide awake and changed his mind. He would trim his beard and ignore Confucius. Shaving in cold water came easily now, but shaving without soap was impossible. He gave up the razor and used a pair of scissors. As he peered in the mirror self examination began all over again. The man incapable of resolution had given place to the reckless would-be hero seeking redemption. The siege had subjected him to one test after another. He had been through such ordeal by fire as was seldom the lot of ordinary men and there stretched before him, almost within his reach, a region of calm. It was as if, psychologically, he had left the security of surface reality and been drawn down by events into the deepest levels of his unconscious where guilt lay festering. There he had re-encountered long-imprisoned impulses and, facing them for the first time, had changed and reassimilated their nature so that as the weeks went by and he rose to the surface again he carried with him a new integration of all the characteristics which went to make up the person of Kevin Kershaw.

The twitch at the side of his mouth was still there, reflecting some last unassimilated element. Could it be his love for Lucy? No — that was absurd. But their relationship remained a threat to the realization of — what — his whole self? It sounded so inadequate. And what the hell did it mean? As he trimmed his beard Kershaw began to seek a way of assimilating Lucy — or of excluding her. For all her talk of total love, would she ever become the wife of a minor Chinese official bent on changing a culture entirely alien to her? For that was the destiny Kershaw now saw opening up in the not very distant future, if such a future existed.

CHAPTER XX

"I've suddenly become old," Lady Mainwaring said peering into the left-hand mirror of her triple-mirrored dressing table. The other two mirrors were cracked from the impact of direct hits on the Residence. Only one long crimson curtain remained in place at the sandbagged window. The other had long ago gone to the hospital to cover many a bloody casualty.

"Look at all these wrinkles — three new ones round my mouth — and my neck like a piece of leather — and look at my eyes — pits, black pits."

Sir Archibald was shaving in the bathroom. Somehow he had managed to avoid growing a beard and his fine moustaches were immaculately in place.

"Are you listening?" Lady Mainwaring called.

"Yes, I am listening."

"Well, say something sympathetic."

"I'm sorry, my dear, but we have far worse things to cope with."

"Nothing is worse than a woman losing her youth!"

"Really, my dear — that's overstretching it a bit, isn't it. Neither of us is young."

"It suits a man — it doesn't suit a woman. I doubt I'll ever be the same again."

"I doubt any of us will," he muttered.

"What was that you said?"

"I said I really must get on — oh, damn!"

He had cut himself.

He came out of the bathroom in his shorts. The beginnings of a paunch had long gone. His torso was taut and his face thin, white, tired.

Lady Mainwaring saw the blood on his face in the mirror. "Self-inflicted wounds are a bit out of place here, aren't they?" she said.

She went over to him with a small scrap of white cambric. Dabbing at the cut she said, "It's nasty, isn't it."

"Where are the children?"

"They're playing in the drawing room. I must hurry. We're doing the rounds at eight o'clock."

She sighed heavily. "I'm so tired, I could die. I don't think I can take much more of this. And Lucy's in a bad state too." She called suddenly. "Andrew — come here."

There was no reply. "Did you say the children were in the drawing room?"

"Yes."

She pulled on her dressing gown.

"I've made a pact with Lucy," she said.

"A pact — what d'you mean?"

"If they ever break in here we're going to — " she stopped.

"Going to what?"

"Shoot one another."

"They'll never break in here."

"I wouldn't be so sure. How many times have the Army promised to relieve us — and failed."

"Yes — they do seem to be making a hash of things, don't they."

"People are giving up hope."

"They'll come — eventually."

"When we're all dead. I read those figures on your desk last night."

"That was a silly thing to do."

"Sixty-seven soldiers killed. One hundred and sixty-seven wounded. Two weeks' supply of bread. And how many Chinese dead of starvation?"

"Yes — they're the worst hit."

"How many was it?"

"Stop thinking about it."

"Hundreds."

"You really must not interfere with official documents," he interrupted, pulling on an old pair of trousers.

"I know the food facts, too," she said. "Two and a half ounces of meat left per person. And the hospital's in a terrible state. One thermometer left unbroken — wounds full of gangrene —"

She sat down slowly on the satin stool before her dressing table and buried her head in her hands.

Swiftly pulling on a shirt he went over to her, put his arm round her and said, "Why don't you spend the day sleeping. You must get more rest."

"I can't sleep — you know that. And I feel guilty."

"Guilty? Why in heaven's name should you feel guilty? You've been wonderful."

"They asked for volunteer nurses to help with an operation yesterday. Everyone else was worn out. They were going to — " she paused and then plunged on hurriedly " — saw off a man's leg with an ordinary carpenter's saw."

"That's no job for a woman."

"I couldn't face it — Lucy did. She collapsed in the middle of it. Archibald, when is this going to end?"

She hammered her fists on the dressing table and the gold-topped jars jumped. "Those terrible smells everywhere — it's unbearable!" She swung round on her husband. "Can't we at least do something about the smells?"

"Everything is being done my dear. You've been overworking. Look — take some laudanum. Make yourself sleep."

"The laudanum's gone. There's none left."

"Not even for the hospital?"

"Not even there."

"Things *are* getting difficult," he said.

"Mummy! Mummy!" Both children were yelling from the drawing room. "Come here — come and watch!"

As Lady Mainwaring left the room Sir Archibald combed his thinning hair in her mirror and reflected that one good thing had come out of all this for him. He no longer had the dream about the coloured spheres conjured in the immense fountain with faces resembling his own. The great crimson carpet leading to a splendid dais on which sat Sir Archibald, Minister Plenipotentiary to God, no longer came up to mock him in his deepest sleep. Ambition had vanished, but more than ambition. He had faced up to the fact, now, that he was no longer really in command of the Legation forces. It had long become a war of post-commanders operating on their own. All Sir Archibald's beautiful maps and pins were probably out of date and it was useless trying to devise an overall strategy any longer. But curiously he did not feel a sense of failure. He had survived, the Legations had survived and all that concerned him was that as many people as possible should continue to survive. That was a sufficient and worthwhile aim in life. The means no longer mattered.

As Lady Mainwaring made her way down the corridor to the drawing room she stopped suddenly, shocked afresh by what she saw. Vanessa was bent over a chair, her head protruding one end and her buttocks the other. Standing over her with a long roll of paper in his hand, his legs wide apart, wearing a paper imitation of a mandarin's hat was Andrew, his face set in a ferocious expression.

"Look Mummy," he said as she entered the room, "I'm going to behead Vanessa."

Before she could stop him he had brought the execution sword down on Vanessa's neck and she rolled off the chair, her head flopping helplessly.

"Stop that at once." Lady Mainwaring cried, horrified. She snatched the roll of paper from his hand. "You really mustn't play games like that. It's too horrible."

"Why not?" Vanessa wailed, coming to her feet and beginning to sniffle.

"Because I say so," Lady Mainwaring said. "You've got plenty of dolls in the nursery — why don't you play keeping house together."

"Don't want to play with dolls," Andrew whined. "When can we go out again? It's horrible in here."

The children were still more or less housebound. They looked pale and wan, and sank listlessly to the floor, deprived of their game.

"What shall we do?" Vanessa wailed. "There's nothing to do!"

"Silly old bullets won't hit us," said Andrew, frowning and biting his lip. "Why can't we go out?"

"Very soon now," Lady Mainwaring promised. "It won't be long now."

"Dolls, dolls — too many dolls," Vanessa said.

"What happened to Tea Cosy?" Andrew asked, referring to their favourite black cat. Tea Cosy had, in fact, been shot to provide a meal for a Chinese family but Lady Mainwaring told them, "She got lost in the ruins — we'll find her when all this is over." It occurred to her that in all the horrors of the siege what worried the children was not the safety of their parents or the howling bullets but the fate of Tea Cosy, the cat.

At six o'clock the next morning a shock of earthquake proportions rocked the whole Legation and brought everyone stumbling out into the dawn to confront another crater — much larger than the last — eighty feet across and still pouring black smoke. Another mine, dug even more deeply under the defences, had been fired by the Chinese.

Rumours flew quickly through the Legation. Other and even bigger mines were about to be fired; the Chinese were tunnelling under the very Residence itself; five soldiers, twenty Chinese refugees and many children had been killed; or was it more?

Simultaneously the most ferocious attack they had so far known began. Staggering up from deepest sleep Kershaw said to Lu-Ching, "I have a feeling this is it. If we survive this one we can survive anything."

"Except," Lu-Ching said, "starvation."

"There," Kershaw said, sluicing his face in cold water, "you have the advantage of us."

"You mean that I can survive on a handful of rice?"

"Well — can't you?"

"Perhaps it is one advantage of our civilization."

It seemed typical of Lu-Ching that when the air outside was charged with a rain of lead which withered everything in its path he should reflect on the respective merits of different eating habits.

The clanging of the alarm bell from the tower was only just audible above the uproar.

"Did they give you a rifle?" Kershaw asked.

Lu-Ching shook his head.

"Would you use it if you were given one?"

Lu-Ching sighed. "That would be difficult."

Pulling on his trousers Kershaw observed, "So far I haven't fired a shot." Putting the pistol in his belt he added, "This thing is pretty useless — it doesn't fire straight."

"You dislike the idea of shooting anybody?"

"Yes — Chinese or anyone else."

"You still feel — " Lu-Ching hesitated and sought for a word "— a relationship?"

"Yes — but not with the Boxers. I could shoot a Boxer."

"Perhaps," Lu-Ching said, "that might come within the range of possibility for me too."

"If they break through, what will you do?"

"Commit suicide."

They were silent while they finished dressing. Before they went out Lu-Ching said:

"If you still intend to stay in China I think we might benefit from your advice when we come to deal with the European powers again."

"Do you mean your own yamen?"

"It depends what the Empress Dowager decides to do."

"So you do believe we will survive?"

"I think it is . . . " Lu-Ching spread his hands and left the sentence unfinished.

The next twenty-four hours developed the characteristics of a nightmare. Never before had the fire been so continuous, intense and damaging. On his rounds Kershaw was forced to fall flat and lie prone sometimes for a whole hour. The barricades at several points were falling to pieces under rifle and artillery fire. Around the French Legation and in the Su wang-fu they heard, high above the deafening roar of battle, the ominous snake-like sound — a continuous hiss-hiss-hiss which never ceased. It was made by the new and devastatingly high-velocity, nickel-nosed bullets.

He knew them all now — the rifles, guns, shells, bullets. As he moved around listening to the wild orchestration a word began to form in time to the hiss of bullets. Retaliate . . . retaliate . . . retaliate.

The change in him was once more marked. No longer reckless, no longer abandoning himself to luck, he took cover like a shrewd old campaigner and the thought occurred to him that whatever it might mean perhaps his redemption — was that too high a word — had been worked through, and now he had to face the consequences.

As he ducked at a particularly fierce salvo he smiled grimly. Redemption — hell. It was survival now, and after survival . . . The Chinese guns seemed deadly accurate, tearing down trees, outhouses, bursting through walls, splintering roofs.

"We'll be lucky to survive this time," Captain d'Arcy said as he reached the French lines.

They had been forty-eight hours on duty. The two relief shifts could not get through. It was happening everywhere. The rotation of forces in the front line had become impossible and the firing so fierce everybody was pinned down wherever he happened to be.

"Does Sir Archie know what ees happening in 'is damned operations room? If ee did not ee must be told at once."

A French marine was peering through a loophole, about to fire his gun. Kershaw tapped him on the shoulder, indicating that he wanted to take his place. He felt for the first time in all this long campaign a strange excitement in his blood. He drew the huge Luger and released the safety catch. But immediately after he had tapped the marine on the shoulder the man suddenly keeled over, blood spurting from a terrible wound in a massacred eye. For a split second Kershaw bent to help him and then rage, excitement and kind of lust surged through his whole body and he leapt back to the loophole, desperate to retaliate — retaliate — and there was a Chinese soldier looming up right in front of him and — crack, crack — the big body seemed to leap, dance and crumple, and the sight set the excitement at an even higher pitch and exultantly he went on pulling the trigger until the bullets were all gone and Captain d'Arcy was shouting "*Taisez vous — taisez vous*!" — a curious confusion of slaughter and childishness.

As Kershaw sank down to reload, his hands were shaking, he could not fit the bullets, and the sweat poured into his eyes. Captain d'Arcy, the cool, precise professional replaced him at the loophole, took aim carefully and fired.

There was a pony — one of the last — huddled against a wall and suddenly a shell fragment struck it and seemed to tear it in two. The entrails poured out with a burst of blood and two agonized eyes appealed mutely to Kershaw, lying not ten feet away. Kershaw had just managed to re-load his gun and turned it towards the pony, intending to shoot the animal between the eyes but his hand shook so much he missed, and then of its own accord the pony slumped away into its death throes. The death of the pony became the death of the man, its burst entrails were his burst entrails, the agonized eyes different but the same and the smell of blood and guts from animal and man overpowering. Kershaw had to get away before sick dizziness overtook him.

Everywhere he found the situation the same. Reliefs waited in the background unable to take over from exhausted defenders. The Chinese barricades on the Tartar wall had been pushed forward so close that they could and did heave rocks on to the American lines. And then the miracle happened. There, as if bursting out of the ground in which he had been buried, was the huge fat apparition of Sergeant Winterburn.

Engulfing Kershaw in his big arms he roared at him, "Goddam it you sonofabitch where have you been since they killed me?" Kershaw broke free from the embrace and stared at him. He had a black patch over one eye which had obviously been shot away, and his head was bandaged. But the seamed cheek still glowed, the other eye danced with life and his energy seemed undiminished.

"Blew me eye out of the back of my head — but left a duplicate. I saw you before you saw me. Godammit you sonofabitch you're beginning to look like Jesus Christ."

He shook hands again and again. He talked on without waiting for a reply and before Kershaw could ask a single question at last said: "Gotta get some eggs for the boys — but must talk to you — tomorrow — see you tomorrow at the Watch Tower. Okay? Mid-day. . . . Say you're indestructible buddy. Wouldn't put it past you to survive us all."

He gave one final clump on the back and began to run calling, "Tomorrow buddy. Mid-day. Up yours." He made the necessary gesture.

Kershaw never knew how he finally crawled and scrambled back to report to Sir Archibald in the Residence. Sir Archibald responded instantly. By ten o'clock he had ordered every able-bodied person to the barricades. Sleeping men were armed and given any sort of weapon and everyone was told that retreat would mean being shot. The threat was necessary now, even to hardened campaigners. From the great Tartar wall to the Palace enclosure, thousands of jets of fire were spurting in a vast jagged circle and slowly closing in on all the Legations.

"Reply steadily and slowly. Waste nothing." Sir Archibald issued the order to everybody. Whether they heard or responded no longer worried him. Sitting at his desk he moved his pins and markers on his map and was utterly lost in fighting the battle. Everyone found him cool and ruthless. In these last moments nothing in the battle, theoretical or real, seemed to dismay him. Even his family, locked in the bedroom, took second place.

In the bedroom Lucy took out her revolver and made sure it was in working order. "Who shoots first?" Lady Mainwaring asked, white and intense. "You will have to," Lucy said. The children continued to play happily around them.

Half an hour later Sir Archibald said to Kershaw, "I wonder if either of us will survive."

"Neither," Kershaw replied and in that moment they seemed closer than they had ever been. Suddenly Sir Archibald remembered. "Where the hell is Major Shelham?" Kershaw went in search of him and was alarmed at what he found.

It was one o'clock in the morning. Intoxicated by the living flame of fire, infuriated by the splinters of brick and stone thrown into their faces, Kershaw was appalled to see the British defenders firing wildly and continuously in reply. By two o'clock he realized that if they went on firing like that ammunition would simply run out and then . . . what use were bayonets.

Receiving his report Sir Archibald sent messengers with the urgent request to all posts — "Conserve ammunition — at any cost." Did they ever receive the message?

And then, at dawn, from the Tartar wall, Kershaw suddenly became aware of an entirely new force driving into Peking. It came from the opposite direction. Borrowing Sergeant Winterburn's binoculars and sweeping the horizon, he saw a group of Chinese infantrymen trotting steadily in their sandals. Their uniform was different and as they trotted they frequently looked over their shoulders, away from the Tartar wall. A body of cavalry with gaudy banners followed and then came a long double line of horsemen, flogging their horses with whips.

"My God!" Kershaw cried to Sergeant Winterburn and

stopped, holding his breath. Another sight had come into focus — a series of long country carts laden with men — could they be wounded? — driven by others who stood up whipping the horses on viciously.

"It's the Chinese army," Kershaw shouted. "The other army — in retreat. Seymour's lot has beaten them."

He threw the glasses into Sergeant Winterburn's hands and the Sergeant took one look and said, "Goddam it you sonofabitch, you're right!"

Burning with excitement Kershaw set off down the ramp and almost at once had to take cover. Every brand of gun fired thousands of rounds into the defences in what Kershaw now knew was one last determined effort to wipe them out before the relieving force burst through.

A continuous flame of fire ripped from side to side, deluging the Legation with metal. The accumulated roar of sound was so immense and overwhelming Kershaw suddenly found difficulty in breathing.

How he managed to get down the ramp he never remembered, but moving through the Russian defences he made another alarming discovery. New Chinese troops armed with Mannlicher carbines had been thrown into the battle, and behind a veil of light entrenchments had reached to within ten feet of many positions. From that range the Mannlicher fire was so tremendous it drove right through bricks and sandbags.

And then, as he dipped, swerved, lay flat and raced off again, he suddenly felt fire burn its way down his thigh in a momentary flash. He ignored it, but when at last he burst into Sir Archibald's headquarters his leg was streaming blood and Sir Archibald said — idiotically — "You're wounded."

Kershaw delivered his report which astounded Sir Archibald. Everything seemed in confusion. His aides had been on duty continuously for sixty hours. Reports coming in contradicted one another with steady consistency. But no message had been received from the Tsungli yamen.

Momentarily Sir Archibald stood before his desk, bewildered in the pandemonium, his body drooping with weariness. And then Major Shelham — still alert and carefully studying the pins on the maps — nudged Kershaw and said,

"The carpet."

The uproar drowned his voice. He raised it and repeated, "The carpet, old man."

Kershaw looked down. Blood had run down his leg and formed a widening stain on Sir Archibald's carpet.

"Yes," repeated Sir Archibald absently. "The carpet."

The tableau was momentarily fixed in stupefaction. Nothing they could do now would alter the course of events. Suddenly sitrring himself, Sir Archibald said, "For God's sake, Kershaw, go to hospital."

The pain had begun and was insisting on its presence, but getting to the hospital threatened certain death.

"Can I use the bathroom?" Kershaw asked, and made his way down the corridor, leaving a steadily increasing trail of blood. He knocked on the bedroom door and Lady Mainwaring said, "Who is it?" her voice full of apprehension.

"It's Kershaw — can I use the bathroom?"

"Yes — use anything."

In the bathroom he found the wound relatively superficial. A piece of flesh, six inches long and a quarter of an inch deep, had been gouged out by a ricochetting bullet, in one neat strip. He washed the wound and blood poured away. His handkerchief was quickly soaked and useless. He looked for some form of bandage. On the bath rail hung a voluminous cotton slip with the initials L. S. worked in blue silk into a corner. It was Lucy's. He tore the slip into strips and using remembered skills bound the wound securely. The pain was now acute but as he made his way back down the corridor he stopped suddenly.

A boom so deep and powerful that it broke into and even dominated the roar of fire came from the middle distance. Kershaw held his breath and strained his ears. A moment later came another boom, different from anything the Chinese army was hurling against them. Kershaw found himself biting his lips, partly with pain, partly to stop a ridiculous leap into the long expected but entirely wrong conclusion.

Boom! it went again and then ten seconds afterwards three booms — one, two, three, perfectly spaced. There was no doubt about it. A battery of six guns was coming into action somewhere in the middle distance.

Kershaw hurried back to Sir Archibald's study. but it was empty. He went outside and found him with Shelham, trying to get the exact meaning of the new artillery. And then a Chinese stretcher-party hurried by and one of the Chinese shouted, "*Tai ping laitao liao*" — the army's arriving.

"I think he's right," Sir Archibald said. "But we must be sure."

It was three o'clock of a black cloudy night, with the temperature reaching ninety degrees but as the booming was followed by heavy machine-gun fire a new stir ran through the whole Legation. Everyone came pouring out into the compounds, shaking hands, laughing and women threw themselves into each other's arms.

"The guns! The guns! The army is coming!"

At the barricades the defenders had picked up the cry, *tai ping laitao liao*. They hurled the words across at the enemy — the army is coming — their voices roaring up to a hoarse ecstasy.

The buildings in the Su Wang-fu had been packed with Christians praying hour after hour throughout the night. Now scores of women and children, in sober blue gowns, sitting with hands folded before a single dim lamp, came to their feet and poured into the open, chattering, laughing, thanking God in a mad medley of relief.

Lady Mainwaring and Lucy emerged to join the men gathered on the verandah.

"Is it true?" Lady Mainwaring asked.

"I think so," her husband replied.

Monsieur Bleriot came carefully into the open, Sir Robert Hart and two of his clerks followed and then the Russian and Japanese Ministers joined the group, one full of lively confidence, the other still elegant in a spotless white tunic. Soon more Ministers and their wives had ventured out. They all stood there uneasily, afraid to grasp the reality of relief in case once again it turned into fantasy. The firing continued and increased in intensity and the booming of heavy artillery became a majestic music.

At that moment Lu-Ching appeared and taking his place beside Kershaw stood in silence. Kershaw turned to shake his hand.

It was then that the local firing broke out fiercely again and everybody ran for cover, and once more the certainty of surviving to greet the relieving army began to waver.

CHAPTER XXI

NO ONE SLEPT much that night. The following morning the renewed attacks on the Legation began to falter again. The relieving bombardment drew closer. The mid-day meal of two ounces of pony meat was eaten without enthusiasm. Many people were so utterly exhausted they simply fell asleep where they were, beside a lookout post, repairing defences, even in the lavatory. In the crowded Fu emaciated Chinese women flapped weakly at the flies which settled on dying babies. Down at the Water Gate more people collapsed in starvation comas.

Suddenly, at two-thirty, the uneasy torpor of the compounds was shattered. In a dozen languages the cry went up, "They are coming! They are coming! They are here!"

Confusion overtook everything. Those at the barricades rushed to the compound, the men and women in the compound hurried to the barricades, men rushed up the ramp to the Wall and rushed down again. Every vantage point was crammed with people, all milling around indiscriminately. And then, all at once, as if appearing on a stage, the tennis court was full of Indian troops, and as the crowd flowed in on them a kind of sobbing cheer came from hundreds of throats — a strange uncontrolled sound like the baying of hounds after a successful kill.

More sepoys poured through the Water Gate, up Canal Street, and into the tennis court; tall, turbanned, sweating men, their legs coated with mud from the Canal, their faces grey with exhaustion. Women crowded in on them, touching their arms and hands and some tried to embrace and kiss them. But the fierce-eyed Sikhs simply pointed to their mouths, saying with the humility due to the presence of so many memsahibs, "*Pani! Pine ki pani!*" Thirsty! Thirsty!

Kershaw standing on the edge of Sir Archibald's group was almost mown down as a great clatter of hooves preceded the magical appearance of a full-blown general with genial eyes and flowing moustaches. It was General Gaselee, who had led the relieving troops.

Kershaw watched the general bend from his saddle, grasp Sir Archibald's hand and shake it with such vigour that Sir Archibald almost winced. "Splendid! Splendid!" he was saying, but his voice was hoarse and he clearly had difficulty in controlling his emotions. Sweat poured down his face into his immaculate tunic. Smaller men with different turbans, were already smashing down barricades, clearing a road for the troops to press on. The confused mass of marines and soldiers continued to swell, with some women crying as they patted their sweating faces.

A strange contradiction slowly became apparent to Kershaw as he watched the swirling groups form and re-form round the ever-growing ranks of soldiers.

It was as if the last intense twelve hours before the relief had so drained the garrison of all emotion that after the initial burst of hysteria they subsided into inertia. Their emotions over six weeks had been subjected to such extremes of fear, hope and horror that they no longer had any reserves with which to respond.

It was the rescuers who were excited, enthusiastic, showing the expected response, and even the hard-bitten General Gaselee could not contain his emotions. The effect was heightened by the ladies of the Legation. Anticipating the relief, and horrified at the idea that they smelt, a great flurry of baths, ironing and hair combing had produced toilettes which reminded Sir Archibald of the last Royal Garden Party he had attended.

Above all Kershaw was surprised to discover how many male civilians had been skulking anonymously in every available hideout in the Legation buildings. They now came pouring out, some flawlessly attired in starched shirts with glazed collars, fancy flannel suits and many-coloured ties. Some had not been seen for weeks, others might have been dead, so successfully had they erased their presence from the threat of active service.

Lady Mainwaring excelled herself. She wore a spotless

lemon-coloured dress with a big cartwheel hat trimmed with roses, and carried the most frilly parasol he had ever seen. As she received salutations from General Gaselee she said, patting his horse with a white-gloved hand, "What a treat it is to see a real horse again."

No one would ever have known that twenty-four hours before, on the verge of collapse, she had been perfecting the organization of a double suicide with Lucy Shelham.

And Lucy . . . she stood there in the same dishevelled frock which she had worn all the week. She looked dazed and confused. Suddenly seeing Kershaw she began to make her way towards him but before she reached him Major Shelham intervened, took her by the arm and swung her round.

"You look disgusting," he said.

She stiffened and tried to shake off his grasp but he tightened it. "Get clean dress," he ordered, and began leading her back towards the Residence. "General Gaselee receiving us at one o'clock."

Half-way towards the Residence he released her and she went on walking somnambulistically, but no sooner was she within the porchway than she stopped and turned round.

Kershaw was lost in the crowd but her eyes went on searching until at last she glimpsed him on the far side of the tennis court talking to Lu-Ching. Mingling with the outer fringes of the crowd, she edged her way along until she reached the small arbour on the far side of the tennis court. There she waited her chance. As Kershaw approached with Lu-Ching she reached out her hand and touched his shoulder. . . . At first he walked on and then stopped and turned round. "Darling," she said passionately. "We've got to talk."

"Are you mad?" he said. "Everyone's watching."

"I don't care," she hissed. "Tonight, same place, same time."

"I must go."

"So must I."

Swiftly she headed back towards the Residence, trying to blend in with the surging crowds. Lu-Ching had automatically paused with Kershaw and he listened to their exchange, but now as they walked on he said nothing.

Presently people were at a loss what to do or say, any more, and inexplicably there came a rush towards the lines connecting the American Legation and the Tartar wall. Cheering and counter-cheering burst out, followed by a ragged rendering of the Star Spangled Banner and the reason for the rush became clear. Column after column of American infantry in khaki suits and slouch hats were pressing in until the open squares were choked with men and arms. Soon there was such confusion and excitement that all order disappeared.

The looting began the same night. The Allied commanders quickly divided Peking into different districts and appointed military patrols, but stopping the looting proved impossible. Men who were caught said they wanted only a few trifles but as soon as they were released set off again, their looting fever unabated.

Reluctantly Kershaw agreed to go with an American patrol led by Sergeant Winterburn, who needed an interpreter and insisted on having him. "You're my buddy," Winterburn kept on saying. "We went through it all together." Torn between keeping his assignation with Lucy and this opportunity to escape, Kershaw decided he could simply fade out of the patrol once he had made up his mind. As ten o'clock approached he felt a sense of desperation. If he disappeared in the maze of ruins and went in search of Lucy he knew he would change his life irreparably.

At that moment, a huge Russian convoy debouched into their area to the north of the Tartar wall. It was a curious mixture of green-painted Russian army wagons and captured Chinese carts, and each vehicle was overloaded with every kind of loot. The convoy had come in from the direction of the Summer Palace and was protected by a small escort of Russian infantrymen. As it approached, the ropes binding one cart worked loose due to the hideous bumping of wooden wheels on the rough road. The contents began spilling to the ground. The Russian driver, looking over his shoulder, became furious. Repacking the lost items would have meant a major piece of work and he decided on the simpler method of jettisoning any loose items. Three enormous porcelain vases and some bulky pieces of jade were simply pushed to the ground and smashed in a hundred pieces.

Sergeant Winterburn said, "Say buddy — just put your hands up and stop wrecking the place."

The patrol of six Americans was immediately challenged by five heavily armed Russians, and Kershaw swiftly intervened. For a long-drawn-out minute it looked as though the Russians would shoot it out. The production of an official parchment, signed and stamped by General Gazelee's Adjutant, stopped the threat of violence but not the argument. The exchanges were halting and fierce and at last Sergeant Winterburn said, "Tell them if they piss off we won't arrest them. But they'll have to surrender the loot."

Ten minutes of steadily increasing angry argument, and Sergeant Winterburn said, "Tell them we have orders to shoot looters who resist arrest." His huge body shook with rage as he spoke and the Russians hesitated. Slowly in ones and twos they began to fade away into the surrounding ruins.

As Winterburn's men took over the carts and turned the horses in the opposite direction, Sergeant Winterburn roared with laughter. "Listen, Kershaw. We've got a little stockpile of our own. I want you to come with us."

"If you mean what I think you mean," Kershaw was furious. "It's no deal."

"Now don't try and play the high horse with me," Winterburn said. "Everybody's doing it. Why should we be left out?"

Kershaw remembered what he had seen the day before in Prince Tuan's palace: thousands of pieces of porcelain and baskets full of jade images smashed to pieces by the Allied soldiers. When he asked the eunuchs why the soldiers did not carry off the loot instead of smashing it the eunuchs replied, "They want gold — they understand only gold."

Kershaw became aware that the Russian wagons were heading in the wrong direction.

"Where are we going?" he asked.

"A very nice little place we've got," Sergeant Winterburn told him. "Just follow the carts."

As they walked on, Lucy's image never left Kershaw's mind. He thought of her body, her corn coloured hair, the terrible passion which could possess her and in an instant he peeled off and was walking diagonally away from the convoy.

"Hi — where do you think you're going!" Winterburn said forcefully.

He pulled himself up and turned back to the carts.

"We can't have you wandering about with all these thugs around," said the Sergeant. "You might get yourself hurt."

Ten minutes later they were deep in the ruins, far away from Legation Street. Sergeant Winterburn called a halt.

"Now listen buddy," he said to Kershaw. "Are you with us or aren't you? We share the proceeds equally — that's the deal. Everybody here's with us. The question is, are you?"

Stalling for time, Kershaw replied, "What have you got to share?"

There ran swiftly through his mind the appalling contrast between the hundreds of fat eunuchs in the Imperial Palace, guarding the myriad rooms packed with the Dowager Empress's priceless collection of jade and china, and the thin pigtailed peasants struggling with elegant sedan chairs which contained even fatter merchantmen or dignitaries. Loot. Was the Dowager Empress's wealth loot? Did the mutilated men who grew fat on corrupt patronage deal in loot? Were the craftsmen's skills looted for a beggarly price to decorate the lives of the rich and privileged? It was a word of multiple meaning. Socially sanctioned looters were everywhere in everyday life. What did it matter if a handful of ignorant soldiers ingratiated themselves into the habits of their elders and betters by cruder means for a brief saturnalia? Had he any right to moralize? Simultaneously Lucy's image came up again. He glanced at his watch but it was too dark to see the time. He moved out of the shadow of the ruins into the moonlight. Five minutes to ten.

"Make up your mind," snapped Sergeant Winterburn.

"Go ahead," Kershaw said. "But you keep my share."

"Now look, buddy . . . " Sergeant Winterburn began and Kershaw interrupted:

"I'm not moralizing," he said. "I just don't want to be lumbered with a lot of loot I can't carry."

"You mean we can rely on you not to report us?"

"Yes."

Sergeant Winterburn took Kershaw's hand in his huge grip. "That's dandy," he said. "Just dandy. But wait until you see what we've got and you'll sure as hell change your mind."

Kershaw was counting down the minutes. He had no eyes for the astonishing array of loot laid out in the cellar because he was fighting the urge to run, to reach the rendezvous before Lucy left, to take her in his arms, feel the reassuring warmth of her body.

"Well — for jumping Jesus' sake say something," Sergeant Winterburn said. "Damn fine collection, don't you think?"

It was an Aladdin's cave. Silks, jewels, porcelain, jade, all neatly stacked and lit now by the light of the candles which threw back multi-coloured reflections in a dazzling array of brilliant surfaces. Two permanent guards were on duty.

"We'll be setting up business when it's all over," commented Winterburn. "Stock so far estimated at a million bucks — plenty more for the taking."

He slapped Kershaw on the back. "Better get on with the patrol," he said. "Gotta catch those dirty bastards — can't have looters bustin' in everywhere."

He roared with laughter.

Outside Kershaw glanced at his watch again. Five past ten. He saw her in his mind's eye, almost hidden in the corner of the three walls — the same white wraith, waiting.

As they moved out on patrol again he felt that he had lost control. His mind no longer functioned. Everyone was laughing, joking at their latest haul but he heard nothing and was merely an automaton playing out his role while his mind re-built the details of Lucy's image with loving care. Suddenly the fantasy blazed with the living reality and he heard her voice saying something.

He stopped abruptly. "I've got to go," he said, but Winterburn took his elbow. "Now don't get all upset — that's not like you, Kershaw. Just carry on with us — we'll look after you."

Fifteen minutes later they arrested four more looters and in the hopeless scrimmage which followed Kershaw had to draw his revolver and threaten to shoot one man. Lucy's image retreated into the background.

When it was all over he glanced at his watch yet again. And then his heart leapt and his breathing stopped because he heard the words so distinctly. She might have been beside him. "Kevin — where in God's name are you!"

He began running then, and Sergeant Winterburn bellowed after him, but not even the shots fired with such skill that they tore up the thick black Peking dust without hitting him stopped him in his headlong rush, and even his bursting lungs and streaming sweat passed unnoticed in the demonic need to reach the rendezvous, reach it before the figure faded away altogether.

Ten minutes later he was there at the outer wall, gasping "Lucy — " but no one answered. He entered the three-walled room and stared at the corner. There was nobody waiting. He went over to the corner and in his despair ran his hand over the wall. No one — nothing.

There was an official sight-seeing visit to the Imperial Palace by the British Legation for a very select handful from the staff. It included among others Lady and Sir Archibald Mainwaring and Major Shelham. Kershaw agreed to play the role of interpreter once more simply because he hoped to encounter Lucy again. But when they all gathered in the drawing room of the Residence Major Shelham said that his wife was indisposed and would not be coming.

They passed into the Imperial City by the northern entrance and found themselves in the middle of a big Russian encampment. The soldiers were taking it easy in the hot sun, stripped to the waist, sluicing their bodies in ice-cold water from the marble-enclosed canal. Scores of clean white men with flaxen hair and blue eyes seemed completely out of place in the barbaric splendour of the Palace grounds through which the Empress with all her cortege had fled twenty-four hours before.

Next came another gate supported by pillars of teak with elaborate fretwork panels and huge marble tigers, the pillars painted in brilliant vermilion. They passed through four more gates, each smaller than the last and all protected by fierce Russian guards. Sir Archibald's official pass was frequently scrutinized for several minutes. At the ultimate gate two sentries lowered their bayonets and challenged them. Then they were into the enormous maze of gardens and buildings surrounding the Palaces.

They moved on up a flight of marble steps and made their way along a terrace with fantastically carved trees set in beautiful porcelain pots, interspersed with enormous bronze braziers. As they turned towards the end of the terrace the party stopped suddenly at the sound of a few soft screams and a scuffle of paper-clad shoes hurrying away as fast as bound feet would permit. There was a quick vision of brilliantly coloured silks and satins and rouged faces and then, as high tittering laughs began, a very fat eunuch interposed his bulk at a side door.

There were ten people in Kershaw's party, five of whom were women who covered their embarrassment by falling silent. The men talked on, and Sir Archibald asked Kershaw, "Where are the Empress's apartments?"

Kershaw was wondering at that moment whether destiny had not laid down for him a clear cut path which it would be madness not to follow. Every twist of accident and luck was keeping Lucy and himself apart, tempting him towards the Chinese way of life. He had discussed it at length with Lu-Ching. They had formulated a plan, but with Lucy the plan became impossible. Without her . . .

"I don't know what's the matter with you today," Sir Archibald was saying. "You seem miles away.

"I'm sorry," said Kershaw. "What did you say?"

"Where are the Empress's apartments — that's what we want to see."

"I don't know. I'll ask."

There were three huge eunuchs guarding the next door and they refused to stand aside, but Kershaw continued to argue with them. Their leader was a man with several chins drooping down over his chest to be met by an enormous paunch, his eyebrows heavily painted and his rubbery lips rouged. He spread his arms across the final ornate doorway. Kershaw consulted with Sir Archibald. "I think," he said, "if I waved my gun at him . . . "

"So long as you don't shoot." Sir Archibald smiled wryly.

It worked at once. Two of the eunuchs fell on their knees kow-towing elaborately and the third drew aside with a half-bow. They entered two lofty rooms with camphorwood boxes ranged along the walls, every box filled to the brim with coats and trousers embroidered in gold and pearls. Other boxes held sable coats lined with white fox fur and on the single long table in the second room were dozens of foreign clocks all ticking noisily and unevenly in the silence.

And then at last they were in the Empress's bedroom. On the air there was still an exotic scent unknown to European nostrils. Twenty-four hours before, the hunched up Buddha-like woman known as Tzu Hsi, with her nails six inches long and her body smothered in ornate skirts and tunics, had lorded it over two hundred million people, the most powerful woman in the whole of Asia. Then, disguised as a peasant woman, with pigtail and nails cut short, she had fled. But her presence was still in the room. There was a great rectangular bed with heavily embroidered hangings shutting off its interior. Ranged round it were ornate chairs and stools, all carved from polished woods, lacquered in elegant patterns. Once again a high table held an array of jewelled clocks, all ticking at different times. Lady Mainwaring strode over and pulled aside the hangings round the bed. On the rich coverlet lay an embroidered coat of black satin and peeping out from beneath the bed was a pair of Manchu shoes. Two large boxes of silk handkerchiefs were overturned. A handful had been hurriedly snatched from each. The party talked and fingered, carefully watched with growing apprehension by the three eunuchs. And then Lady Mainwaring led the way to a corner with a compartment cut off by rich yellow curtains, and pulled the thick golden tassels which controlled them. There, revealed to every embarrassed eye, was nothing less than a pot de chambre cast in solid silver.

Ten minutes later they were still moving round the ante-rooms when Sir Archibald noticed that his wife was missing. He sent Kershaw in search of her. One room gave on to another with such frequency it dawned on Kershaw he must be careful to note some characteristics of each or he would be lost. And then — silently — he came upon a room with a high ceiling, carved wooden frescoes and beautiful scrolls hanging from the walls. Half-a-dozen delicately made lacquered tables, each one holding jewelled rings, vases and ornaments were placed in a circle at the centre of the room. In the middle of the circle stood one magnificent jar which held his attention. As he stood there gazing diagonally into the room from one side of the doorway, he saw Lady Mainwaring snatch up one exquisite ring and slip it in her handbag. Her eyes lit up and she seemed to listen intently. A moment later she snatched up a small jade Buddha and slipped that into her handbag too.

Returning to his room at mid-day Kershaw found, propped on the table, a note from Lu-Ching written in beautiful Chinese characters. "I am returning to my yamen at Fengtai. Why not follow me."

CHAPTER XXII

Lu-Ching found the small town of Fengtai in confusion and his yamen in complete disarray. Communication with the outside world had broken down and the four garrison buildings were wrecked and looted. Of two hundred horses, over a hundred were missing and many of his cherished possessions destroyed. But his secretary was overwhelmed by his reappearance and would have prepared elaborate celebrations with a great feast, but for one fact. Shivering with apprehension, he revealed that none other than the Dowager Empress herself was in the Huai-lai district and had sent a message which no one dared read.

Hurrying into the reception room, there laid out on the table was a handful of coarse paper without even the protection of an envelope. With the aid of his secretary Lu-Ching unravelled the paper and smoothed its innumerable creases. Revealed as a long strip, they deciphered a list of names, beginning with the Empress Dowager and the Emperor and ranging downwards through Princes and Counts to Grand Councillors, Secretaries and Officials. Beside each name was a request for immediate service in many forms. The Emperor and Empress must have — a table and full feast. For Prince Ch'ing, Prince Li and Prince Tuan, a table and a kettle of food. So it continued, the requirements diminishing in descending order of importance.

The secretary's hands were shaking as he held the last part of the long strip for final examination and he repeated several times, "How can we in this humble town prepare for such a grand body of people? How can we in this humble . . ."

Lu-Ching closely scrutinized every detail of the paper, fearing that it could be another trap elaborately devised by the Boxer chiefs who were still at large, but the date was impressed with the seal of the magistrate of the Yen Ch'ing District, and he knew that seal well.

Several assistants came in to welcome Lu-Ching and congratulate him on his survival but all were confused about what action should be taken on the royal edict. If their preparations to receive the Empress were inadequate they risked a scolding, a caning and even, for some more serious shortcoming, beheading. One urged Lu-Ching to abandon his office and flee. The risk of causing displeasure with their limited resources was too great. Another suggested consulting the magistrate of the Yen Ch'ing district, a man known to Lu-Ching, but Lu-Ching reasoned with them thus . . . It was his bounden duty to remain in and protect the Huai-lai district, and since he had partaken regularly of the Imperial grain, how could he not now respond to the Empress's appeal for help when she was in such ultimate trouble? Choosing between disaster and happiness in such a situation was not for him, and there remained only one course of action which his ancestors would have taken — to fulfil his duty.

Once more, with the help of his secretary, Lu-Ching calculated that the Empress and her entourage would reach Yu-lin Post Station, sixteen miles away, on the following day; and now he summoned what remained of the yamen's cooks and butchers. Normally he could muster nine cooks and three butchers but now there were only four cooks and two butchers. Two of the four cooks were carefully instructed to carry a stove, sea savouries, fruits and rice to the few officials stationed at Yu-lin post and to warn them on pain of severe consequences that a meal-cum-offering must be prepared to present to the Empress on her arrival. No time was to be lost.

When that was accomplished Lu-Ching suddenly felt a desperate need to sleep. The accumulated weariness and strain of all those weeks in the Legation had overwhelmed him, and now, when he should have been able to relax and sleep, he was confronted with this new crisis.

Half an hour later the two cooks returned in a state of great distress. The Head Boxer had refused to let them leave the town. Consulting with his secretary, Lu-Ching devised a simple plan to outwit the Head Boxer. The cooks would, by stealth of night, mount the city wall and swing down to the other side by ropes, carrying their apparatus in basketwork jars. In the morning more cooks and butchers would follow in their wake.

As the new strains mounted, Lu-Ching began to wonder whether his physical strength could sustain itself long enough to see him through this new and desperate situation. Facing death at the hands of the Boxers or in the Legation had drained his resources, but to insult the Empress by not appearing punctually with all the privileges which she demanded meant the kind of humiliation which would be worse than beheading.

Lu-Ching now dressed with great deliberation in his official robes, with the richly brocaded tunic, the mortar-board hat and the sleeves obliterating his hands and arms, but just as he was about to leave to meet the Head Boxer, his secretary came in to say a man was asking for an audience on urgent matters which he said were of the greatest moment. Moreover the man claimed to be a friend of the honourable magistrate.

"I cannot see him now," Lu-Ching said and mounted his horse, but as he was riding through the gate a figure came running beside him in the likeness of a Chinese peasant. Suddenly the figure broke into the English language.

"Lu-Ching — it's me."

And there was Kershaw so successfully disguised — with pigment rubbed into his already pallid cheeks, a wig with perfect pigtail surmounting his head, and a filthy tunic encasing his body — that Lu-Ching could not believe his ears when the English words fell upon them.

He dismounted at once and did something he had never attempted before in his life — embraced Kershaw with both arms, saying, "But you must hurry — hurry — do you still have your revolver?"

Kershaw pointed to the inner band underneath his tunic. "But only — " he began.

Lu-Ching swiftly explained the situation. They returned to the yamen, removed Kershaw's pigtail and re-dressed him in the robes of a yamen assistant, examining him closely in the mirror for any traces of his American origins. Then, at last, since he could not ride, he was asked whether he would walk, holding Lu-Ching's stirrup. This, in the event, proved unnecessary because, to the alarm of the scholars, officials and secretaries of the yamen, the Head Boxer suddenly arrived with scores of "associates" and demanded audience with the Magistrate. The Boxers were far less vociferous now but still powerful, and audience had to be granted. Swiftly Lu-Ching arranged for Kershaw to sit on the right hand of his black chair in the Judgment Chamber, with orders to shoot the Head Boxer if he showed signs of becoming violent.

It was a very different Kershaw who sat there coolly waiting any eventuality with his folded hands concealing in his long sleeves the ugly old Luger pistol which he had only fired once before. He felt calm and confident, and the idea of killing this man no longer troubled him.

"Why," the Head Boxer demanded of Lu-Ching, "are you leaving the town?"

"I go to meet the Sacred Chariot of the Empress Dowager."

"But how is this!" the Head Boxer demanded, his voice loud and arrogant. "She has fled long ago. Why do you still call her the Empress Dowager? She is not worthy."

"The Emperor on behalf of the Empress must make a tour of investigation every three years," Lu-Ching replied. "If as a district magistrate I also go on such a tour you cannot say I have fled."

The Head Boxer, bewildered by this logic, simply shouted at his associates, "Do you feel the breath of a Secondary Hairy One? Must he be killed?"

"Shoot to kill," Lu-Ching whispered to Kershaw who brought the barrel of the huge Luger out of his sleeve and directed it between the eyes of the Head Boxer, who took fright, turned about and fled, his associates following in disarray.

Lu-Ching drew breath deeply. He had learnt another European habit which now overtook him spontaneously. He shook hands with Kershaw, to the amazement of his assistants, who had never witnessed such behaviour in him before. Simultaneously his secretary intervened. "They will come back," he said. "We must hurry."

"How many horsemen have we?"

"Twenty."

"Tell them to take arms and be ready to use them. We will leave by the West Gate and shoot anyone who dares to hinder us — shoot to kill. And you, Kershaw, is it your wish that you come with us?"

Kershaw hesitated a long moment. He had seen opening before him as an assistant to Lu-Ching a way of life which would absorb him back into Chinese roots but he had not taken account of violence in that way of life. He had seen an escape from the ambition and harassment of the West which should slowly release him into that serenity which went with an ordered life devoted not to private but public service. And now at the outset the worst characteristics had broken into that vision.

"I will come with you," he said, because Lucy still deeply troubled him and this new situation offered once more a solution. He could not expunge her image from his mind even as they rode out of the West Gate under heavily armed guard, and he had no sense of danger because of her deeply felt presence.

In the Residence Lucy Shelham buried her face in the pillow and began silently weeping. She was still weeping twenty-four hours later, but no sound accompanied the tears. On the following day she seemed to retreat into herself and had no communication with the outside world. She moved like a robot through a number of simple routine actions, but people said she failed to hear or if she heard understand what they said. This was particularly so with her husband, Colin.

At nine o'clock the same morning Lu-Ching, Kershaw and two assistants arrived at Yu-lin to find it deserted, the Boxers and everyone else having fled because news of the Empress Dowager's arrival had spread fast. Quickly, they surveyed the available inns and selected the largest as a resting place for the Sacred Chariot when it arrived. This was hardly done when Prince Su came clattering up on horseback covered in sweat and dust. "The Empress Dowager is travelling in the four-man chair of the Yen Ch'ing magistrate," he said breathlessly. "Behind her are mule litters carrying the Emperor and Prince Lun, the Empress's daughter, Ta Ah-Ko, the heir apparent and the Head Eunuch. Only when the chair and first litter have passed may you rise from your knees."

Kershaw's Western independence began to reassert itself from that moment. He had not foreseen falling to his knees in respect for an Empress who clearly at that time qualified as one of the wickedest women in the world.

Six horsemen rode up five minutes later to announce that the Sacred Chariot was arriving. Almost immediately the beautifully lacquered and embroidered chair, carried by four sweating officials, was seen approaching the selected inn and Kershaw watched as Lu-Ching fell to his knees.

"Down!" Lu-Ching whispered fiercely. "Down!"

Kershaw slipped slowly and reluctantly to his knees. Lu-Ching was chanting, "I the magistrate of the Fengtai district, kneel to welcome the sacred Chair of the Empress Dowager."

"Repeat after me," he whispered fiercely to Kershaw, but when Kershaw tried he muddled the words and for a moment the surrounding horsemen looked on him with suspicion. But everyone showed signs of hardship and hunger and, in the confusion of princes, dukes and officials all fulfilling one role or another around the Sacred Chariot, his clumsiness was forgotten.

The largest room in the inn had been cleared and decorated with the necessary emblems. Ten minutes later a eunuch called Ts'ui Yu-Knei, with an enormous stomach, came out and demanded imperiously, "Which is the Huai-lai magistrate?"

Lu-Ching acknowledged his identity with the correct degree of humility. Familiar as he was with the abject respect which ascended from the lowest to the highest in the royal hierarchy, it seemed to Kershaw that when the object of that respect had revealed such evil, then the whole system had converted Lu-Ching into an unthinking courtier. He did not like his friend in this role.

It was only later that he learnt from Lu-Ching what happened when he entered the Empress's presence. He had found her hunched up, worried, and dressed in simple cotton clothes with her hair done in a most unsophisticated knot on top of her head. She had, he learnt to his amazement, escaped through the fighting disguised as a peasant woman. Now she enquired into his heritage, history and precise rank, and at last she wept openly as she said, "We have travelled in great danger for hundreds of miles without stopping to be greeted by a single subject. Now it is good to meet one dressed in the official robes and hat of a magistrate."

Lu-Ching was in great fear, he told Kershaw, because the feast of meat he had prepared for the Empress had been stolen and eaten by runaway Boxers. "Only one kettle of green bean and millet porridge which was intended for your soldiers are left," he had said, his voice trembling. "The food I greatly fear is much too coarse for your Highness to eat."

But the Empress demanded the millet porridge at once and devoured it like a Chinese peasant.

The words re-echoed in Kershaw's mind as he listened to Lu-Ching's story — like a Chinese peasant.

"Surely these things must begin to change," he said.

"Change?" Lu-Ching looked puzzled. "In what way?"

"How can respect continue to be given to such an evil woman and the peasantry continue to starve?"

Lu-Ching was amazed at such thinking. "Nothing will change," he said. "Among the many ranks of our philosophers only one expresses the views you have expressed, and he cannot possibly prevail. He is very unpopular. When cultivating a garden from a trapeze you need a very long spade."

"I would like to meet this man," Kershaw said, but Lu-Ching grew uneasy and worried for his safety.

"It would be unwise to meet him," he warned. "Your hold on our culture is very fragile. You must remember that and behave accordingly."

CHAPTER XXIII

NEW YORK, WITH sights and sounds which assaulted the senses, New York of the immense concrete towers which crowded out the sky as Lucy threaded her way through the streets. When the afternoon merged into dusk, the lights flickered to life, the buildings became disembodied, and a fairyland of sparkling minarets overwhelmed material ugliness.

It was all new and not new to her. It had all changed on the surface but was the same underneath. The city of daylight, harsh, driving, relentless, and the city at night, a place of magic and murder. Morning and evening, the concrete warrens poured out their myriad workers sold to property or advertising, journalism or clerking in the multiple devices of commerce.

The atmosphere was electrifying after Peking. It should have brought her alive as it did in the old days but she no longer responded in the same way. Some part of her was still dead, beyond even the reach of New York to revive.

She never knew whether her period was psychologically delayed by overwhelming stress or whether she had had an early miscarriage. She persuaded herself it was a miscarriage. *She had lost Kevin's child.* Shelham never knew. Trying to bring her out of depression he had manoeuvred to achieve her lifelong ambition, a posting in America. Now from a window on Central Park West they could look out on New York City. Both had suffered from cultural shock in the first few weeks. Both found the elegant blue-bloods, burghers and social tycoons who lived in apartments cheek by jowl with flop-houses at twenty-five cents a night, bewildering. Driving through the crowded streets in one of the new Oldsmobile motor cars was exciting but Lucy preferred to wander on foot. It was exhilarating to be hurled up and down buildings in elevators but she preferred the older buildings with their modest height, better design and slowly negotiated stairways. Only reluctantly did she shed certain relaxations which went with the reflective way of life and handcarts of far-off Peking.

And then, after six months of slow adjustment, Major Shelham woke at seven o'clock one misty morning with the river steamers hooting in the background, and reached out a hand to caress his wife's back. As she shivered awake under his touch he turned over on his side and brought his body symmetrically against hers, his hand reaching round to settle gently on her breast.

She lay still for a long moment feigning sleep but she could not remain completely quiet and as she straightened her curled legs he began kissing her. Turning round, she returned his kisses. They made love for fifteen minutes and from long practice she finally sank back on the pillows with every appearance of a satisfied woman. He no longer smelt of drink or stale cigar smoke in the mornings. His hair had gone completely grey, his cheeks were no longer rosy and he treated her now like a woman and not a sexual object. There was no mistaking a kind of love in his final kiss which was free from anything but tenderness. Ten minutes later he ran her bath and she climbed slowly out of bed to subject her face to its morning scrutiny in the mirror. The ten years had left its mark with streaks of grey in her hair, spreading rapidly. The colour had never returned to her cheeks since the day the siege ended. Indeed, she had never been quite the same again, Colin said.

She began to massage the puckered lines under her eyes and was fumbling for her lipstick when Colin brought in the *New York Times* and threw it on the bed. She picked up the paper and said, "I think, darling, I'll have my bath later. Let's have some coffee and talk."

"Have hurry down office," he said. "Must shave fast."

The maid brought coffee, toast and orange juice and Lucy decided to go back to bed, eat her breakfast and idle through the newspaper. Life had settled into a comfortable routine. Everything ran so smoothly she scarcely noticed the passing of the days, each morning dealing with the maid, the housekeeper, the post and invitations. Shopping in the afternoons and taking old-fashioned English tea in that exclusive little patisserie on 42nd Street where it was *à la mode* to play the role of an English lady. As Second Secretary at the Embassy, Major Shelham lived a wide social life and she had become adept at the right dress for the occasion, the precise word in the right place and every nuance of protocol. Still a handsome woman, she had perfected the deflection of all those mild flirtations which might in the old days have led into such devious pathways.

She was still sipping her coffee when her eye caught two paragraphs on page two of the *New York Times*.

AMERICAN DECAPITATED

"Yesterday afternoon Mr Cyrus K. Kershaw, a Chinese-American who had been living in Peking for the last ten years was ceremonially beheaded in the city of Yu-Lin. Six months ago he was charged with being an American spy carefully infiltrated by the American Secret Service into the Chinese Civil Service. He was also accused of associating with a secret society which had revolutionary aims. His activities were said to be subversive despite his claim that he was a reformist, not a revolutionary. A spokesman for the State Department said that they had no record of any agent named Cyrus K. Kershaw anywhere in China."

The *New York Times* slipped from her hands and she sank back on the pillow. The shock left her paralyzed.

She lay there a long time, staring at the beautiful moulded ceiling of the old-fashioned mansion apartment.

As the pain at last began to free itself she knew it would be too much for her and she dressed so hurriedly and left the apartment in such haste that she failed to give the maid instructions for lunch.

She began walking. Down from Central Park West, round Columbus Circus, into the rush and roar of Broadway. She felt she was fleeing from something but could not clearly identify what, and so intense was her need to escape that she took little heed of where she went and only when she found herself stumbling amongst the bums on the Bowery did she recoil, hurrying back to the civilized centre of the City. Her feet were sore, her body exhausted, but she went on walking.

When she did not come back by midnight Shelham alerted

the police. At three in the morning the Missing Persons Bureau reported picking up a woman half asleep on a bench way out beyond 91st Street.

It took her a whole week to recover. Shelham never knew what mysterious illness so drastically changed her in a single week because it was not simply a matter of one week. For months afterwards she was no longer the same person and there were times when he felt he would never really communicate with her again.